"You're awfully helpful for a man."

"That might be because I'm trying to make a good impression." He grinned at her over the rim of the glass. "Is it working?"

"It depends on the impression you're trying to make."

"Why, showing you the kind of husband I'd be to you." He smiled sheepishly. "Useful. Considerate. I hear the ability to fetch things is a good trait in a husband."

"No, that's in a dog," she teased.

"Right." He laughed at himself. "I've been making myself look like a fool, haven't I?"

She shrugged, unable to agree. He wasn't a man practiced in courting, but he was sincere. He had taken care of her more in the short time she'd known him than her own mother had in her entire lifetime.

He had made her dream again with a single touch of his big, rugged, working-man's hands....

* * *

The Horseman
Harlequin Historical #715—August 2004

Praise for Jillian Hart's recent books

High Plains Wife
"Finely drawn characters and sweet tenderness tinged with poignancy draw readers into a familiar story that beautifully captures the feel of an American romance."
—*Romantic Times*

Bluebonnet Bride
"Ms. Hart expertly weaves a fine tale of the heart's ability to find love after tragedy. Pure reading pleasure!"
—*Romantic Times*

Cooper's Wife
"A wonderfully written romance full of love and laughter."
—*Rendezvous*

DON'T MISS THESE OTHER TITLES AVAILABLE NOW:

#716 A SCANDALOUS SITUATION
Patricia Frances Rowell

#717 THE WIDOW'S BARGAIN
Juliet Landon

#718 THE MERCENARY'S KISS
Pam Crooks

THE HORSEMAN

JILLIAN HART

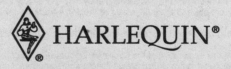

HARLEQUIN®

TORONTO • NEW YORK • LONDON
AMSTERDAM • PARIS • SYDNEY • HAMBURG
STOCKHOLM • ATHENS • TOKYO • MILAN • MADRID
PRAGUE • WARSAW • BUDAPEST • AUCKLAND

ISBN 0-373-29315-1

THE HORSEMAN

Copyright © 2004 by Jill Strickler

www.eHarlequin.com

Printed in U.S.A.

Please address questions and book requests to:
Harlequin Reader Service
U.S.: 3010 Walden Ave., P.O. Box 1325, Buffalo, NY 14269
Canadian: P.O. Box 609, Fort Erie, Ont. L2A 5X3

To Ernest Fraijo,
who gave me the inspiration for the Spirit Horse.
To Tony and Ryan, who will always be heroes to me.
Thank you.

Chapter One

Montana Territory, 1882

I should be holding my baby now. Katelyn Green sat up in bed and buried her face in her hands, unable to hide from the grief. Pain filled her up, cold and dark as the night. She didn't want to feel it; the loss was overwhelming. She was empty, her stomach strangely quiet.

By all rights, she ought to be cradling her daughter, safe and warm in her arms.

But instead she had this horrible sorrow, deep like a well and as dark. With a groan she shifted carefully, ignoring the physical pain the early birth had brought her. She climbed from the bed as if she could escape her sadness, but it followed her like the gloom to the window where she leaned her forehead against the frosty glass.

If only the baby hadn't come early. If only she had lived.

Try not to think of it and maybe you'll be all right. She willed her heart to be as cold as the glass at her brow. As icy as the frigid world outside her window. As quiet as the hard frost that painted the black reaching limbs of the leafless trees a solid snowy white and coated the vast Montana prairie with a frozen hush.

The moon was out, a bright round disk that warmed the ice-cold light from a thousand stars scattered across the void of night. The silvered light glinted across the prairie, as if more stars had tumbled to earth and still shone where they had fallen in the rises and draws of the high plains.

Like a lure, the night beckoned her, as if in those deep shadows where the moonlight and stardust did not reach, Katelyn could hide forever in the cold and night. Surely the grief could not follow her there.

"What are we gonna do with her?" a man's deep voice demanded from the kitchen down the hall.

A voice hard and violent with anger. Katelyn shivered, her insides coiling up into a hard knot. She feared her stepfather, Cal Willman, but not as much as the husband who'd cast her out.

"She's not staying with us much longer." Cal sounded adamant and forceful, the way he always did when he'd been drinking.

"She's my daughter. I guess I have to help her." Her mother's voice answered, perplexed and put-upon, sounding thin and torn.

Katelyn could picture her mother in the parlor, hands to her stomach, helpless to know what to do. Katherine Lyn Willman was not good at decisions or seeing past her own needs. It was a weakness of character and one of heart.

Katelyn knew what her mother would say next. She'd learned from the hard experience of growing up in this house. And from similar conversations her parents had had about her since she'd arrived five weeks ago.

"But we must consider our reputation." Mother's words vibrated with the worry of it. "I've had plenty of sympathy from my friends. They say it's terrible how her husband set her aside."

"Terrible? It's scandalous. It's ruining my business, that's what it's doing, and I can't have much more of it."

"Yes, but if we cast her out, think of how that would make us look."

"But she's useless, nothing but a burden—"

Useless. That's what Brett had called her, the man who'd vowed in front of God to honor and cherish her. Katelyn squeezed her eyes shut, soaking in the cold draft seeping through the single-paned glass.

If only she'd had someplace else to go. It hadn't been easy coming back. Walking the mile from town after a difficult birth and surgery three days after losing her baby, a girl child and not a son. *You're useless to me,* Brett had told her. Worthless and replaceable.

He was a judge, and he'd found a way to dissolve the legal ties of their marriage.

"No decent man will have her." Her stepfather sounded deeply disgusted. "It's not as if we can find someone to marry her. She's barren."

"When she's well, she could help with the housework. We'd be able to get by without a second housemaid."

"Did you hear me, woman?" Cal's disdain rang bitter and cold as the night outside. "I don't want to cast my eyes on that daughter of yours. She's a disgrace, and I have my business to think of.''

Katelyn covered her ears, refusing to listen to her mother's answer, for it would be filled with her own selfish worries, as always. This was no home, no refuge, the way it had always been. This place was only another form of hell that she'd married to escape.

And the joke was on her. Marriage had been worse than this place, and now she had nowhere to go, no one to turn to, and her future was gone, vanished like a puff of smoke in midair, evaporating as if it never had been.

Her stepfather had said it. No decent man would want her. And she had to wonder if there were any decent men, husbands who treated their wives with tenderness and honor.

Maybe there were no men like that, like the princes in the fables she'd read about as a child, or heroes in the novels she so loved to read. Heroes of heart and courage and integrity were fiction, and nothing more.

What am I going to do? She couldn't stay here, and she wasn't yet strong enough to leave. Hopelessness lashed through her, smarting like the tip of a bullwhip against the inside of her rib cage.

I can't stay here a moment longer. She had to escape, even if only for a few minutes. Her fingers glided over the glass panes. She unlatched the lock with a flick of her thumb.

''There is another course.'' Her mother's voice sounded again. ''We send her away. Find a situation for her and wash our hands of her. All anyone needs to know is that she's gone to stay with relatives.''

The night breeze was blessedly cold and as welcome as a wish come true. Katelyn sucked in the cool scent of winter and held it deep in her lungs before she tugged her quilted housecoat from the closet and pulled it on over her nightgown.

It was the darkness and not the starlight that drew her as she climbed through the window. The bitterness of her parent's voices dulled to a mumble, their words becoming indistinguishable and then nothing at all as her feet hit the ground beneath her bedroom window.

She hated the weakness that shivered like water through her limbs. The weakness that made her feet heavy as she shuffled through the dormant rose garden. The shrubs were bundled in cloth with straw tucked around their shadowed bases. Hibernating. Envious, she kept on going.

The last of the fallen leaves crunched beneath her slippers as she ambled toward the open prairie. Pain sliced from her stomach down to her knee with each step. The doctor had said it would take a long while to heal. She'd lost a dangerous amount of blood during the birth and after.

She limped across the yard, the grass crisp and dead beneath her slippers. She could feel the night around her, somehow alive and magical, as if the moonlight laid down a path of silver for her feet and the white ice of the stars glittered like hope in the velvet sky.

The last time she'd felt hopeful was for the one moment in her bleak marriage when she'd first felt her baby quicken in her womb, that faint, incredible flutter of new life. *Gone*.

Her hands covered her stomach, empty and hollow.

She should have died with the child, she thought, turning her back on the moon and stars, closing her eyes so hard the tears of sorrow could not escape. She was dead in all the ways that counted.

It did not matter what her mother and stepfather decided to do with her. Whatever situation they would find could not be worse than this pain she was in. A pain so deep it was a perfect darkness, like a night without moon or stars or end.

She heard him before she felt the change in the air, like the whisper of an archangel, then she heard the booming crack of thunder so loud it shook the despair from the night. The drumming crashed through the silent yard growing closer. It echoed along the eaves of the house and the long row of stables and outbuildings.

A high, sharp neigh trumpeted a warning an instant before the black shadow galloped into sight, front hooves pawing the air as he reared into the sky, nostrils flaring, ears pinned back, fury in his cry. The sight of him lured Katelyn closer, despite the pain of each step.

She could feel the wild rage of the stallion, the untamed power of him as he called out again, a warning neigh that pierced her ears like a bugle's call to battle. She hugged the flat board rail of the paddock fence and watched, spellbound, as the magnificent creature leaped a six-foot-high fence in a single bound.

He's magnificent. She held her breath as he landed, skimming the ground. He flew with effortless grace toward the far stables. The night slowly disguised him until there was only the beat of his hooves on the frozen earth.

The door to the bunkhouse slammed open and the sharp smack of wood striking wood shot through the yard like a gunshot. Light spilled into the darkness from the open doorway.

"What in the blazes?" a man's gruff voice asked in confusion.

"It's the devil, he's back." Old Pete, one of the longtime ranch hands, answered as he shoved his way through the door. "I know how to handle this one. Stand out of my way."

A metallic rasping resounded in the dark. The sound of a rifle being cocked.

No! Katelyn watched in horror as the shorter, stockier man lifted the gun. Horror washed over her, launching her forward onto the bottom rail of the fence. She had to stop him—

A shot rang out, piercing the night. She clung to the top rail, helpless to do anything more than watch as the stallion neighed fiercely. He lived.

Relief left her dizzy. She'd had enough tragedy. She'd seen enough harm.

"Are you crazy?" a man's voice boomed like winter thunder, deep and confident and angry. In the lit doorway across the row of paddocks, the strange man held the rifle by the barrel, as if he'd ripped it out of the old ranch hand's grip. "You could have killed the beast."

"That was the notion. He killed my only son last year, and I swore an oath on my boy's grave that if that bastard dared to come back to these plains, I'd shoot him dead."

"Get back to your bottle, old man." The stranger jerked on the back part of the gun and the rattle of bullets clinked into his palm. "No one harms an animal as long as I'm here. Is that understood?"

"You wranglers come and go and think you know everything, but you'll see that I'm right. The only way to handle a beast like that is with a bullet." The old man shook his fist, as if in warning, or as if casting a curse, and then hobbled through the lit doorway and into the shadows of the bunkhouse.

The man was alone in the yard, standing with his shoulders broad, feet planted and the rifle in hand.

A dangerous man. Fear caught in her chest, watery and weak. Tonight, he'd made the choice of protecting the stallion.

The old man had called him a wrangler. He must be the new horseman her stepfather had hired some time back. Katelyn had overheard him discussing it more than once. He was a drifter by the sound of it, a man said to have been everywhere, done everything and have a rare touch with horses. It was rumored he had Indian blood in his veins.

The wind shifted. The shadows deepened. Katelyn felt the horseman's gaze shift to her and focus with the same threat as if he'd loaded the rifle and aimed it straight at her heart. The hair prickled on the back of her neck. Her flesh rose in goose bumps as the night expanded around her.

The stars seemed to snuff out one by one until there was only the two of them. The powerful, intimidating man with a rifle and her, in her housecoat and slippers. If he was a dangerous man, she was alone with him. Perhaps that wasn't the wisest course. She could simply turn around and scurry back the way she'd come.

She took a step back, knees weak. Scurrying wasn't as simple as she first thought. The pain was worse, knifed down her legs in fine, cold slices. Maybe she'd stand here and rest up before heading in.

The man was staring at her. He looked like trouble. Although she could not see his face, there was something about him. Something raw and mighty, as if he were made of iron and not flesh and blood.

He stood in the faint shadows. The light gilded the broad strength of him, but his face remained in darkness.

She did not doubt his would be a hard face, one weathered by time and sun and violence. But why would such a man save a wild animal?

The stallion was calling again, pawing at the closest stable. He bugled a sharp protest. What was he doing? Then a gentle nicker answered from inside the stable.

The stallion lifted his head high and arched his proud neck. As if showing off for the mare, he pranced the length of the paddock. The fading starlight worshiped him, glinting like precious silver dust on the graceful line of his back and shoulders. A dream come true.

No man was a dream. Disenchanted, Katelyn turned away. Her uneven steps crackled through the frozen grasses loudly enough to pinpoint her location. The night silenced—even the wind fell still—and she felt the horseman's presence as surely as the icy ground beneath her feet.

Something touched her cheek. Feather soft. Brief.

Abrupt. She jumped, the fight rising up in her like a storm. She was alone. There was no danger as a second snowflake brushed the tip of her nose. A third caught on her left eyelash.

She felt foolish for being so jumpy. All around her was the whir of a million snowflakes, tumbling from the sky to tap against the ground. They filled the silent night like a symphony and softened the darkness.

There was the horseman. He was more than shadow now, and close. Too close. He was four fence posts away, leaning on the corner post without hat or coat. The stolen rifle rested against the long length of his thigh. He looked invincible standing there like a warrior of old.

It was the horse he was after. Not her. Katelyn stopped, grateful for the chance to catch her breath. She was quaking from fear and cold, but she could not tear her gaze away from the man, barely visible in the dark as he braced both forearms against the top rail.

"Hello, boy." When he spoke, it was like harmony, low and sure and true. "Lookin' to go courtin', are you? You're out of luck tonight, man. The stable's locked up tight."

Katelyn couldn't believe her eyes. The stallion stopped pawing the ground and stilled. He swung his big head to stare at the man who dared to talk to him. The stallion's ears pricked as he scented the stranger, then he snorted in obvious disdain of the human.

The man didn't seem offended by it. "Folks tell me they call you the devil for a reason."

The stallion bared his teeth and laid back his ears in answer.

"I see. You're a tough one. Me, too, so I understand." The easy friendliness in the man's voice and posture remained. "It isn't often a man comes across a mustang like you. Those are pretty distinct markings you have. Do you know how valuable that makes you?"

"Five hundred gold eagles," called another man's voice from the direction of the bunkhouse. Another one of the hired hands.

That seemed to get the horseman's attention. "Why? Is he someone's lost horse? Is there a reward on him? He looks wild to me."

"Cal Willman wanted him caught and broke to ride. A stallion with markings like that would be worth something in stud fees, even if he is a cayuse. That horse put up a fuss and killed Old Pete's son before he broke free and took a few prized Arabians with him. Cost Willman a bundle, I'll tell you. Near about ruined him, far as anyone can tell. He fired a whole bunch of us, and we've been runnin' this place with just a few hands ever since."

"Wonder if Willman still has that reward out for him," one of the hired men asked. "Reckon we can collect on it?"

"What do you mean 'we'?" the other ranch hand argued. "I'd like that money for myself."

So, that's why my stepfather sold the house in town. Curious, she couldn't help creeping through the shadows and swiping the snow from her eyes, edging close enough to better hear what the men where saying.

But it was the horseman her eyes strayed to. The way he remained motionless, snow accumulating on his dark locks, the width of his shoulders, his attention trained on the wild horse, his focus never wavering.

He's going to catch the stallion. But how? If the animal had leaped into the paddock, he could easily leap out before he could be cornered. The fence could not hold him. What could? The magnificent beast's hooves beat out a swift rhythm along the length of the stable, as if he knew it, too, and he wasn't afraid.

Run, she silently pleaded. *Run while you can.* The stallion skidded to a halt, shaking the snow from his coat. He turned to face the horseman, nose up, ears forward, nostrils flaring wide to scent the man who watched and waited.

"We are going to be partners, you and me." The horseman's promise made the men behind him guffaw.

"Keep on dreamin', Hennessey," one of the men called. "You're not man enough to get your hands on that big fat reward. Bet you'd like to."

"I wouldn't mind if I did. It wouldn't matter if I didn't." The horseman climbed onto the rail and eased down into the paddock. He approached the stallion slow and sure, like a predator stalking his next meal, confident of the outcome. "You are a handsome one, aren't you, boy?"

The stallion nickered, a low warning sound that sent shivers down Katelyn's spine.

"We've got lassos ready," one of the ranch hands said as he led the others toward the fence. "Stand back, Hennessey. Let the real cowboys take care of this one."

"Fine, Ned, but you boys will scare him off." The horseman lifted a coiled whip from his belt. "Go ahead. You catch him. I'll just lean back, take a few minutes to rest and watch you rope him in. It shouldn't be too hard for a seasoned wrangler like you.''

''You're a son of a bitch, Hennessey. There isn't a horse I can't break.'' Ned crawled through the fence, then shook out his lasso.

Dillon Hennessey had learned long ago how to manage fools like Ned Ritter, so he was careful not to let anger get the best of him. He had a quick trigger when it came to the way men treated horses. It was just the way he was. He believed in respecting animals.

And women, too.

He'd noticed her before tonight. What man wouldn't? He'd caught sight of her in the windows of the house, quiet and pale and moving slowly, as if in pain. She'd lost a child. That was hard on a woman. He could understand that.

What he couldn't understand was why any man would have set her free.

She was beautiful. Probably the most beautiful woman he'd ever laid eyes on. She was delicate, refined and as fragile as those china dolls he'd seen in the store window in town. She was far too fine for the likes of him. *Why are you even looking at her, Hennessey?*

Because while he tried his best to make wise decisions, he made mistakes. And watching the owner's daughter out of the corner of his eye had to be the worst mistake a man like him could make.

''You're spookin' him, Ned.'' Dillon couldn't believe his eyes. What were the four men going to do?

They could toss all the rope in the county around that stud's neck, and it wouldn't do any good. They couldn't hold him.

The truth was, nothing could hold that horse.

Nothing except his loyalty. A stallion like that one decided if he'd trust a man or not. That was the secret to dealing with difficult animals. That, along with no small bit of kindness, did the trick.

It was a secret Ned didn't seem to know as he tossed the fat noose through the air. The hemp smacked the horse in the head.

With one great shake, the stallion knocked the rope aside. Another sailed through the air and he pivoted, a blend of shadow and substance, and fled.

"I got him! I got him!" Ned braced his stance and whipped the lasso tight.

"Hold on, Ned!" the hands advised.

This ought to be good. Dillon settled back to watch, wondering how long Ned would last. Thirty seconds at most. The stallion bunched up into a powerful jump that sent him sailing like Pegasus himself over the fence railing, hauling Ned into the fence with a crash.

Ned's groan of pain was followed by a long string of vile curses as the end of the rope sailed out of sight along with the horse. The stallion returned to his herd of mares and galloped for the foothills of the Big Horn Range, until there was nothing but the faint drum of their hooves. Then nothing but wind and storm.

"You stood there, you lazy cuss!" Ned moaned, finding his feet and swiping the snow from his backside. "If you would've helped, I could've held him."

"You said to let the real cowboys handle it, and I

did.'' That comment only made Ned mad, but Dillon didn't care. He ignored the ranch hand's tirade.

What Dillon *did* care about was the stallion. He was a runaway, was he? From this ranch? Interesting. Dillon figured he'd find out about the reward. And why the stallion had returned to this spread.

A mare's nicker sounded from inside the stable, lifting on the rising wind, and it was a sad and lonely sound.

A female. It always came down to that. When she was special, what was a poor male to do?

Suffer, that's what. Dillon glanced over his shoulder to the shadows near the far fence. She was gone. There was only shadow and a thin blanket of snow. Fat flakes tumbled relentlessly, covering over her footprints.

Dillon stared down at the imprints. Small and delicate.

Just like her.

Warmth filled him. It was a strange thing. A dangerous reaction.

He was lonely. He wanted a wife. But there was no chance in hell that beautiful Katelyn Green would want a man like him.

Yep, he knew when to draw and when to fold. He stood in the storm a long while with the snow falling all around him and thought of her, as elusive as that stallion in the night.

And twice as unreachable.

Chapter Two

Katelyn carried her morning cup of tea to the dining-room window to watch the snow fall. Peace. It covered the landscape in a blanket of white, the gentle rolling whiteness covering up the mud and dirt and the season's dead grasses, making the world new and beautiful. Heavy ice-gray clouds hung low on the horizon, masking the proud peaks of the Rocky Mountains on one side and the Big Horn Range on the other.

With the snow falling, it felt as if the sky was so close to the ground that if she went outside, she could almost touch heaven. Wishful thinking, she knew, but it remained a hard longing within her. Probably because she wanted to escape this house and this pain.

"I told you, hot tea in the mornings. *Hot,* not tepid. This is entirely unacceptable." There was a clatter from upstairs and an angry tap of shoes on the staircase that echoed through the downstairs room.

It didn't sound as if Mother was in a good mood this morning. Katelyn cradled her teacup in her hand and hobbled to the kitchen. She was still too tender to hurry, but she ignored the shooting pain that radiated from her midsection as the beat of Mother's angry footsteps knelled closer. Thankfully the kitchen doors swung shut behind her a second before Mother entered the dining room.

"She's in a mood this morning." Effie stirred scrambled eggs on the stove. "I don't blame ya for wanting away from her. Stay here with me, and I'll give you the best bits of bacon I saved. With all you've been through, you need to eat. Else how do you expect to gain back your health?"

"Just the tea for now, thanks." Katelyn brushed a kiss along the older woman's cheek. Effie Kerr had been a fixture in this kitchen for as long as she could remember and more kindly to her than her own mother could dream of being. "I'm too upset to eat."

"And little wonder, with the way they was carryin' on, as if you'd done somethin' bad." Effie put down her wooden spoon to brush a handful of blond locks from Katelyn's face. "That husband they made you marry is the bad one. Everyone knows it. Never heard of such a thing, undoing the marriage the way he did. Suppose he knows how to do it, but it ain't right if you ask me."

"Don't work yourself up, Effie." Katelyn caught the older woman's callused hands in her own and gave a squeeze. "I wasn't happy being a wife to that man."

"I should think not." She returned to the stove, shuffling like a woman far older than her years, her back beginning to stoop. Her sadness was as palpable as the heat radiating from the stove.

Losing her son had been hard on her. Katelyn recalled how Old Pete Kerr had wanted to kill the stallion, and remembering that majestic creature made her breath catch. He'd been remarkable, like poetry moving in the darkness, something bold and beautiful and striking like William Blake would have written, a wild animal burning in the night.

"Sit down, child, and finish that tea if nothing else." Effie pulled out a chair at the small table in the corner. "Maybe some of my biscuits fresh out of the oven will tempt that appetite of yours."

"They smell good." Katelyn obliged, grateful to rest in the comfortable chair. The cushion was soft, and the view remarkable. She leaned her elbows on the edge of the table, since there was no one to reprimand her, and stared out at the world of white.

If only the world could stay like this, comfortable in a cold layer of snow, and made new every morning. Although she knew the temperatures were bitter outside, sitting with her back to the stove and tea warming her up was the most pleasure she'd felt during the years she'd been married to the county's most respected judge.

She shivered, remembering Brett. Her stomach coiled into a tight ball and the peaceful moment was ruined. Breathing in the sweet spicy tea, she tried to banish thoughts of him from her mind. She needn't think about him or any man ever again.

She was better without a husband. Without a ring on her finger. Safer.

"It's good to see you feeling better, dear. To have you up and about." Effie slid a covered basket onto the edge of the table. "Don't be afraid to eat them all. Go on, now."

The warm yeasty scent of fresh roll with melted butter, sugar and cinnamon made Katelyn's mouth water. Her stomach growled in anticipation. "Maybe just one."

"Thata girl." Satisfied, the cook ambled away. The bang of pans against the stove filled the kitchen with a merry sound.

Katelyn took one sticky roll from the basket and tore off a bite-sized morsel with her fingers. The gooey icing reminded her of when she was a little girl, sitting at this same table and unrolling the coiled cinnamon roll so it was one long strip of sweetness.

Something stirred in the white downfall outside and distracted her. She absently placed a bit of roll in her mouth and chewed, squinting through the smudged windowpanes. All she could see was the steady cascade of snow falling like rain outside, obscuring the mountains and the plains, giving her only a view of the yard directly outside the window.

There it was again. She held her breath as a blur of dark color moved closer. A deer, perhaps? An elk? Or what if it was a moose? She'd missed the wildlife coming to visit, living in town for so long. At least that was one blessing. She'd grab her coat, head straight to the barn and snatch a bag of grain. Maybe the animals would come close enough so she could watch them eat.

But it wasn't a deer or an elk or even a moose that broke through the veil of snow and into her sight. It was Dillon Hennessey riding a big black-and-white mustang. Sitting tall and straight in the saddle, he looked rugged and as invincible as a warrior of old. As if nothing could defeat or diminish him.

A strange tingle began at her nape and slid down her spine. What kind of man was Dillon Hennessey? Why did she want to know? She didn't like men. She wasn't interested in them. Not after what she'd been through.

So, why couldn't she tear her eyes from him? Why did that tingle in her spine strengthen when he rode so close to the window?

He was dressed well for the weather, and she couldn't see his face. Couldn't see anything more of him than she had last night in the dark. But the wide cut of his coat suggested a man of muscle and strength. The shadowed profile hinted at a man hard as stone.

She shivered. He was probably a harsh man. Weren't they all? Stronger than a woman, and he was probably the worst, breaking horses with whips and spurs and cruelty.

The image of Brett's raised fist flashed into her mind and she shook harder, willing it away. She was safe from him here. Whatever happened to her now would not be as bad as being married to that man.

She wrapped her hands around the teacup and lifted it to her lips. The dark liquid sloshed up to the rim but didn't spill. She took a deep breath. She had to relax. She didn't need to be so jumpy. She was safe, remember?

She felt something, a strange sensation like the brush of a feather against the side of her face. She snapped her head up. There, on the other side of the glass, the horseman was staring at her. He'd turned in the saddle, his face shadowed by the brim of his hat, and in the storm all she saw was his dark blue gaze, compelling and calm, before the snowfall swallowed him whole. Leaving her watching the flakes tumbling past the window and with a strange quickening in her chest.

"Effie, do you know anything about that new man?"

"The wrangler?" The wooden spoon scraped on the steel fry pan. "Came in about a month ago. Your stepfather brought him in to work with his new mares. Dillon Hennessey's supposed to be the best. There ain't a horse he can't break."

"How unlucky for the horses." Her stomach tightened and she stared at the roll. She was no longer hungry.

"Horses aren't useful for much if they can't pull a buggy." Effie dropped the empty pan on the counter, untroubled by the clatter, and rescued the sizzling bacon from the heat. "I hear he comes up from Texas way, but worked in Wyoming for a spell. Been all around. California. Colorado. New Mexico. He always comes back to Montana. Folks say this here territory is his home."

"I thought you said he was from Texas?"

"I don't rightly know. He isn't given to talk much, and you know my Pete is as deaf as a turnip. Can't hear anything right, so that's probably what he *thinks* he heard about Hennessey. Haven't spoken to the man myself. He keeps to his own."

A loner. A drifter. Katelyn remembered how he'd stood apart from the men last night, and it hadn't only been the distance between the others that separated them and made him distinct, as if he were above those other men.

And yet how could he be? He was no different, being a wrangler, a man who wore spurs and dominated wherever he could, and at whatever cost. Like any man.

"Eat up, girl, you haven't eaten enough to keep a bird alive." Effie thrust a plate of bacon and eggs onto the table.

Katelyn wrinkled her nose. "I'm not hungry."

"It doesn't matter. Eat. Or there will be hell to pay." Effie's stern words were forceful enough to echo in the small kitchen, but her eyes shone with kindness.

Hers was the only caring Katelyn had known since she'd been a little girl. Grateful, she lifted the fork off the edge of the plate. For Effie, she'd do her best, even if her stomach felt as if it were tied into a hundred knots.

Effie's attention drifted to the window. "Was there any reason you wanted to know about Dillon Hennessey?"

Was it Katelyn's imagination, or did Effie sound unusually pleased? "It was idle curiosity. So much has changed since I've been gone."

"True. You were married how long?"

Effie knew full well how long. "Five years. A lot has changed. I wondered if my stepfather has been any more successful in keeping his hired men."

"Not a bit. If Pete wasn't your mama's cousin, we'd be long gone ourselves. Cal Willman is a tough man to work for, I'll grant you that. A man like Hennessey, he's a drifter. He moves from ranch to ranch. Gets paid well, I hear. We had a year and a half wait for him, he's got that much work. That ought to say something good about him, wouldn't you say?''

''I suppose.'' Katelyn stared at the eggs in front of her. She never should have asked a single question about the horseman.

Effie snatched the pot from the counter, moving casually, but there was nothing the woman did without purpose. ''He's pleasing to the eye, wouldn't you say? A woman can't help but notice Dillon Hennessey's about as tough as a mountain and good-looking to boot.''

''I hadn't noticed.''

''You are a terrible liar, dear heart.'' Effie sounded as pleased as a new mother as she tipped the pot, warming up Katelyn's cup. ''Even at my age, a handsome man still catches my eye. He's not truly handsome, though, is he? Rugged. Striking. That describes him better. He looks like a man who could protect a woman from any threat. Any danger. Now *that's* what a woman needs in a husband.''

Katelyn groaned. ''Stop, please. I've had one husband. I will never want another.''

''But whatever will become of you?'' Effie set the pot on the table and drew up a chair. The sharp scrape of the wooden legs against the floor came as harsh as the fear on the woman's face. ''I've heard what they've been saying, the two of them, when they think no one can hear. They intend to find a situation for you, and it won't be a pleasant one.''

''I don't need them to find anything for me. As soon as I'm well, I can leave.''

''What if they ain't planning to wait that long? And

where would you go? This is a cruel world for a woman alone."

"It can be a cruel world for a married woman."

"No, only if the woman marries the wrong kind of man. I promise you, you could do much worse than Dillon Hennessey."

"What? Effie, I asked you to stop. I can't stand it." She laid down her fork and rested her aching head in her hands. She was still weak from one man's beating. Did Effie think that she couldn't wait to give control of her life to another man?

"There, there." The cook's hand lit on Katelyn's shoulder blade, a gentle, comforting touch. "Didn't mean to overset you. But keep in mind, you need a situation better'n the one your stepfather will find for you. The best way to get out of here is to marry a man of your own choice. One that'll treat you good, the way you deserve."

"Oh, Effie." Tears burned behind her eyes, blurring her vision, and Katelyn blinked hard, refusing to let them fall. What would she do without Effie? She'd be all alone. Utterly, completely alone. "The food will get cold. You'd best go. You know how my mother gets."

"Well, I do." With a dramatic roll of her eyes and a heaving sigh, Effie hauled her bulk from the chair. "Now you think on what I said. Mr. Hennessey has never married, at least that's what they tell me. At his age, a man wants to be settled and have sons to pass on his wisdom to."

With a smile of approval, Effie hustled from the room, snatching two platters of food on her way out.

I can't give him sons. Effie knew that. *Everyone*

did. Hadn't it been the topic of gossip around the ranch for the past month? The doctor had told her she couldn't give any man a child. Not that she wanted the horseman—she never wanted to be at a man's mercy again—but the fact that she would always be completely alone without a child, without a family, hurt like a mortal wound.

She opened her eyes. There was no use in spending the morning in sorrow. Sadness couldn't change the past. Nothing could. The only course open to her was to move forward. To make what she could of today and of the solitary future ahead of her.

Resolved, she stirred the tip of her fork through the fluffy scrambled eggs. They'd tasted delicious, for Effie was a remarkable cook, but she wasn't hungry. How could she be? She felt dead inside and nothing, especially a plate of food, was going to change that.

But food *would* help her regain her strength. She wanted out of this house more than anything. Determined, she took a bite of eggs and chewed, even as her stomach recoiled. She fought to swallow and keep it down.

When she was done, she sipped her tea and watched the snow fall. Now and then she thought she saw a movement in the relentless shower of white, a dark shadow, *his* shadow.

But she was wrong. There was no formidable man riding through the storm like a legend born.

Why was she thinking about him again?

She didn't need another man in her life. What she wanted was to be left alone.

She rubbed the space on her fourth finger, where a slight indentation was the only reminder that she'd worn a ring. That she'd made vows to honor and cherish and obey. What a mistake that had been. A mistake she would never make again.

She drained the last drop of tea from her cup and set it down with a clink. She was stronger today. Better.

Maybe she'd go spread some grain in the field. That should draw out any animals, and then she could enjoy the peaceful sight of the beautiful creatures. Perhaps the serenity of it would ease some of the ache from her soul.

And keep Dillon Hennessey from her thoughts.

As he had expected, with the snow falling hard and heavy, Dillon saw no further sign of the stallion. Still, he'd had to try. A true horseman couldn't let a stud like that slip out of his fingers.

Something told him that the horse would return. So, he may as well head back and grab a hot cup of coffee from the stove in the bunkhouse. That sounded mighty good, seeing as how he was frozen clear through.

It was hard to give up the hunt. Hard to nose his gelding toward home and turn his back on the chance of finding that stallion. What a magnificent animal. He couldn't forget him, the same way he couldn't forget the woman, Katelyn Green.

How could he? She'd looked like an angel come to earth this morning, framed by the window and brushed with a golden radiance by the lamplight. She was beyond beautiful. She looked like goodness in a woman's form, with that softly spun blond hair she wore down so it cascaded around her heart-shaped face. A face dominated by eyes a rare, exotic blue, a small, delicate nose and a mouth so perfect it would shame every rosebud in existence.

If he closed his eyes, looked deep into his being and pulled out his vision of the perfect woman, it would be Katelyn Green. He'd never seen anyone like her, and it wasn't her beauty that drew him. That was the plain truth.

It was something else. Something about her, and her alone. He didn't know what it was, and he wasn't a man who was good with words or feelings, but he did know people, the same way he knew animals. When he'd locked gazes with Miss Green through the snow this morning, he'd seen the quiet gentleness inside her. Rare, indeed.

Back on the acreage he owned next door to his brother, he had a mare like her with big scared eyes and it had taken nearly two whole years of work before she'd let him stroke her neck without flinching.

Not that a woman was like a horse, but it was horses he knew and not women. Yep, women were pretty much a mystery to him. His ma had died when he was a small boy. He had no recollection of her, and that left only his pa and his five brothers. Pa had never remarried, never tried to replace the love of his life, and so there was no woman's influence in Dillon's life as a boy.

And as a man, he was bewildered to think about beauing one of those pretty creatures in soft dresses that swept the floor whenever they walked, giving the impression their dainty feet did not touch the ground like mortals. Women were different entirely and far too fine for the likes of him.

Even if he could catch a lady's attention, what would he do then? He wasn't given to fancy language and insincere flattery to make a woman like him. Hell, it would probably take more than a mountain of flattery to do that. Even if he could manage to speak instead of remain tongue-tied, what would he say? He wasn't citified and he wasn't educated. The only thing he knew was horses and horse breeding.

He couldn't imagine walking up to Katelyn Green and asking her opinion on which stud should service the thoroughbred mare that was coming in heat.

The same mare the wild stallion had wanted last night when Katelyn Green had been out wandering in the dark in her slippers and housecoat, her hair down and unbound and billowing around her in the wind and snow. He wanted to know what she'd been doing. And why, when she was infirm, was she up, limping in obvious pain?

He had little doubt her parents had no compassion to spare. Cal Willman's hard countenance and heartless manner told Dillon all he needed to know. He'd met a hundred rich men just like him over the years, and they were all the same. Every last one of them. Ruthless and cruel, men who cared only about themselves.

As for the wife, she was as harsh as a Montana blizzard. It was clear in the way she ignored her own daughter.

Dillon wished he knew what had happened. He couldn't help feeling sorry for Katelyn. He didn't seem able to stop wondering about her. Maybe he'd round up enough courage to ask one of the hands what had happened to return her childless and wounded to her parent's home and what would become of her next.

Not that he had a chance, but he *was* a man. He noticed a pretty, available woman. He was lonelier than he wanted to admit. He'd been wanting to get married for a long time, but he'd never been able to talk to a lady, much less court her.

That proved a terrible problem. He had a house he didn't live in. A bed he didn't sleep in. A life he didn't live because he had no one to share it. He would give anything for a kind, gentle wife to call his own.

He would give his soul and more to marry a woman like Katelyn Green.

But even if she was recovered from her loss, she'd hardly glanced at him. He'd lay down good money that she didn't know his name. And if she did, what could come of it? He would be gone in a few weeks, when his work here was done.

The new stallion—a pale comparison to the magnificent black stallion—was progressing fine. And the problem mares were responding to him. They'd come around soon. His work here would be done and he would leave, as he always did, with a pocket full of cash, heading in the direction of the next ranch in need of him.

He didn't like the notion of leaving at month's end. Not that he was fond of the place. The truth was, he couldn't stand Cal Willman or his wife. What he would miss, even more than the horses here, was the pretty blond woman who made him very aware of being all man.

Was it his imagination, or did he hear something?

A female's voice lilted on the wind as sweet as a song. "That's it, don't be afraid. Come closer. I won't hurt you. I promise."

That *had* to be Katelyn. Who else could it be? Not Effie, the cook—the tone and cadence were too soft for her. Not Mrs. Willman, who talked with enough venom to poison a rattler. Not the housemaids, for both were Chinese and spoke very little English.

"That's right. See? You're perfectly safe."

Katelyn had to be just beyond that rise. Ten yards away. He jerked the horse to a stop and ignored the gelding's protest. Normally he was steady with his horse, trustworthy and calm, but the thought of seeing Katelyn Green was enough to make him break out in a cold sweat.

She was here alone. What should he do? He could keep on riding and wave at her as he went by. Or he could stop and talk with her. Hmm, that could work. But what would he say? The thought made his throat close shut. His tongue had become paralyzed and wouldn't work. Dang his shyness.

He could picture the impending disaster. He'd ride on up to her, stop his horse, brace his fist on the saddle the way he'd seen other men do to look tough, and stutter and stammer like a fool.

Wouldn't that impress her?

A rugged man like him shouldn't be shy. He ought to be bold. Be brave. He should talk to her the way he talked to anyone.

He was tough. He'd faced down killer stallions and an attacking cougar. He'd been kicked, bit, stepped on, bucked off, crushed against fences and thrown to the ground more times than there were numbers to count with. He was one of the best at what he did.

A pretty, delicate little woman shouldn't terrify him.

You can do it, Hennessey. Just ride on up to her and smile. Then say howdy.

The wind seemed colder as he pressed the gelding into a fast walk. The ground was too uncertain and the snow too deep for anything faster, but if he could, he'd gallop full tilt past the beautiful woman and never think of her again.

She came into view as he rode over the rise. He eased the gelding to a halt at the crest, gazing down the gently sloping field of white to the slim woman wearing a dark blue cloak, buttoned tight from ankle to throat. A small feed pail dangled from her left hand.

What a sight. Joy filled him. Snow dappled her like a Christmas angel, clinging to the woolen cap and the rippling sheen of golden hair flowing down her back. White flakes hugged the delicate line of her shoulders and the rise of her breasts. Snow clung to the curve of her waist and hips and caked the long hem of her cloak, a womanly shape of grace and loveliness that made his chest tight. Awe swept over him, sweet as a morning breeze.

Just then came the slightest movement in a grove of trees tucked into the lee of the slope. A predator? God knows cougars didn't like to hunt in the snow. Dillon *had* spied cat tracks a half mile to the north. They preferred their warm dens on days like this, but that didn't mean, if a lone cat was hungry enough, he wouldn't go in search of a meal.

And that meal wouldn't be Katelyn. She was all alone out here, unprotected. With that pail on her arm, she was probably putting out feed for the birds and unaware of the danger stalking her.

Fierce protectiveness surged through him, spilling hot in his blood. Careful not to make a sound, he eased the Winchester from its holster and covered the cocking action with his free hand to hide the chink of metal. A cat would hear it and bolt, and that was unacceptable. There was a threat to Katelyn Green and, damn it, Dillon Hennessey *would* stop it.

He held the rifle steady, aiming just at the edge of the trees, anticipating that first glimpse of a shadow. He hugged the trigger, ready and alert, as the shadow nosed toward Katelyn.

It wasn't the fast strike of a cougar. Dillon took a breath, waiting, as Katelyn's melodic voice lifted up to him on the wind.

"That's it. See? No one's going to hurt you. You're safe. Come closer. That's right."

Sweet as a hymn. She could coax the wildness out of a cougar, he figured, with a voice like that. It wasn't just the voice—it was her, the goodness in her, the heart of her. He could see it as plain as the woman and she waited while the first doe broke from her cover and eased forward to eat the grain Katelyn had spread on the ground. Grain, not birdseed.

Dillon couldn't believe it. The wild deer came right up to her. Two smaller animals joined her—yearling fawns, he figured, judging by their size and markings. Young, not fully grown. They, too, scented the air, considered Katelyn standing as still as a statue and bent their dainty heads.

Shrouded in snow, like poetry and fairy tale, the woman watched the delicate creatures eat. The wind gusted, ruffling Katelyn's long gold locks against her back, caressing the curled ends like a lover's fingers.

What would it be like to touch her hair? Dillon lowered the rifle, thunderstruck by the notion. He imagined lowering his fingertips to that lustrous fall of gold, and he knew she would feel as soft and fine as silk, the fancy kind in the stores only the rich could buy. She would be like that, and satin everywhere....

Whoa, now, that was not a respectful thought. He took a deep breath, banishing further inclinations from his mind. He was a man and he couldn't help desiring her, but that didn't mean he ought to give those thoughts free rein. He had no right to look upon her like that. She was not his wife.

She never would be.

No, she'd find herself courted by one of the rich dandies in town. The kind with an enormous house on Elm Street, the finest lane with the fanciest homes. The sort of man who sat inside all day, didn't wear Levi's and smell of horses and leather. The sort that sipped brandy after dinner in the parlor.

Not the kind of man who drank a pint of ale in the bunkhouse.

It saddened him. If he had a dream, then it would be Katelyn Green.

Chapter Three

Dillon couldn't talk to her. The tightness was working its way up from his chest into his throat. By the time he made it to her side, the tightness would have worked its way up to his paralyzed tongue, and there would be no way in hell he could make an intelligible sound.

He'd be best to keep quiet, turn the horse around and ride the long way back before he made an embarrassment of himself.

The saddle creaked as he shifted his weight to draw the gelding around, and the sound traveled like thunder above the whisper of the falling snow.

Katelyn jerked in his direction, her eyes wide with the same surprise and fear as the deer, frozen, ears pricked, heads high, scenting him. Woman and animals stared as if he were evil incarnate.

Katelyn Green's gaze scorched him like blue flame. "What do you think you're doing?"

She sure sounded mad. She looked it, too. Dillon's mouth opened, but nothing came out. And it was a good thing, too, since he didn't know what to say anyway. Did he apologize for intruding? Was that why she was so angry?

"How could you? What kind of man are you?" She marched toward him, pure fury, and he had no notion what he'd done.

"I, uh…" *Damn it, Hennessey. You can do better than that.* "I'm, uh, sure am s-sorry, ma'am."

"Sorry? For trying to kill the deer when I was feeding them? What did you think? That I wouldn't mind if you just started shooting?"

"No, uh—" Dang it all, but he was tongue-tied. She flustered him worse than any woman ever had, the way she was flying up the hill toward him, focused anger and indignation.

She was pure beauty, with her face pinkened from the cold and high emotion, her small fists clenched, her hair flowing out behind her like a mare in full gallop. The passion in her showed.

No wonder he was speechless.

Then he realized he was holding the rifle still aimed in the direction of her deer, which had already fled into the trees and disappeared. There was only the two of them, and, flushing, he eased the hammer back and slid the weapon into its leather casing. "S-sorry about that, ma'am."

"You're sorry?" She looked ready to hurl sharp objects at his head. Good thing there weren't any handy. "You ought to be ashamed of yourself, taking advantage like that. You're a man. I guess I shouldn't be surprised—"

He knew what she thought. "You're wrong, ma'am. I s-saw some cat tracks back a ways and thought…" He couldn't find the right word. What the hell was he going to say? She lifted her chin, staring at him expectantly with those fiery blue eyes accusing him of being the worst sort of man, and he just couldn't think.

"I, uh, didn't want to see you get hurt, ma'am," he finished, but it wasn't what he intended to say.

Had she noticed? All that stammering *had* to make him look bad.

"A cougar?" She seemed to be debating whether or not he was telling the truth.

Well, that was progress. Leastways she wasn't ready to give him a lashing. And she wasn't staring up at him like he was a stammering numbskull. That had to be a good sign. He sat straighter in the saddle.

"I'm Dillon Hennessey. I'm the horse trainer your stepfather brought in." He tipped his hat.

White tumbled down his face and fell in a heap on his lap. Damn. He should have knocked the snow off *before* he tried making advances at the pretty lady. Had she noticed?

Sure she had. Her top teeth dug into her lush bottom lip to keep from laughing, and her eyes crinkled at the corners with amusement.

He withered a little inside. He'd acted like this before with women, but not in front of one that mattered so much. If he didn't get over this blasted shyness, he would never find a wife. Never have a family of his own.

"Well, thank you for protecting me." She was trying to be polite. A different light sparkled in those blue depths and the sadness in them, the pervasive sorrow he'd noticed before, had ebbed. "I'll just fetch the feed pail and head home. I wouldn't want to be cougar food.''

''Guess you probably don't need to worry about that. Seein' as you'd be too sweet for 'em.'' Good job, Hennessey. He moaned internally at the words that just popped out of his mouth.

He had *not* said what he just said. He would never say anything as ridiculous as that. Right? If he tried hard enough, maybe he could forget he'd said it.

First he couldn't speak, now he couldn't shut up. He might as well have said, *I'm sure interested in you, Katelyn Green.* It would have left him with more dignity.

''I mean, I'll keep watch as long as you're out here.'' He cleared his throat, trying to sound gruff, because he was a fearless rugged man, raised in the wilderness, half Nez Percé and a warrior.

She picked up her feed pail and brushed a lock of gold behind her ear, looking up at him through her thick lashes. ''Then I guess I should apologize for being angry at you. I saw the gun and thought the worst. I'm sorry.''

She lifted her face, and in the soft daylight he could see plain as day the faint impression of a bruise on her far cheekbone the size of a man's fist. The wind ruffled her hair and a thick shank of hair fell forward, hiding the mark.

Rage came to life in his chest. Hot and hard, like a kerosene fire until it threatened to burn out of control. His jaw clamped tight. His hands fisted. If the man she'd been married to was here right now, Dillon would be glad to teach him a lesson.

"I should be getting back." She turned, avoiding his gaze, letting him know she wasn't interested.

She walked away into the veil of falling snow. He couldn't stand it, the way she was leaving like that.

"The deer must like you," he called out, and grimaced. If he kept this up, she'd simply run away from him and his terrible attempts to talk with her. "I mean, it's rare for them to come up to a person."

Katelyn glanced over her shoulder, considered him, but kept walking.

"My grandfather could do that. Deer would approach him."

Why did he keep trying to talk to her? Katelyn wondered. She kept walking, limping, because the pain was still with her. She felt the horseman's eyes on her back like a touch.

"He had a way with animals."

Had he taken a sparking to her? Katelyn turned toward him at the same moment he shrugged one big, snow-lined shoulder, and a row of snow tumbled off that broad perch to startle his horse. The mustang sidestepped, startling the rider.

"Whoa, boy." Instead of sounding irritated or angry, the wrangler's voice rumbled low and as warm as buttered rum. He stroked his sizable hand down the gelding's neck, a gentle gesture for so powerful a man.

Katelyn shivered, wondering if his touch was as tender as it looked. But she knew there were no heroes made of honor and strength and tenderness in this cold, hard world.

Dillon Hennessey might be strong and seemingly kind and a little awkward when it came to speaking to a woman, but he was still a man and, like the cougar prowling these prairies, he would strike when he wished. He was more ruthless at heart. It was simply his nature.

Or was it? Every time she glanced over her shoulder, there was the outline of the man on his proud mustang, waiting on the crest of the rise, watching as the storm droned on, the rifle at his shoulder, ready but not threatening.

A protective warrior who remained steadfast and vigilant as she ambled carefully through the deepening snow.

Katelyn may not have had much time with the deer, but a quandary had been solved. At least she knew more about Dillon Hennessey. Remembering how he'd stammered and looked lost, that giant mountain of a man, made her smile.

She lifted the latch to the front gate. She was home, for now. When she turned to wave a thank-you to him, she saw only snow and wind and prairie.

The horseman had gone.

His image remained throughout the day and into the evening as twilight came early. After a slow bleeding of the sun, and the gray shadows had wrung all the light from the sky, darkness descended. Katelyn kept to her room with a single candle lit. She took supper on a tray but could not eat. She hadn't been hungry in so long.

There was so much to consider, so much to think about. Fear nibbled at the corners of her courage, and she eased out of the chair in the corner and lifted the rug at the foot of the bed. There, beneath the floorboard she'd loosened, was her future. She unwrapped the cloth bundle carefully, cradling it in her hand. Even in the faint light from a single candle, the diamonds flashed and sparkled. The cold, multifaceted gemstones were framed in the gold of a necklace and two rings, gifts from her wealthy husband to his beloved wife.

Or, that's what he told others at the dinner parties where he pretended to others that he was a fine, loving husband. And she could not tell the truth.

She hated every one of those stones. The wedding ring, the anniversary ring, the necklace he'd given her when she first learned she was pregnant and could be carrying his son.

Tears flooded her eyes and she willed them not to fall. The diamonds blurred into a rainbow glitter of pure, white light as she covered the jewelry, secured it well and tucked it back into its dark safe hiding place. As much as she hated the gems, they would buy her future. She planned to sell each piece and take pleasure in the knowledge that Brett couldn't touch her, that she didn't need him.

She didn't need anyone.

She would make a new life. Alone. The way she wanted it to be.

"Katelyn?" Her stepfather's voice on the other side of the door sounded harsh.

She dropped the edge of the fringed rug and stood, pain shooting through her as the door hinges whispered open, but it wasn't fast enough. Cal Willman stood in the doorway, his cold eyes narrowed, his mouth pursed in thought. Or in calculation.

How much had he seen? She would have to find

another hiding place, just in case. Her stepfather was the kind of man who took what he wanted. He was a big man, imposing, taller than the horseman, but all brute, and she shivered. She felt small and vulnerable, and she hated feeling so ill. Another week to recover and she would be gone, slipping off into the night as if she'd never been. She never need see him again.

"Is there some good reason for bursting in on me?" she said quietly.

"This is my house."

"That may be, but you have no right entering my bedroom without knocking first."

"My name is on the deed. I will go wherever I wish."

"Yes, but my father built this house with his own hands. I watched him lay every board and hammer every nail." Her father had been a good man, at least he'd been good to her, and thinking of him brought up a faint memory, as it always did, of a tall, brawny man with a broad-rimmed hat shading his face as he worked in the sun, talking with her while he'd built their home. She'd been five. "Is Mother unwell?"

"Your mother has not been well since you knocked on our door and collapsed on the parlor floor. It wasn't as if we could take you back. I saw you walking around today. If you're well enough to walk in the field and try your wiles with one of my hired men, you're strong enough to get the hell out of this house."

"You think I want another man after all I've been through?"

"Isn't that what all you women want? A man to pay for every little thing?" The muscles in his jaw jumped and bunched beneath his smooth-shaven skin. "If it's a man you want, I will find you one."

"I have no need for a husband."

"And I have no need for you. Understand this. If you bring more shame to my family name, I will make you regret the day you crawled back to this house. Do you understand me?"

"It's not my shameful behavior you need to be concerned with." She spoke quietly but with steel. She'd not be bullied in the house her father built.

Cal's hard blue eyes iced over, like a pond in winter. Hands fists, feet braced, jaw tensed so tight he could break teeth, a cold anger took him over. "I'll not be judged in my own house, missy. Remember that, or you will be out on your backside faster than you'll know what hit you."

She wasn't welcome here. How could she be? She was in the middle of their constant fighting. She was a sore reminder of the family name being soiled.

"This shocking scandal has cost me half the business at the bank. How will you make it up to me, I wonder?"

He'd figured out she had something to hide. Something of value. The brief flicker of satisfaction at his severe mouth told her to beware.

He'd demanded whatever money she had on her when she arrived, broken and homeless. She'd lied about the jewels, carefully hidden in her smallest skirt pocket.

She'd find a better hiding place than the floorboard, that was for sure. Those three pieces of jewelry might not be worth thousands, but they were valuable enough to buy her the chance to start a new existence somewhere else now that she was regaining her strength.

Cal stormed from the room. The candle's flame flickered in the wake of the slamming door, and snuffed out.

She stood in darkness, lost, so very lost. Outside the window, the first glow of star shine misted on the frozen sheen of snow. The silvered light drew her toward the frosty panes. There was the horseman, sitting tall in his saddle, one hand on the saddle horn, holding the reins, the other resting on his thigh. He was a formidable shadow against the velvet-black sky and glittering gray meadows, like all that was good in the world.

He's a man, Katelyn. Don't be fooled by appearances. All men are the same within.

And yet he still made her breath catch and her pulse skip through her veins. He drew his horse to a halt at the paddock gate and seemed to be peering at her bedroom window. Instead of a prickle of fear, a jolt of heat arrowed through her, like lightning striking from sky to earth. Could he see her, even through the darkness? Was he watching her?

It was as if the entire world silenced. The anger at her stepfather faded. Why did it feel as if there were only the two of them, and no one else, in existence? And how, when she could not even see his face?

Seconds passed, and they beat within her as the shadowed man looked in her direction, and she in his. What was this strange tingle in the center of her chest? And why were her palms damp from heat, not fear?

He agitated her, that was true, and drew her like a

falling star to the ground. Her feet shifted, moving her toward the window. She clutched the cool sill and watched as he lifted one strong arm to tip his hat, a polite countryman's greeting, before he nudged his mount from the edge of the fence and rode off. Back straight, shoulders proud, becoming one with the night.

The bond between them snapped, and Katelyn's senses filled again with the world around her. The icy draft from the windowpanes, the scent of hot candle wax and the sharp voices arguing in the other side of the house. A booming crack told her the argument had become violent.

What was it with men, that they had to be in control? In charge of his own castle, as Brett used to say. And what did that make the women they married, the women they courted so gallantly to wed before God with vows to cherish? The horseman, despite his shyness earlier and the mythical look of him this night, could be no different. He wore spurs, didn't he? He broke horses' spirits with lashes from a whip.

Disappointed in him, she sank into the wooden cane rocker in the corner. The book she'd been reading slipped to the floor with a thud, but it was hardly audible over the voices rising and the sound of violence piercing the walls. *This* was marriage. Most of the marriages she'd seen, including her own.

She buried her face in her hands. She would *not* remember. She would not allow her thoughts to drift backward. Agony twisted through her, braiding her into a tight, hard knot until she couldn't feel anything. Not one thing. It was better this way, not to feel.

When she lifted her face, she saw him through the

window. This time he was a distant figure, a man and his horse, small against the great steeple of the sky but not insignificant. He rode tall and straight in his saddle. He looked as if nothing could scare him, as if he were in authority above all living things on the plains. She felt the charge of it like the burn of a fire to her fingertips. Like a flame reborn on the blackened end of a snubbed-out wick.

What was it about this man? She was no longer a schoolgirl, wishing for the magic of a man falling in love with her. It made her feel old and disillusioned to remember how once she'd melted and sighed in hope that a man might truly love her. A fine, wealthy man like Brett Green, with the finest set of high-stepping bays in the county. A man who had treated her with respect, courted her with gentle words and romantic intentions, and who had proposed to her with a bright sparkling diamond when her other girl-friends wore plain gold bands.

There was no romance. No gallantry. No man's love to gain in this world.

Bitterness soured her mouth and ached like a wire barb in her chest. Why did she still dare to hope? With a wrist wrapped in a splint and bruises fading from her face, with a barren womb and an obliterated heart? Why did she sigh when she gazed at the horse-man?

Because it was human nature, she supposed, to want to be loved and loved truly. No matter how severely Brett had hurt her and no matter how broken her heart, she wanted to believe that a great, worthy man existed. And that he could love her.

That she could be lovable.

The horseman drew her attention again. He'd come back. He was not alone.

Awe filled her as Dillon dismounted in a slow, smooth movement and, dropping the reins, stepped away from his mustang. The starlight revered him, blessing the bow of his head and honoring the gentle invitation of his opened palm.

The wild stallion eased out of the shadowed draw, bold head held high, ears pricked, tail high, every muscle poised for flight. The stardust shimmered along the glossy slope of neck, back and hindquarters, and the only movement was the wind flicking the long mane and buffeting the brim of Dillon's Stetson. Man and horse faced each other, both as still as statues.

She couldn't believe her eyes when the stallion moved. He lifted one powerful hoof and stepped forward, toward the still horseman. His hand remained extended in offering. Why wasn't the stallion running?

Katelyn's fingers had curled around the top rung of the paddock fence before she realized she was outside, the window open behind her and the bitter night's chill creeping through her flannel petticoats. She shivered, but she didn't care if the blood froze in her veins. She had to watch. She had to see what would happen.

The night around her waited as well. A hooting owl silenced, as if listening to the low, melodic rumble of the horseman's voice.

Rising now, slow and peaceful, the faintest strain of sounds she couldn't put into words. What was he saying? Whatever it was, it held the stallion transfixed, and she, too, was drawn by the masculine baritone and gentle sounds. She'd never heard the like of it. In his words tolled a tenderness, a respect as holy as the starlight, and Katelyn slid down the top rail and into the paddock. She was drawn to the horseman's voice just as the wild stallion was.

The animal nosed forward, stretching the magnificent length of his neck. The white mane lifted and fell in rhythm with the breeze, and his tightly coiled muscles trembled and flicked beneath his dappled coat. The Appaloosa leaned an inch toward Dillon's steady hand.

Katelyn's slipper crunched on a twig in the grass, and the crackle jerked through the stallion. She froze, but it was too late. The great animal pivoted, springing sideways as if under a cougar attack, already fleeing.

The horseman spoke, a cautious and interested sound, a combination of vowels Katelyn had never before heard. Whatever the meaning, the stallion halted, turning again to take the man's measure and listen to more of that soothing language.

As if he were unaware of her, as if he hadn't heard the crack of wood that had startled the animal, Dillon remained as he was, feet planted, spine straight, focused solely on the horse. He was like a strange, lone, rugged magician casting a spell that held captive the wild animal more completely than hobbles and a noose ever could.

What a man. She'd never seen the like. The gun at his belt remained untouched. The leather-gloved fingers of his free hand were not inching toward the lasso at his hip. He simply lured the stallion closer, not to catch him, but to know what it was like to be near him.

The Appaloosa took a wary step closer. Only a few feet separated man from beast. Both stood like legends cast in pewter and glazed by star shine.

The lure of Dillon's words was like sunrise after a cold, bleak night. A kind, gentle light she hungered for, when her defeated heart hurt with darkness. Her chest ached, as if a bullet had torn her apart. Deep and sharp and raw.

The sight of the wild stallion reaching out to the humble man made her want to reach out, too. She longed to place her hand in Dillon's open palm, to know the warmth of his touch and lose herself in the beauty, the gentleness. Could there be one man worthy enough to trust?

Come on, stallion, come closer. Please. He was almost there, a handful of inches from Dillon's bared fingertips. Cautious but mesmerized, the wild beauty stretched his long neck, closing the gap. His nostrils flared, inhaling the horseman's scent.

A crack thundered through the night, shattering the spell. The stallion streaked into motion, his neigh a sharp trumpet of fear and pain. A second gunshot thundered, resounding across the wide expanse of prairie as the Appaloosa took flight. Blood stained the white snow, leaving behind a gleaming trail.

He'd been shot. How badly? Katelyn's knees gave out and she fell to the ice-hardened snow. The impact rattled through her bones. Who would shoot such a beautiful creature?

"Damn it, Hennessey." Her stepfather's fury raged like a full-strength blizzard. "Why didn't you shoot that worthless piece of horsemeat while you were standing there? I couldn't believe my eyes. What were you going to do? Rope him first?''

Katelyn turned away, hiding her face. Had what she'd witnessed been real? Or had the horseman lured the stallion close just to capture him? Dillon wouldn't have harmed the animal, would he?

"I hadn't figured on roping him," the horseman answered.

Her stomach lurched. Horror lashed through her, sharp as the sting of a bullwhip across the span of her back. The horseman was not made of legend and moonlight. It had only been the glow of the starlight, nothing more, and her own fanciful imagination. A foolish imagination that still wanted her to find a good man to love.

Still. After all she'd been through, she ought to know by now no such man existed. Like a slap to her face, she felt the cold punch of air on her exposed skin, the cold burrowing in her bones. The ache of it in her joints as she knelt at the base of a scrawny cottonwood, as desolate as a night without stars.

"Then what's wrong with you?" Cal demanded. "Mount up, boys, he can't be far, not with that bullet I put in him. The first man to bring him down gets a five-hundred-dollar bonus."

"Paid with what?" Old Pete argued back, and several hands guffawed in agreement.

"In trade, if that's what you want." Cal's pompous tone fooled no one, least of all, her. Her stepfather's financial troubles had to be extensive.

His pride was more important, apparently, as his next words came from the direction of the stables.

''Saddle up my gelding, Ned. I want that problem eliminated. I'm sick and tired of that mongrel stud coming after my purebred mares.''

Katelyn watched in horror as the horseman wasted no time swinging into his saddle. Determination made him fierce as a warrior as tiny bits of snow sifted down like sorrow.

Hennessey looked neither right nor left as he sent his gelding soaring over the somber prairie, taking the last remaining shard of her innocence with him.

Chapter Four

Katelyn could not sleep. Restless, she tugged the counterpane over her head, blocking out the bold moonlight spilling through the gap in the curtains. Total darkness didn't help. She could still see the horseman mounting his mustang like an ancient warrior, armed and ready for battle.

Her stomach sickened. What was she doing lying here? She may as well get up and brew a pot of tea. Something soothing to help her relax.

But chamomile, she suspected, wouldn't keep Dillon Hennessey from her thoughts.

The kitchen was dark as a cave, and her nightgown rustled around her as she opened the belly of the stove and stirred the covered embers to life. They gleamed orange in protest as she added a handful of kindling. The snapping and popping told her the dry cedar had caught fire. She left the damper open and the door ajar, the strange growing light flashing and writhing as she located the ceramic teapot from the cabinets and dug through the crocks on the counter.

A reward for destroying the wild stallion. The rage

she felt burned to life like the flame inside the stove, stronger and brighter and all-consuming. Who could harm such a beautiful animal? In her mind's eye she could see the regal stallion, skin over taut muscles flickering with fear, daring to touch the horseman's extended hand.

How dare he trick the stallion? Katelyn slammed the tea ball on the counter, ignoring the echoing chink as she rummaged in the drawers for a spoon. If the horseman were here, she'd have a good mind to tell him exactly what she thought of him. Of him and his deception and his spurs and his guns and his vicious nature well hidden beneath his shyness and his quiet nature.

Oh, she could have a list of faults in the time it took for the water to heat. His faults, Brett's faults, her stepfather's faults, every man she'd ever met, in fact. They were all so pleased with their own power and in imposing it on others. Regardless of the cost. Regardless of who suffered and who died…

The dam broke, and her eyes burned. Her vision blurred. The crack of pain in the center of her chest sharpened and spread, like wood breaking one splinter at a time, then faster and faster until she was on the floor, sobbing so hard she couldn't breathe, couldn't see, choking on the grief set free. She was drowning in the sudden wave of it, sweeping her away, and she was dying, too.

Her arms were so empty. Her heart so empty. Her body, her soul, her life. All she wanted was the baby she loved. The round-faced little girl with the tuft of black hair and button nose and…

The back door squealed open on tired hinges. The

muted rap of a man's boots followed. Her stepfather! Katelyn swiped at her face with her sleeve, but the tears kept falling. She stood, fumbling to close the oven door and the only light in the kitchen faded.

But not fast enough. He was behind her in the threshold, bringing the cold breeze from the night with him. Chill radiated from him, and in the darkness she shivered, wiping at her face and clearing the tears from her throat.

"Just making some tea. I couldn't sleep."

She knocked over the lid of the crock. The clatter, as it rolled to a stop, wasn't loud enough to obliterate the sound of her broken breathing or the catch in her throat.

"I get like that sometimes," Dillon said. "Tea helps me to settle, too."

The kitchen was dark, but he didn't need light to see her.

Another clatter rang as she dropped the spoon on the floor. She gasped a brittle sound of distress as she knelt, her nightclothes whispering around her. She wore a nightgown with ruffles at the hem. He remembered seeing her last night. Of course she'd have ruffles. She was a dainty, high-quality lady. Probably had ruffles at the sleeves and collar, around the soft swell of her bosom.

Remembering his manners, he swept off his hat, holding it in one hand. "Smells like chamomile."

"Yes." Her back was to him, but she wasn't hiding a single thing from him.

He'd been a horseman all his life. Reading another creature's emotions was simpler than the book of poetry he read in his bunk every night. He'd heard her crying, and he could feel the raw emotion like a pain in his own heart.

Sympathy welled up in him, so stark and bright it surprised him. Laid him bare. Made him brave as he took one step forward, but only one step. She was easily startled, and the last thing he wanted to do on this earth was to scare her.

Hat in hand, he planted his feet and let the seconds tick by as she set the tea to steep. "What would it take to get a cup of that?"

"A loaded gun pointed at my head."

Funny thing, she didn't sound so easy to scare. "That seems mighty drastic. I'd be willing to trade you a favor. Judging by your stepfather, you might need a helping hand now and then."

"What kind of favor would I need from the likes of you?"

"Oh, I don't know, a saddle horse so you could ride into town."

"I can saddle my own horse, and I'll thank you to leave me be."

She *definitely* didn't sound afraid of him.

She sounded mad, and that didn't make a lick of sense. Not at all. "How about a saddle horse in the middle of the night, with my word no one would know you were leaving?"

That did it. Her reaction was like the snap of a bullwhip. She tensed. "How did you know?"

"Easy guess. Your stepfather doesn't seem to want you here, and you keep gazing off down the road." That was better—he had her attention now. He hung his hat on the edge of the chair back. "Seems to me a woman with her eye on the door has plans to leave.''

''Am I that obvious?''

''Maybe to someone watching, but Cal Willman isn't observant.''

''Oh, good.'' The relief in her voice was the briefest sigh.

Dillon felt it as if it were his own. His chest squeezed tight until it hurt. How bad was it for her here? He knew she was grieving the loss of a child and her marriage, but was there more?

Remembering the fading bruise on her cheekbone, he knew there had to be.

''How about it?'' Gentle, that's how he'd be to her. Let her see right away the kind of man he was. ''Do I get some of that tea?''

''No.''

Not the answer he expected.

It was probably the one he deserved. *Whoa, Hennessey, you know the lady isn't interested in you.* It disappointed him. A lot. The weight of it settled on his shoulders and in his heart.

Sad, he snatched his hat off the chair back. ''Guess I'll leave you be. Good night, ma'am.''

''Good night.''

''Sure hope the tea helps you to sleep. I'm so tired I'll sleep like a dead man.''

What did she say to that? Katelyn winced as the spoon she held bit into the crease of her knuckles. She ignored the stinging pain, loosening her strangulation grip on the utensil. To think he could hunt down a beautiful creature, the same one he'd tricked into trusting him, and then be able to fall asleep?

The horrible man! She hated him. She hated every-thing about him, everything he represented. She had a good mind to hurl the spoon at him. She would, too, except for the fact that he was much stronger than she was and much bigger. He would certainly exact revenge, as any man would.

Still, it was the thought that counted.

She'd had enough of brutal men. Enough of them to last her a lifetime. With her jewelry to sell, she wouldn't have to be dependent on anyone. She would get a good job and her own little place to live and no one could hurt her. No one.

She might be lonely. She'd sleep alone. Eat alone. Live alone. Spend every holiday alone.

She watched the breadth of Hennessey's shoulders as he ambled away, probably in search of Cal, and she listened to the ringing authority of his gait. She knew with all the certainty in her soul she didn't need any man.

Loneliness was a small price to pay for safety. For peace. For the chance to be, if not happy, then con-tent.

It was the most she could hope for.

The warm, honest scent of chamomile brought her out of her thoughts of the future. She had to concen-trate on regaining her strength. She was too weak, and still too sore, to leave. Dillon had made her realize all she needed to think about. Would she take a horse to town? It would be faster than walking, she knew.

She could still take the train, as she planned, and leave the animal at the livery. Where would she end up? She didn't have a train schedule, but she could hear the whistle from town. She knew when trains arrived and departed. She'd take the first one, even a freight train making a water-and-coal stop, during the night. And make her decisions from there—

"Hennessey! Is that you?" Cal's fury cannoned through the sleeping house.

Katelyn dropped the spoon again. Damn! She plucked it off the counter, vowing not to make another sound. She couldn't face her stepfather one more time tonight.

"Yep, I just got back." Dillon's easy drawl sounded friendly.

Why not? Katelyn figured they were cut from the same bolt of cloth. Tears of anger stung her eyes, and she wrapped her arms around her waist, comforting herself, the handle of the spoon cutting into the meat of her palm.

Maybe, if she didn't make a sound, Cal wouldn't know she was here. That was the best course.

"Guess I owe you five hundred when you leave. Not pleased about that, horseman, but I am grateful to you for solving that problem for me."

"I see. A man with a reputation for fine horseflesh wouldn't want an Indian pony mating with his expensive broodmares."

"Glad you see my point. I won't forget about the five hundred. You got the animal strung up? We got a cougar problem. Wouldn't hurt to set a couple of the men up with guns and use the carcass to draw the cat out. I'd be most obliged."

Obliged? That was a civilized way of saying it. A moneyed way of dealing with a problem. Disgust soured Dillon's mouth, leaving a bad taste he couldn't tolerate. He liked to avoid confrontations when he could. Most situations weren't worth fighting over.

Some were.

He took a breath, remembering the woman in the other room, and kept his tone low so he wouldn't scare her, but serious. Deadly serious. "I have trouble seeing how the boys will be able to do that."

"Oh? Tired, are they? I suppose tomorrow night will do as well." Perched at the top of the impressive cherry-wood staircase, at one with the shadows, Cal might have figured he looked intimidating.

Dillon braced his feet and planted his hands on his hips. "Nope. As I see it, tomorrow night ain't going to work, either."

"Why's that?"

"Two reasons. The first being the men aren't back yet. They're still out there looking for that Indian pony." Defiance strengthened the horseman's baritone and it rang like winter thunder.

Katelyn crept to the doorway, keeping out of sight. She could see a sliver of the horseman, the jut of his elbow and the steeled length of his upper arm. The rounded tip of his right boot.

But she could feel his presence like a swiftly approaching storm, the crackle in the air, the sting of anticipation and the bridled force.

"What's the other reason?" Cal demanded.

Katelyn knew what the horseman would say. The money wasn't enough—he wanted more than five hundred. She knew how men worked. He and Cal would argue about it, trade insults, show their tough sides and Dillon would hand over the stallion he'd caught and had hidden for the right amount of cash.

Why was she listening? She ought to take her tea, creep up the backstairs and never think of the horseman again. He was no different from her stepfather or from those other hired men who were riding by the light of the moon, hunting a wounded stallion for their own gain. It was a shame.

"The real reason I can't do it is simple." Hennessey grabbed the knob of the newel post and his glare was an unmistakable challenge. "I didn't catch the stallion."

"What do you mean? You were right there. I wounded him. He couldn't have outrun you."

"He's a tricky devil."

Oh, so that's how it was going to be. Hennessey was planning to bargain now, get the price he wanted first, then bring in the stallion.

Nauseated, Katelyn turned away, her step a whisper on the boards, her disappointment as heavy as an anvil. She didn't want to hear anymore.

"I don't give a damn how clever that piece of dog meat is! I want you to bring me that stallion."

Katelyn froze. What had happened to the stallion? Her pulse hammered through her chest, a staccato beat that coursed through her veins and she waited, aching with the faintest hope the animal had escaped.

"Can't do it. Sorry, sir."

Katelyn felt dizzy with relief. Or maybe it was the extreme emotions warring in her. Pride in the injured stallion for eluding the horseman. How strong and brave of him. Fury at Hennessey for hunting the horse in the first place. He was a son of a bitch, that's what he was. A strong man hurting the weaker, the more vulnerable. The very nature of man made her sick and she padded away, careful to remain quiet.

"Then get the hell back out there!" Cal's fury echoed in the silent rooms. "Out! Now."

"Won't do it." There was no apology in the horseman's words.

Hope returned. *What* did he say? The stallion was alive?

"I won't allow that stallion to be harmed. Not if I'm standing. When I hired on, we made a deal, Willman. I told you, no harm. I won't inflict it. I won't stand for it. Only a coward hurts an animal."

He stood like an errant knight at the base of the stairs, washed in light, framed by darkness, a solitary soldier that fought for all that was right.

It was fanciful, Katelyn knew, but she'd been wrong. Dillon hadn't hunted the stallion, and the power of it left her trembling. Her chest filled. Her eyes burned.

She'd been mean to him. Again! Remembering his fumbling attempt to speak to her in this kitchen, and how she'd expected the worst of him, she covered her mouth with her hands. She'd been wrong. She'd been wrong about the stallion. What about the man?

"No, Willman," Hennessey was saying, his rage a controlled, quiet warning. "Not for all the money you could beg, borrow or steal to pay me. It's time to end our business."

Cal's swearing tirade made Katelyn wince, but it didn't seem to intimidate Dillon. He did not shrink or cower, but faced Cal with confidence.

"If you can't find the greenbacks, I will take my

salary in trade. I've got my eye on three of your broodmares. I'll be happy with that.''

"Why you greedy bastard. You take those horses, that's theft, and I'll have a noose hanging around your neck. We still hang horse thieves in this county.''

"Taking what you owe me isn't theft. Any jury will agree.''

"Who needs a jury? You'll do the job I paid you to do.''

"Then pay me what you owe me, or I'll make you get out that noose. You're not man enough to get it around my neck.''

"Fine. I'll be rid of you, but that won't save the stallion.'' Cal stormed down the stairs and pushed past the horseman, knocked him hard in the shoulder as he passed.

Hennessey didn't move. The blow didn't register. He stood like a granite mountain, as if nothing could harm him.

He was the only man she'd ever known who would stand up to her stepfather.

A door squeaked open at the far end of the hall. Not the door to the library, where her stepfather's safe was hidden, but her bedroom door.

No, not the jewelry. Horror filled her as the air was pulled from her lungs. Her hands flew to her throat as she gaped, fighting to breathe. Her plans died before her eyes as her stepfather approached, holding something that winked and glittered in his outstretched hand.

"Here. Take it. It's all I have. It ought to be worth a few hundred. A drifter like you couldn't be worth more.''

"I'm not interested in a lady's jewelry. I told you, I want greenbacks, or I'll take the mares. It's your call."

Katelyn sank to the floor, her face in her hands. This couldn't be happening. How could she have forgotten to move the jewelry? It was because of him, the horseman. *He'd* been the sight that drew her from the room, making her forget everything but him. It wasn't fair. Not after all she'd been through.

"I can't let you have the mares, Hennessey. They are all that's keeping me solvent. If I had the money in hand, I'd pay you." Cal closed his fist, crushing the necklace in his cruel hand. "I have a fine house, with many treasures here. Surely I have something you might want?"

"I have no use for a fancy painting or expensive candlesticks. You have until morning to come up with the greenbacks, or I'll take this matter to the sheriff."

"No, wait. There is something you can have. I know you want her. I've seen the way you look at her."

Katelyn's hands slid from her face. Her head jerked up, seeing at the same time the cruel triumph curling Cal's upper lip and the horror on the horseman's.

"You would sell me your daughter?"

"She's my stepdaughter and of no use to me. Take her. She cooks, she cleans, she'll warm your bed. Surely that's worth three hundred dollars."

Chapter Five

Dillon couldn't believe it. Was he hearing the man right? Or imagining it? Men didn't sell their daughters.

Not good men, he amended. It hadn't been the first time he'd seen such a thing. From penniless farmers to gamblers desperate to stay in a poker game, he'd seen it. "Are you really that low of a bastard?"

"At least I'm not a worthless drifter. Take her and go." Willman gathered up what remained of his dignity, shoved the string of gold and diamonds into the pocket of his fine black-striped house robe and disappeared up the stairs.

I despise that man. Dillon jammed his brim low, pivoted to face the door and caught the faint shadow of her face through the dark kitchen. He'd forgotten she was there, that she'd heard everything.

He stopped, torn. Did he go to her? And if he did, did he reassure her? Or offer the one thing he knew she wanted, the chance to escape this house?

And if he did, why would she want the likes of him? As soon as she was well, he had no doubt there'd be men knocking at the door. Gussied up in their Sunday best, with their hair slicked back and their manners in place for the chance to court lovely Katelyn.

He heard a whisper of fabric, the hush of a footstep, and she was gone. Somewhere in the back of the house a floorboard groaned beneath her weight. She was going pretty fast. *Guess that's your answer, Hennessey. She doesn't want the likes of you.*

Fine. He'd wait until morning to settle the matter. He wasn't about to treat a woman like goods to be bartered. Except it sure would be something to have a wife.

Then you'd have to talk to her. Kiss her. Figure out what to say at the supper table. He may as well try to jump to the moon. His few attempts at conversation with Katelyn had to make her think he was a bumbling fool.

And now, the sort of man who would buy her.

It just went to prove his philosophy in life. The problem wasn't with the horses but with the owners. Every single dad-blame time. The longer he was at this, the crazier it seemed folks were.

Maybe it was time to settle down. He'd been thinking of it hard on and off over the past year. Missing the land he owned. Missing a sense of permanence.

Reason he traveled was because he had no one to anchor him. No woman of his own. A house was mighty lonely day and night without end, to a bachelor too shy of women to court one.

He wouldn't have to court Katelyn, he reasoned. She'd be already his.

Don't even consider it. Buying a wife. What sort of a man did such a thing?

What would *she* think of that?

Remembering the ghostly shadow of her face in the kitchen, how she'd seemed so withdrawn, pulled in on herself. It was a purely protective stance, he knew. A deep wounding.

No, she wasn't about to trust another man so easily. And a man who worked with his hands for a living? It was crazy thinking, that's what it was, and he'd do best to figure out where he was headed next. And which mares he wanted, since Cal Willman was too financially troubled to come up with a few hundred bucks, the bastard.

The night had turned brutal. Sharp chunks of snow punched from a hostile sky as he waded through the accumulation. Frigid air speared through the layers of wool he wore to freeze against his skin beneath, but he was too damn het up to let it bother him. His breath rose in great puffs.

Anger built with every step he took, a rage he fought to control. What a pompous, heartless son of a bitch to think he could barter a grown woman like a broodmare in his paddock.

Ned appeared out of the blackness, sidestepping his gelding to get the hell out of the way. "Whoa, what put you in a fightin' mood?"

What had happened in that house was no one's business. What Willman had offered him seared like a raging flame in his guts. Another man would have taken him up on it. It was a free country, sure, but women were at the mercy of the men responsible for them. Cal Willman wanted to be rid of his stepdaughter; it was plain and simple for any man to see.

Who would he offer her to next? Ned? Or Rhodes? There was the cold-eyed cowpoke, following Ned out of the storm. The small, mean-spirited man held his rifle still, cocked and ready. Eager to earn what he considered a fortune at the unholy killing of that mystical stallion.

What if Rhodes had found the Appaloosa and Willman had offered Katelyn as the prize?

Dillon's guts twisted so hard he missed the bottom porch step. The thought of the cowboy's grimy, stubby fingers on her creamy satin skin made his vision blur. Rage roared through him like a firestorm, obliterating everything as he kicked his boots off in the corner and jammed wood into the potbellied stove with enough force to dent steel.

She wasn't his to protect. He knew it.

It went to show how much he sparked for her.

"The horseman's in a good mood," Rhodes quipped as he stomped into the bunkhouse, snow crumbling off his boots and onto the plank floor. "Pissed you didn't get the reward, I reckon. Good, 'cuz it takes a real man to take down a piece of horseflesh like that. Knows these prairies, and where to hide. Don't worry yourself none, 'cuz I plan to draw him out."

"If you figure on taking one of Willman's prized mares with you, one in heat, don't figure on it working." Dillon couldn't believe how dumb some men could be. That animal had been wounded. He'd be doubly hard to hunt down now. "Take off your damn boots. I'm not sweeping up that mess."

He jammed the door shut, needing a target for his

anger and knowing the danger in that. He couldn't remember the last time he had felt this furious. A raging mad that whirled inside him like a hurricane, growing inside itself until it threatened to break down his control. And all because of a woman.

He was a sad, sorry man. He ached for her as he washed the hard ride's grime from his face and brushed his teeth in front of the cracked mirror in the necessary room. His reflection confirmed it. Lines on his face, the deep furrows in his brow. He was troubled, no doubt about it.

His bunk was damn cold. The sheets crackled with frost as he hunkered down between them. The old tin lantern cast a sputtering light, enough to read by if he squinted some. The brazen words of William Blake drew him into the poem but did not take his mind from her.

He could see the light of her bedroom window, if he leaned to the left and craned his neck just right. The ranch house was dark except for one faint gleam in her window. A single candle, he wagered, flickering around her as she stood at the foot of her bed. He felt like a criminal watching her.

No decent man peered into a lady's bedroom window, but he looked anyway. She'd left the curtains open, and he saw the graceful curve of her back as she stooped, folding something with care. The way she bent, elegant and slender, the perfect rounding of her spine elongated her neck and accentuated the alluring curve of her full breasts.

Desire pulsed through him like a whip's lash. Fast. Unexpected. Fierce. The snap of it surprised him. He was rock hard, his long johns straining, suddenly tight at his groin as he leaned toward the small grubby window that gave him a view of hers.

The faint light caressed her sweet woman's form, stroking her like a dedicated lover. His hands curved, wishing. He ought to be ashamed, lusting after her. But it wasn't only lust he felt.

She sure was something. Longing tugged at his heart, at every inch of his being. Down to his very soul. *I want her so much.*

Ned's rough voice rang at the far end of the house as he uncapped a bottle of whiskey and a few more of the boys crowded inside, stomping ice from their boots, growling at the weather and the damn horse that had eluded them. The noise reminded Dillon where he was. He wasn't about to be caught pining over a woman clearly too good for him.

He leaned into the pillows and held his book up to the light. He read, but tonight the bright images and powerful words did not move him. He was too tired, too cold, too distracted. Maybe it was best to call it a night.

He put down the book, blew out the light and huddled beneath the blankets. Gradually the covers warmed from his body heat, and the rest of the hired men stumbled to their frosty beds. The bunkhouse was dark and filled with the sounds of drunken snoring and the scouring snow against the outside walls.

Exhaustion settled on him like a dead weight, but he couldn't sleep. Blood pumped through his veins, and he was still hard. He refused to think of her. Wouldn't resort to lusting after her. He had too much respect for her for that. And yet...

He leaned toward the window. Yep, her light was

still gleaming like an invitation in the night. Was she in bed, beneath frilly lace-edged sheets and a fancy blanket? Was she wearing that white ruffled night-gown that had to feel as soft as her skin?

That way of thinking was only making his situation worse. Uncomfortable now, he sat up, shoving away the covers to let the frigid air cool his sizzling blood. Surely that ought to help.

Even as his teeth chattered, and he shook from head to toe, he still had that particular problem. It didn't look likely to go away any time soon.

He sat up and rested his face in his hands. He had a big day tomorrow. He had to be ready for it. If only he could stop wanting her, then maybe he could at least get some sleep.

Maybe, what he wanted tomorrow couldn't wait.

Tonight's conversation with Willman troubled him. He remembered feeling Katelyn's shocked silence in the dark kitchen. Dillon wasn't the kind of man who'd buy a wife, that was for sure. But if she were willing…

Had he gone plumb loco?

A movement through the window snagged his attention. What was it? The faint shadow flashed briefly in the impenetrable storm and vanished before he could hop off his bunk and scrape at the frosty glass with his thumbnail. It was her. A thin wisp of a woman, hardly more than shadow and night, but she called to him. Made his heart move in a way it never had before.

Katelyn couldn't go back to her bed. She couldn't sleep after that. She couldn't stand to be in the house, as weak as she was, and headed for the back door.

She'd already been out of bed too long today, and pain gripped her chest. She let the dark and cold scud over her. Welcomed the freezing wind into her soul as her stepfather's words echoed over and over. Anger hammered through her, blurring the world of night and shadow into one blackness. The bastard had taken her jewelry, all she had in the world. All she'd been wearing when she'd left her husband's house. She had nothing more of value. She had no other family, no friends, nowhere to go.

Forcing back those horrible memories, she made it to the stable, grateful, sagging against the door before she opened it to catch her breath. If she could leave, she would. She'd buy a ticket on the train and hurry far away.

The doctor had told her she had to rest. He'd told her the complications he feared, and she closed her eyes, willing away the panic of remembering the blood staining the nightgown and sheets and—

Don't think of it, Katelyn. She willed the image away, but the truth of it remained. She shivered deep, afraid, while the wind gusted her as strong as a human touch to her back. Well, she'd heeded his advice. She'd been too weak to do little else, and where had it gotten her? Now that she had regained some strength, however tenuous, she was penniless.

What would become of her now? She was still too weak to travel.

"Ma'am." A deep baritone penetrated the force of wind and snow.

It was his touch on her back, she realized. The horseman towered over her, shielding her from the brunt of the cold.

"We best get you back to the house where it's warm. It's mighty cold out here. A man well bundled would freeze to death in no time. It isn't safe for a little fragile thing like you."

"I can't go back yet." She didn't know why she told him that. He wouldn't understand.

"Pretty bad in that house, is it?"

"It always was, that's why I married. I thought any place would be better than living with those people." *I was wrong.* She kept back the truth. There was worse. Living with a man who wanted a son more than anything. Anything. And watching how that had destroyed him, and then her.

"Desperation can bring out the bad in a man," the horseman said thoughtfully. "Or it can bring out the best. It tests the mettle, anyhow."

"The best? That I'd like to see." She didn't believe it. Had stopped believing in anything.

Why hadn't she moved that jewelry? Mad at herself, mad at Cal, it felt near to breaking her. Without her health and anything of value, she was at the complete mercy of her stepfather. The man who'd offered her to Hennessey like a horse to be traded.

The horseman reached over her head and dragged open the heavy wood door enough for the comforting warmth of hay and horse to float through. "You don't believe in a man's goodness?"

"No."

"Never? You think there isn't one good man in this entire territory?"

"There was one." Affection warmed her, chasing away the cold and pain and taking her back to a simpler part of her life, when the summer had seemed to last forever and when she'd known kindness. "My father was a good man."

"Is that so? Come inside, out of the wind, why don't you, and tell me about him."

She saw what he was up to. The steadiness in his voice, the interest. He wasn't here out of the goodness of his heart. No man did anything for free. Not without expecting something in return.

And she feared what it was. What had gone on between the horseman and her stepfather? Had Cal paid Hennessey with cash? Or not?

"What are you doing out on a night like this?" she asked instead, tucking her memories away to keep safe.

"Couldn't sleep. Have a lot on my mind."

"Your next job, perhaps?"

"No. I figure I'll head home for a bit. I'm not worried about my next job. They tend to find me." He nudged her elbow, guiding her into the darkness.

She inched away, refusing to lean on him. She knew what he was thinking. "You would be better off with the horses. Even with the jewelry. It would fetch you a few hundred if you were to sell it."

"I don't want a lady's bracelet. I've got enough horses."

Why didn't he have a wife? The dark hid him from her, and he moved with the slightest sound into the aisle. She listened to the rustle as he moved, to the tap of his solid boots on the floor and the scrape of metal as he found the lantern.

A match flared, and light danced across his rugged

features. *My, he's handsome.* She'd always thought he was nice looking, but this close, he was devastating. A generous forehead over dark, expressive eyes. The high, sharp cheekbones of his native ancestors and the same proud look. A straight nose that wasn't too big, but fit his face well. Over a mouth that was hard enough to be cut in stone, but suited him and didn't look harsh. A jaw as strong as he was, and he clenched it hard so that muscles bunched in his throat while he studied her.

"I've been cast aside, you're aware of that." It was only the truth. "I did not make a good wife."

"I suspect that's a matter of opinion."

"I don't want to marry again."

"What? If your stepfather offered you to me, he may do the same to someone worse. Ever think of that?"

Her stomach rolled. It was logical, of course. The horseman was right. She hadn't considered the possibility. Cal had said he was looking for a situation. One that suited him financially, no doubt.

While her stepfather could not force her to marry anyone, he could make her life so miserable she would choose anything as an escape. Just as she'd chosen Brett. As an escape. As the one chance at happiness she thought she'd ever get.

"Come on up to the loft. There's a good view from up there."

"I don't want to sit with you. I came here to be alone."

"Me, too. We can be alone together. Come on." He carried the battered lantern with him, sending light swinging back and forth across the dirt floor. Horses inside their shadowed stalls snuffled and shifted in protest, for their sleep was disturbed. Hennessey stopped at the end of the aisle. "Why don't you come on up and make me understand why you won't at least consider the proposition I have for you."

"Why? It won't be in my best interest."

"You can't know that. You're assuming I'm no better than your stepfather or that bastard who hurt you." He held out his hand, palm up, just as he'd done with the stallion. "At least come tell me no and be done with it."

She found her feet moving forward. "I can tell you no from here."

"Yeah, but if you reject me here and now and I go back to the bunkhouse to lick my wounds and leave for home come morning, then you'll never know what happened to the stallion." A gleam of triumph widened his smile as he climbed the ladder, taking the light with him.

That man! She found her feet moving forward, taking her to the small glow of light, trailing down the wooden ladder from the loft above.

Hennessey gazed down at her, one brow cocked. "Interested?"

Wasn't that what she'd expect? Men liked to dominate. They liked to control. Be in charge. Use leverage. The very reason why she could never marry again.

But you have nowhere to go. That truth weighed like a thousand-pound anvil on her chest as she curled her hand around the sanded rung.

"That's it." The horseman gripped her wrist, then her elbow, aiding her up with hardly a strain to those muscles of his.

Reminding her how strong he was. Not as big as Brett, but bulkier. Iron hard. The latent power in Hennessey's tall, lean form frightened her. It was his touch that soothed like steaming hot chocolate on a cold day. Like a toasty hot bath before a crackling fire.

She pulled away, her feet solid on the hay-strewn boards. She skirted a pile of hay just to get away from him.

"The snow's letting up." Hennessey's baritone rumbled along the rafters she had to duck to miss bumping her head.

"Sure is a bad sign, getting a hard snow this early. Likely to be a cold, long winter. The old-timers say that, too." Like a touch, his voice drew her closer. "That means your stepfather's situation is going to get worse. This hay won't last him through a long winter. He pinched pennies this summer by trying to get by with fewer hired hayers. It might cost him big."

"I know what you're trying to do."

"Fine. I'm not denying it. But it's a free country, and I do have the right to ask."

She remembered how he'd looked on the midnight prairie. Remembered how he'd watched over her when she'd been feeding the deer. *I'm not afraid of him,* she realized. It wasn't much, but it was the reason she followed him to the edge of the loft, where he threw open the haying door. The night air rolled in.

"Are you cold?" he asked. "I'll give you my coat."

Already he was shrugging out of it. It was a soft calfskin jacket lined with fluffy sheep's wool. How warm it would be, she realized, and how it would smell of his salty male skin. "No, I'll be fine enough. I don't plan on staying here long."

"We'll see what I can do to change that." He shoved his fists into his pockets, looking oddly nervous and vulnerable for a man who towered over her, pure strength and might. "Look at the storm break. Sure is something."

He wasn't a polished lady's man, that was for certain. Katelyn leaned her shoulder against the door frame. The rough-textured wood caught on her sleeve. It would be best to be honest with him. He looked as if he was suffering. "I know what my stepfather offered you."

"I'm sorry you had to hear that. Had to make you feel pretty bad. I mean—" He hesitated, swiped his big hand over his face. "You're not an animal."

He really wasn't eloquent, was he? She bit her lower lip to keep from smiling. That was a change from the men she knew, friends of her stepfather's, friends of Brett's. "No, I'm not livestock to be traded. I'm glad you understand."

"Good. Then come and sit with me. You might as well enjoy the view while you're up here." He eased onto the floor and hung his feet over the edge. He held out his hand, palm up, to help her down. "You aren't in a hurry to go back into that house, right?"

"Right." Hennessey might not be sophisticated, but he was perceptive. He'd said the exact words to make her stay with him. At least he understood. That was what mattered. He wasn't going to take Cal at his word.

Her relief felt as endless as the night sky, where the storm clouds ripped and shredded apart to show a thin curve of moon. The prairie stretched in a frozen hush as if in waiting.

Or, maybe that was the way she was feeling. Not relieved because the horseman understood but worried over what Cal would do next. Where he would send her, before she was strong enough to strike out on her own. Who would her stepfather offer her to next?

Cal was desperate, she realized that. Stretched tight and hurting for money. He was proud and cared only that it looked as if he were doing well. What he had to do to maintain that facade, well, he would do. Even sell her to the highest bidder.

She shivered, repulsed, afraid. The calm after the storm, the gloss of the moonlight on miles upon miles of snow made the world look like a prized pearl. So beautiful it hurt to look at it. She ached, wondering where her horizons lay, what the morning would bring.

What if one of the other hands found the stallion? Would one of them take her instead of diamonds and gold, when there was no money behind Cal's reward offer?

The only option left her was to run tonight, in the bitter cold. She was not yet strong enough for travel. And without funds, she couldn't take the easier journey seated on a passenger train. That left more arduous forms of transportation. She would not survive a stagecoach rattling her across Montana Territory.

"Want to know what happened to the stallion?"

Her head jerked up. "You said he got away from you."

"No, I said I didn't catch him. I wasn't honest. I trapped him in a small canyon in the mountains. Made sure he was safe and hid my tracks on the ride back."

"How badly is he hurt?"

So much concern. Dillon figured he liked the woman even more for her softheartedness. He could spend the rest of his days counting the pretty, privileged women he'd come across in his work, who saw their prized matched teams as little more than an extension to their fine, fashionable buggies and surreys.

He always figured a horseman's wife ought to at least like horses. "The bullet hit him in the shoulder, I think. It was hard to tell in the dark and it happened fast. When I corralled him in, he wouldn't let me close enough to patch him up. From what I could see, it was nothing serious now, but if the bullet's still in there, he'll need care."

"And the other ranch hands won't find him?"

"Not if I get him moved right away."

"You'll capture him, then, and tame him. Break him," she corrected, adding the last words with a heavy disdain.

Or sadness. He could feel both. "I don't break animals. I train them."

"Isn't that the same? Just because you're not wearing your spurs now, you use them. You carry a whip."

"I don't wear spurs."

"All the hired men wear spurs."

"Then where are mine?" He held up his boot as proof. "My grandfather was a great Nez Percé warrior. He could talk with horses. A rare gift. He taught me what he knew. Gentle voice, gentle hand, gentle treatment makes for a gentle horse. Haven't you seen me working your father's mares?"

She shook her head, looking away toward the horizon. Appearing so lost and frozen inside.

"How about I make you two propositions?" He stood, because she was still standing, and watched her eyes narrow, felt her stiffen in distrust as he approached.

She smelled like beauty. Spring flowers and starlight, and the impact beat through him. Hot. Hard. Fast. He wanted her with a fierceness he'd never known and he couldn't believe he was standing here, about to offer for her.

Hell, how was she ever going to say yes? "I don't have much to offer a woman like you," he began, because it was the truth and he didn't want to lie to her. Ever. She had to know the man he was, good and bad. "I do have a house and three sections of land a far piece northeast of here. Good, rich land. I've got a herd of mares, ones I've picked up here and there. My brother keeps an eye on them. His land is next to mine."

"He's a horseman, too?"

It was a good sign she hadn't run for the hills yet. "He is. My house isn't what you're used to. It's stout enough to keep out the brutal north winds. It has a view that is just as good as this one. I promise you, on my honor, on all that I am, that it's one place where you will be safe. No one, I mean no one, will ever hurt you there. Marry me. I'll never give you cause to be unhappy.''

She turned away, grimacing as if he'd caused her harm.

What hopes he had slid south until they crashed to the ground in little irretrievable pieces. *She doesn't want me at all.*

He was a man. He was strong. He could live with that. Taking a shaky breath, he tried to be logical. It wasn't as if he had a real chance anyway.

''What's your second proposition? You said there were two.'' She sounded hollow and tired.

She wasn't interested in him, he knew that. He was a practical man. So he told her what she wanted to know. ''To help me with the stallion.''

''What would you do to him if I don't accept your proposal?''

Was that fear in her eyes? ''I would never hurt him, don't worry. His welfare doesn't depend on you marrying me. Your welfare does.''

''I can't. I can't ever marry anyone again.''

''Why not?''

Because I'm afraid. Because I'm barren. What man didn't want a son? Gossip traveled on a ranch. Hennessey had to have heard the rumors, and he was here, in front of her. Why? What did he want? Did he think she had money?

''I know you were hurt. I know what happened.'' The horseman laid his palm against the side of her face.

His touch made her hurt inside, like frost burning on bare skin. Maybe it wasn't only his touch that hurt, but the compassion in his voice. Compassion wasn't something she was used to. No man was like this in real life, was he? He had to want something. That was it.

She steeled her emotions, fought hard to be less vulnerable because this was the proof. He thought she was well-off. It would be reasonable. Brett was a wealthy man.

"Sure, you're ready to walk away. You don't think a horseman would be a good match for a lady like you. You may be right. But right now you're about as frail as a woman can be. You need time to recover, but what about tonight? Your stepfather doesn't want you here."

"I know."

"Then why are you here?"

"Because I had nowhere else to go." She hated hearing the words. Hated how alone they made her feel.

"And now?"

She shook her head. Nowhere. No one.

"The way I figure it, your stepfather is in a monetary bind. He made me an offer, but other bills are going to come due. He's going to have to hire someone to replace me. He has no money to pay them. What about the coal bill? What about the wages? How long will it be before he offers you to someone else?"

"It has occurred to me."

"If you stay here, then what? You want to be standing in front of Rhodes with a minister? The truth is, your stepfather doesn't care what happens to you, but I do. You could do a whole lot worse than taking me as a husband.''

No. She started to tremble, a fine, cold quivering that began in her soul and overtook her. She couldn't trust a man. She couldn't do it again.

Like a gallant knight, graced by moonlight, Hennessey knelt at her feet and cradled her hands in his.

''Marry me.'' Deep and true, his words rang like a hymn in the stillness. ''Please, Katelyn. Be my wife.''

''No.'' She tugged, but he had a tight hold on her hands. ''I don't have anything. My clothes and a few books are all I own. Cal stole what little I took with me when I was forced from my own house.''

''After childbirth?'' He rose, his face twisting. ''I'm sorry. That's damn horrible.''

His hand curved around her nape, and folded her to the hard plane of his chest. She breathed in the scent of night and snow on his coat, fighting the sensations that were overtaking her. The soft tanned leather against her cheek. The heat of his body. The hardness of it. The sound of his breathing, the rhythm of it.

''I will keep you safe, I swear it.'' How fierce he sounded, how sure. As if he'd move mountains if he had to, reshape the earth and raise the endless prairie to keep his word. She could feel it in his touch, in his body as he held her tight, held her safe, made her feel sheltered.

She *almost* believed him. ''I truly don't have anything of value. Not even this land. It will be handed down through Cal's side of the family.''

''I told you, I have my own land. I don't understand. Do you think that matters to me?''

"Why else would you be proposing to me?" She pulled away, out of the refuge of his arms.

"That is what you think. Do I look like the kind of man who'd marry a woman for what she's worth?" Dillon couldn't remember being more mad. Not at Cal Willman. Not at anyone. "Do you really think so little of me?"

"I wanted to be honest."

"Honest? You look at me and think I'd harm an animal, so why wouldn't I marry a woman for my own monetary gain?" He was ashamed, how wrong he'd been. "I think you are the most heavenly woman I've ever had the privilege to meet. You are beautiful and gentle, and I know I'm stepping out of place, a workingman like me asking for a wealthy man's stepdaughter to be my bride. Even if she has nowhere to go and no one to help her."

"You asked out of pity?"

"No. I asked you because I couldn't imagine a man like me being so lucky as to have a wife like you. And if you married me, I'd be grateful every day of my life."

"It's not what you do, Mr. Hennessey. I just can't. I can't." The pain remained frozen, a hard icy clump deep in her heart as she watched him stalk away. Heard his boots snap against the wooden ladder rungs and then pound through the stable.

If you married him, you wouldn't be here. You won't be alone. She heard the stable door bang shut, caught on Hennessey's emotions and a gust of wind. She didn't need him. She wasn't interested in his proposal.

So, then, why did she watch for him to cross

through the barn's shadow below and into sight? He'd called himself a workingman. She could not forget his words. His kind, obviously sincere words. *You are the most heavenly woman I've ever had the privilege to meet. You are beautiful and gentle.*

He was wrong, but oh, how nice it was to hear kindness. She didn't receive a lot of that.

There he was. Striding hard, but in control. Head up, shoulders set, back straight. He was angry, yes, but had she hurt him?

Chapter Six

It was nearly daybreak, and Dillon was still feeling like a fool.

Why else would you be proposing to me? He could remember her confusion as handily as if she was still standing in front of him in all her beauty and grace. *I truly don't have anything of value. Not even this land.*

She'd thought he'd been wanting to improve his circumstances in life by marrying a wealthy man's daughter. Well, not so wealthy at this particular time, Dillon thought wryly as he grabbed the iron poker from the hook in the hearth.

Good going, Hennessey. His first proposal to a woman and it could not have been more of a ruination. Maybe he should just keep away from women entirely. Then he couldn't act like a fool. Then he'd at least keep his dignity.

He doubted Shakespeare himself could find the words to describe how humiliated he felt this morning. And he hadn't stopped there. He'd tossed and turned in his cold bunk thinking of her.

It had been a long shot, proposing to her, sure. But he remembered when she'd first come to the ranch. Over a month ago now, he had finally been making some progress with that blood-bay mare. She'd been mishandled something fierce. Effie had made her way from the kitchen with some treat, and Dillon had overheard it then.

It was hard not to eavesdrop when Effie gossiped, since she saw no cause to lower her voice to a whisper when she did. Half-dead, poor thing showed up on the doorstep late last night, she'd said. The doc came and went and didn't think she'd live.

He'd felt sad for her, hearing of her tragedy. But when he'd first laid eyes on her the night she'd climbed from her window, well, he'd never been the same.

He knocked the ashes from the pile of coals and stirred them. Watched them glow orange the moment air touched them. He opened the damper wide, because he wanted a good hot fire. The bunkhouse was drafty and frigid, although he'd risen first and early this morning. It was a good time to think, and he had some thinking to do.

The bunkhouse was silent, unless you counted the snoring. While the kindling crackled to life and sent hungry flames to lick at the seasoned logs of wood he'd added, Dillon hunkered down in front of the open door and held his hands to the warmth. Damn, that felt good. His fingertips prickled so sharp he gritted his teeth to keep the swearing in.

She'd sure been a sweetness against him. His thoughts drifted backward, to the precious feel of her tucked against his chest. Fragile and female. When he'd folded his arms around her and felt her hair catch on his unshaven chin, something had changed in him. His chest expanded, his blood quickened, his soul woke up and took notice.

He wanted to protect her. To take care of her. To hold her. Never let her go.

Why? He'd seen her a few times. He hardly knew her. He didn't know a thousand things about her, what her childhood was like. Was the good man she'd known her real father? Had she always loved horses? Why had she married a man who wasn't kind to her? What were her favorite foods?

See? He could make a list that would stretch from here to Great Falls of every single thing he did not know about Katelyn Green.

What did he know?

That when he looked at her, the world faded away. Everything he'd ever cared about, everything he was, came alive as if newly awakened. It made him feel better than the man he was.

She didn't think so much of him. She'd thought he wanted money. Then again, maybe that's what she knew. Maybe the man who'd cast her aside had done that. Looked at her and, instead of seeing the woman she was, saw her family's wealth.

Dwindling wealth, he corrected. Times were hard and were about to get harder. He was going to take three mares, unless Cal Willman could cough up enough greenbacks.

It wasn't as if he'd be riding out of here today with a wife. Disappointment raked through him, sharp tipped and hard. It was too bad, because he wanted her. His own wife.

Strange, soft feelings had beat to life within him. He wanted her. Still.

Didn't that make him five times a fool? Wanting a woman who didn't want him?

Grumbling sounds emanated from the back. The boys waking up, pulling on their ice-stiffened clothes and complaining about it. There were horses to feed, stalls to clean and, for him, horses to say goodbye to. Friends that he'd made, the four-legged variety that he understood far better than the two-legged.

Another wall of storm clouds had covered the sky from sight as he waded through the snow. Flakes started to fall, hard, fast, dry. The wind came from the north at a swirl.

Not a good sign.

He pulled open the door enough to slip inside, the same door he'd held for Katelyn last night. She'd shut it behind her. How long had she stayed in the loft? Had she watched the night stars move across the cloud-strewn sky and thought about him? Or had she hurried back to her fancy house and warm bed, glad to be rid of him?

A nicker drew his attention. The sorrel Arabian mare, one of the horses he'd been hired to train, leaned against her stall gate and stomped her right foot, demanding his full attention.

"Good morning, beautiful." He slipped her a broken piece of peppermint from his jacket, as he always did, and offered it on his flat palm.

Pleased, the mare nibbled the treat, her delicate lips whisking over his skin like a tickle.

"I'm taking you, pretty girl," he told her in his grandfather's tongue. The reverent lilt of the language was a sound of peace to all living things. "You are one fine beauty."

The mare leaned her forehead against his shoulder in response. His chest warmed at the emotional connection. Trust. She trusted him. It had been a hard journey they'd taken together, but what a reward. He rubbed his knuckles into a sensitive spot behind her ear. She pushed harder into him, her way of hugging.

Affection filled him, soft and sweet. Yep, he'd take this one for sure. What a fine addition she'd make to his herd.

With the job ending early, would he head home? Would he stay for a spell? Or move on, unable to take the emptiness of a lonely house? To sit alone evening after evening, sleep alone night after night.

Maybe he could remedy that. He moved down the aisle, digging more peppermint out of his pocket, stroking more soft, eager noses. There were all sorts of ways to get a bride. Now that he had some experience with a woman under his belt. Fine, not a successful one, but he'd managed to talk to Katelyn last night without stumbling and stuttering like a clodpate.

There were those magazines where women had placed advertisements in search of a husband. Maybe one of them would be nice. Kind. Gentle as an angel come to earth.

Even as he considered the notion of another woman, his chest seized up. The trouble was, whoever he picked wouldn't suit him. She wouldn't be Katelyn.

I can do this. I can stand up to Cal. Katelyn rubbed her gritty eyes, dry and sore from lack of sleep, breathed deep, steeled her spine and pushed open the library door. It whispered open to reveal a book-lined room draped in darkness.

Cal sat on a big Windsor chair, pushed away from his rolltop desk, his elbows on his knees. His face in his hands. The rounded C of his back powerful and shadowed. The faintest gray of predawn peeked through the curtains, a witness to the sorrow in the room. Defeat hung in the air like dust motes.

She hadn't realized how much trouble he was in. She'd been too hurt to notice. A sense of foreboding beat like a war drum in her stomach.

"Put the tray on the coffee table and leave me." Cal didn't move.

Say it. Just walk right up to him and tell him. Her feet didn't move her through the threshold.

"I said, leave it, damn it!" Sharp, red faced, Cal whirled around, the chair squeaking as it spun with him. When he realized it was her and not the servant standing in the doorway, his impatience changed to hatred. "What do you want? Come to say goodbye?"

Do it, Katelyn. "I'm not going anywhere. I want my jewelry back."

"What jewelry?" He straightened to his full height to glare down at her like an angry deity. "What jewelry?"

"The pieces you stole from the loose board in my room. I saw you offer my bracelet to the horseman." Chin up, she met his gaze. Fisted her hands. Planted her feet. She refused to be afraid of him. Of any man. Ever again. "Those diamonds are mine and I want them back."

Tendons stood out on Cal's neck. "If you've lost

your things, then that's your own fault. Don't come to me and complain.''

''It's theft, and I'm certain I could ask the horseman to verify that you offered him my bracelet as payment.''

''Your bracelet? I took that as partial payment for your doctor's bill, which is sizable. Or do you intend to pay the bill? And what about the room and board and trouble you've cost me and your mother?''

''Return the jewelry to me, and I'll gladly pay my own bills.''

''Can you reimburse me for the business I've lost at the bank? My reputation is everything, and to think the best people in town are moving their money from my bank. Your divorce is a scandal, and it's ruining me.''

''Ruining you?'' What Brett's abandonment had done to her was immeasurable, and Cal wanted to blame his business failures on it?

''Last year, Clemming, my competitor, was losing business, and do you know what happened? He went broke. Had to sell what little his bank was worth and give up his home. He left town a broken man, heading back east to live with relatives. And do you know why?''

Because of his daughter. Katelyn withered. There was no possibility of getting her jewelry. None.

''Because his daughter got into trouble. Folks thought, what kind of banker is he? He can't keep his children in line and behaving well, so how well can he manage a bank? That's what they say. They lost confidence and brought their business to me.''

''Your financial problems have been going on for some time. I'm not the cause of your problems.''

''No, but you will be a partial solution. I've got bills to pay.'' He gestured toward the pile of papers strewn on his desk. Bills due, debts to be paid. Over a few dozen of them. ''There's the coal bill. Over two hundred dollars. Old Hal down at the railroad buried his wife a month ago. He'd be glad to take you. Or how about this one?''

Cal grabbed the piece of paper and shook it open with a snap. ''A note due on two of my best mares. I think Johnson down at the auction house was complaining about his last woman. Maybe he'd take you in trade.''

''You can't sell me and you know it, Cal.'' There was no talking to a man so arrogant. And maybe, she wondered noticing the glaze in his eyes, to a man who was desperate. A man to whom his reputation and appearance of wealth was everything, and he was on the verge of losing it.

Footsteps hustled on the carpeting. The maid, late with breakfast, looked harried. Katelyn moved out of the doorway and let the woman pass, to receive Cal's irritated remarks about her lateness.

She marched down the hall. She was leaving this house today. Somehow. The doctor said she wasn't strong enough, but it didn't matter. She'd pack what she could carry. It wouldn't be much. Whatever awaited her out there, alone, had to be better than staying here.

Dillon expected trouble. The hired men were watching him, keeping an eye out while they worked.

The hairs along the back of his neck itched, a sure sign something was wrong. Dillon tucked his extra halters and lead ropes into the spare compartment of his saddlebag. Almost done.

Good thing he'd worn both revolvers strapped to his left and right thighs. He was handy with a gun, but he was outnumbered. If Willman thought he was an easy target, then he was dead wrong.

Dillon sensed him before the horses stirred in their stalls, alert to the intruder. He felt the man's hatred before he heard the first drum of an authoritative footfall on the hard-packed earth.

"So, you didn't listen when I told you to leave the horses alone." Willman must have thought he was judge and jury with the cold hard judgment that drove his words, for he had brought Ned with him. "If you take those mares, you hang, boy."

"Who are you calling 'boy'?" Dillon didn't bother to hide his disregard or his sneer. "You're the one who needs a hired gun, not me. I'm not about to take your mares. I'm taking your stepdaughter."

Surprise flashed in those cold eyes, then a brief gleam of satisfaction. "Oh? Then take her and go."

"I already have." Dillon freed the hem of his jacket from his right hip, to reveal the loaded Colt .45. "Our business dealings are through. Are we in agreement?"

"I am done with you, horseman." A bead of sweat rolled down Willman's temple.

"No, I'm finished with you. Ned and Rhodes, stand back. There's no need to use those guns you're packing," Dillon said as he settled his left hand over the base of the whip coiled at his hip. "I don't want trouble. Do you?"

Ned shook his head. Rhodes stared, jaw set, and his hand twitching above his holstered Colt .45. The youngster was looking for an excuse.

The hired men let him pass. Feeling Willman's malice on his back like cannon fire, Dillon loaded his packs in the sleigh. His mustangs waited patiently in the wind shadow of the stable.

There was one more thing to do. Not even the hard fall of snow dared to impede him as he headed straight to the main house. He didn't knock. He didn't figure he needed to ask permission to take what was now his. He ignored the spoiled Mrs. Willman seated at the dining room table, fussing over her clothes for some fool women's meeting in town by the sound of it, and marched down the hall.

He rapped on her door and pushed it open.

The room was perfect. The fancy sleigh bed made up in satin counterpane and those fancy matching pillows. A rug and curtains to match. Little breakable knickknacks crowded across the carved bureau and the little dressing stand.

His gaze flew to the open wardrobe in the corner, where every peg was bare.

Katelyn was gone.

By the time Dillon had gone a half mile, the storm had turned treacherous. Good thing he was a damn good tracker. He'd been taught by his great-grandfather, once a Nez Percé warrior, who hunted in the old way. The snow was fast falling, but he'd found a trail.

Yep, he was getting closer. She had to be just up ahead. He brushed the new snow from the faint imprint of a woman's shoe. Katelyn's shoe. He imagined the foot that had made the impression. He thought about the woman as he grazed his gloved fingertip over the curve of instep.

He only had to think of her and softness eased into his chest. It was a strange, expanding sensation behind his breastbone.

It looked as if she was staying close to the fence lines, which pretty much followed the road to town, so she'd be easy to find. The wind kicked hard, making the storm nearly a whiteout. At least she was smart enough to find her way. Plenty of folks got lost in these storms and wandered out onto the vast prairie to freeze to death. The wind gusted and drove through his layers of wool and flannel. Hell wouldn't be this cold if it froze over.

Teeth gritted, gloved hands tucked into his armpits to keep them from freezing. The sleigh's runners squeaked on the snow, and the clomp of the horses' steel shoes were the only other sounds.

Why was he going after her like this? She could be safe in town by now, sipping hot tea in front of a fire at the town's fanciest hotel.

She's mine. That's why. She'd been hurt, he understood that. Hell, wounded hearts was his business. Every horse he'd ever worked with had a damn good reason not to trust men. Remembering the pain in her eyes last night, he knew Katelyn had been more than hurt. She'd been betrayed and abandoned and cast aside.

He'd worked with horses like that, too.

Wait—was that her? He caught the hint of a shadow in the cascading snow.

"Katelyn!" He cupped his hands to his mouth and bellowed so she could hear him above the storm.

She was merely a part of the snow and wind, a brief curve of shoulder before the curtain of white swallowed her then teased him with another glimpse of wool cloak. Head bent, stumbling in the drifts, she had to be half-frozen. That fancy coat she wore couldn't keep her very warm.

"Katelyn," he said again, but the jealous wind stole his words away. She looked so cold. He took her arm and gestured back the way they came.

The curtain of snow dropped again, snatching her from his sight. Swiping snow from his eyes, he swore. This was foolish. They couldn't even speak, the blizzard was bad and getting worse. Why was she out here anyway? Did she think so little of him?

Hell, he wouldn't force any woman to marry him. He was quaking now, frozen clear to the bone marrow, and getting a tad irritable.

He grabbed the soft curve of her upper arm, meaning to show her he intended to take her back to the house, but the moment his fingers curled around her, the storm ceased. The winds silenced. The snow disappeared. The beat of his heart slowed to an eternity as, miraculously, her mittened hand fisted in his jacket.

He felt her question before she yanked her scarf from around her mouth with her other hand and shouted.

He shook his head. He couldn't hear her. He said the only word that counted. "Home."

The fist at his jacket twisted the material more tightly. He could feel her desperation. And it tore at him. "Too cold."

"No." As firm as the earth at his feet, that word.

Was she so desperate to escape him? The fight went out of him. He unclasped her hand from his jacket and cradled it in both of his.

"...town..." he heard her say as the wind fractured and beat between them. "Please?"

God, she was killing him. But he swallowed the pain, pushed aside the wound of her rejection. If only she hadn't said "please" like that, with so much naked grief and need that not even the storm could lessen it. Tenderness seeded in his chest, a thin growing warmth that left him helpless.

Tears were freezing on her exposed cheeks when he took the end of her scarf and gently tucked it back into place around her mouth and nose. He swiped at the tears, rubbing them before they burned her delicate skin.

His eyes had adjusted to the whiteout conditions and he could distinguish the almond shape of her eyes, visible between the scarf and the woolen cap she wore over her head. He felt the unspoken plea as if she'd whispered it to his soul.

"C'mon." He held her arm tight, shielding her from the brunt of the wind with his body the best he could, and led her to the waiting mare. He placed her hand on the animal's warm flank and leaned close to her ear. The ice-flecked wool scratched at his jaw. "Can you ride?"

"I won't go back. I won't." She was as fierce as the wind.

"Fine. Let me help you."

"I don't need help."

"Yes, you do."

Katelyn didn't want him, but could she trust him? Struggling through the snowdrifts and fighting to keep her sense of direction in the confusing swirl of snow and wind was more difficult than she'd imagined.

"You'll truly help me?" she asked, daring to lean close to speak against his ear. "You won't trick me?"

"I'm not that kind of man."

She didn't know what manner of man he was. But she needed help. She could follow the fence line only so far. Could she find the road to town? Every landmark was shrouded in snow and the storm was impenetrable.

She couldn't see the horseman, as close to her as he was, although apparently he could see her as his hand found her elbow and steadied her.

He was offering to help her into his sleigh. She couldn't see the vehicle—sudden pain slammed into her knee—the sleigh. Awkward with exhaustion and cold, she lifted one foot while Hennessey held her steady. She slipped into the seat with a grateful sigh.

Snow pummeled her face like a thousand icy shards driven on a violent wind, but the horseman shielded her with a bundle of blankets. She caught a brief glimpse of him, hat and profile, and the storm closed around her, draping him from her sight. She felt alone in a vast, cold world. Every inch of her ached from the cold. She clenched her teeth to keep them from chattering.

Then he was climbing in beside her. She felt the

iron of his thigh and the hard bone of his elbow as he gathered the reins.

She belonged to him now. She could *feel* it. She didn't have to turn around to see there were no prized Arabian mares tied to the back of the sleigh. She didn't need to ask if he'd accepted the diamonds and gold as payment. He'd taken her.

Miserable from the cold, hurting from the inside out, she felt hopeless. What would her future hold?

But no shelter from the storm rose out of the night. Only the endless howling of the blizzard and the beat of wind-driven snow against her back. Time stretched forever, an eternity of enduring the ice creeping from skin to muscle to bone.

Exhaustion settled in like a heavy steel weight in her midsection, dragging her down. She was too tired to worry about what would happen next. Tucked safe against the horseman, her eyes drifted shut and the welcoming darkness claimed her.

Chapter Seven

Dillon watched her thick curling eyelashes drift shut. Katelyn's breathing relaxed into a quiet cadence. Her fingers slackened on the edge of the robe.

Asleep, she didn't look wounded or wary. She was an angel, the worry and pain gone from her face. *It's all right, darlin', I'm going to take good care of you.* It was a promise he meant to keep.

He nosed the team of horses into the storm. The winds had waned and the snow was less heavy, but it was hazardous traveling like this with nothing but the wide, lonesome prairie to keep him company. With any luck he'd be coming across town by nightfall. His house wasn't far from his hometown of Bluebonnet, so that meant he could be sleeping at home tonight.

Home. Maybe it would be with Katelyn there. Maybe, when she saw the place, she'd want to stay. He had horses there, and a brother he was missing something fierce. In all, maybe he finally had a reason to stay put.

And he was looking at her. She stirred in her sleep,

making the softest sound. It moved through him like poetry, the feel of her warmth next to him, the lean curve of her thigh, the line of her arm, the dearness of her cheek as she shifted, her head rolling into place against his shoulder.

Tenderness took root in his heart. He took his time simply watching her. Listening to the sweet rhythm of her breathing. Memorizing the dip in the center of her lush upper lip. Wondering what her kiss would be like. Rose-petal soft, he wagered.

Would she be his? It was a risk to think she would be. She'd made her feelings about him pretty clear. But a woman in her condition, and alone with no one to help her, might need a friend. Or a place to call home.

Anything was possible, wasn't it?

That meant it was his job to protect her. To take care of her. He was a man who took his job seriously. Concerned about her, he yanked off his glove and carefully slipped his fingers beneath the icy glove on her closest hand.

Her skin was soft, cool, but not deathly cold. A good sign. He'd make sure she was safe while she slept. It was intimate watching her. Seeing the tiny blue veins beneath the delicate skin on her eyelids. Tracing the straight line of her nose. Smelling her faint lilac scent. His chest swelled up tight from watching her.

Was there any chance she could be his? Was there something he could do to change her mind? He sure hoped so.

He brushed the ice from her cap and cloak because he wanted to take care of her. Tenderness warmed him clear through, from top to toes. He had to make sure she was warm enough in these extreme temperatures, so he untucked his end of the buffalo robe around her and left the flannel blankets beneath to shield him from the cold.

He wasn't what mattered. She was. He tucked the robe over her body and beneath her chin. His knuckles accidentally grazed the underside of her jaw. Too bad he was wearing gloves. He'd wager that her skin was the softest thing he'd ever felt.

She's awful fine. A mighty aching swept through him, a forceful tenderness he'd never felt before. He reached out to push a few escaped tendrils into place beneath her cap.

Was this as close as he'd ever get to her? Only time would tell.

While she slept, safe and warm, he shivered, counting the miles.

Katelyn woke with the squealing of the sleigh's runners. It was dark. Where were they? She straightened in the seat, hissing at the sudden shock of pain clamped tight in every muscle of her aching body. The robe slid off her shoulders and onto her lap.

"The storm's too mean to go farther." Hennessey leaned to speak in her ear, and the wind was so strong, she struggled to hear him. "We'll stay here tonight. Fine by you?"

She nodded. Whatever he wanted. She'd never been so cold and stiff. The sleigh bucked, caught in a patch of loose snow. They were in a town, she realized. Not the one she'd expected to wake up in.

This town was smaller. False-fronted buildings

framed the long street on either side. Friendly and tidy, lamplight glowed in the store windows. Snow-draped hitching posts and steps onto the boardwalks. No one was walking or out driving in this storm.

The horses slowed to a stop in front of a cozy three-story building on a corner. A sign above the door read Bluebonnet Inn. Were they that far north? She hadn't thought to ask where the horseman was headed. It didn't matter. This wasn't her stepfather's house. That was all that mattered to her. She was out. She was free.

Well, relatively free. The horseman groaned, moving his long legs, grown stiff from the bitter cold. He climbed out awkwardly, and the shield of snowfall snatched him from her sight.

She had to figure out how to move, too. She felt frozen solid. Could she bend her knees? She tried with some success. Pain streaked through her knotted muscles, but she didn't let that stop her. She was going to get inside and buy a cup of hot, steaming coffee and drink it until she was warm clear through. Surely she had enough coins in the bottom of her reticule to pay for that.

With a warm place to think and something in her stomach, she might be able to make a good decision on what to do next. And how to do it.

She climbed out of the sleigh and pushed to her feet. The wash of pain and weakness dropped her to her knees. Lord, she hurt deep in her belly. She placed her hands there, where she hurt the most, only to discover new pain. Every muscle in her body felt raw with fatigue. Every joint felt swollen. Her head spun. The ground tilted, the snow fell sideways.

She breathed deep and waited until the world went back to normal. *Keep going. You have to do it.*

The six paces to the boardwalk in front of her felt like as many miles. Her knees were water. Tears stung her eyes as she fought to make each step. Weakness left her panting and dizzy. Too damn dizzy.

"Katelyn." The horseman's voice in her ear. His solid touch at her elbow.

Where had he come from? She turned toward him, saw the dark circles beneath his eyes and exhaustion evident in his face. Even then, he was handsome. Stalwart.

"You're as weak as a kitten, darlin'," he drawled deep as a low rumble of a warm kettle. The kind of deep, warm sound a woman could sink into like a steaming bath.

She felt herself sinking, and it was the last thing she ought to do. Even leaning on him now would lead to heartbreak. Hadn't she learned that lesson enough times? She was strong. She could stand on her own feet. She could get up the steps to the boardwalk and into the inn. By herself. Without help from any man.

But he was there anyway, his hand braced around her waist to steady her. How nice it felt to lean on him just a little.

His fingers curled at her nape. His was a tender, strengthening touch. One that felt as welcome as spring's first warm breeze to the frozen ground. A warmth that teased at dead leaves and hibernating roots.

And, like winter's first glimpse of spring, she felt an allure that stirred deep in her soul.

His hot breath fanned her exposed earlobe. ''Lean on me.''

How could she lean on any man? She was too weak to fight the flood of memories twisting together into a brief, quick punch of words and images. She remembered Brett's cutting remarks, his slaps that were to teach her when a woman should speak. And when she shouldn't.

She squeezed her eyes shut, struggling with memories and with the snow that clutched her ankles as if to hold her in place.

''Katelyn, you're exhausted. Here, let me take care of you.''

''I've made that mistake before.''

''Letting a man take care of you? He couldn't have been much of a man.'' Dillon gathered her into his arms and carried her, cradled like a child against his broad, granite-hard chest.

Heaven. Katelyn's eyes drifted shut as her cheek rested against the crook of his throat. His pulse surged like a powerful, slow drum beneath her ear. The stiffness eased from her muscles, the ache from her joints.

When he walked, she felt the stretch and bunch of his muscles and the roll of his gait. The power of him broke through her, like a tide upon the shore.

She'd never felt so safe or so protected, as he leaned the underside of his chin on her brow. Tucked against him, breathing as he breathed, it was as if he filled her. Touched her deeply in some strange, new way.

The snow disappeared as he carried her beneath the awning. He wrestled with a doorknob before he swept her inside the warm, brightly lit inn that smelled of wood smoke and furniture polish. She recognized the echoing expansive feel of a hotel lobby, and that meant being alone with him in a bedroom. Fear sliced through her, keen as the winter's cold, as she wondered what he was going to do. How was he going to treat her?

But his hold on her was strong, not possessive. He looked down at her with quiet intensity. His brows frowned in concern, his expression a strange, warm inquiry, the lines in his rugged face gentling.

"You're cold, I know," he murmured quietly. "All you need is some rest. You'll be fine. All right?"

It was as if he knew her fears. And she hated it, and she appreciated it, and she couldn't explain the two opposite emotions. She didn't have the strength to protest as Dillon carried her up the stairs. His body moved against hers in an intimate rhythm that stirred up more emotions.

She felt so warm and safe, snug against his strength and power. A flickering sconce at the landing cast his rugged features as if in bronze, and as if he were more than flesh and blood, made of tougher stuff than muscle and bone.

He was a warrior, a protector, a myth made real just for her on this cold, dark night.

He kicked open a door and laid her in a bed of soft, sweet linen. Exhaustion pulled her into sleep like a weight at the end of a rope, falling, falling.

The last image she saw was of the horseman bending over her, his face a shadowed oval of concern and integrity, his finger's brush to the curve of her cheekbone a tender awakening.

* * *

Katelyn dreamed of him, of the pain of the penetrating wind and then the brush of Dillon's knuckles against the underside of her chin, the faintest graze of kindness.

She dreamed of being lost in the blinding storm and then of how he brazened into sight. Of how he carried her safe against his chest. Of his touch.

She could still feel his caress on the outer curve of her jawbone. An amazing featherlight caress against the side of her face.

When she opened her eyes, she realized it was the way the pillow was folded, with the stiff end pressed against her jaw.

Not his touch after all. Why was she disappointed?

Katelyn dared to move, and her body protested. But, instead of the mind-numbing pain from her abdomen, as she feared, there was only a sharp ache. Her muscles felt stiff and refused to stretch when she shoved the quilt from her chin.

Was she alone? She peered over the sheet. A meager gray light peeked around the sides of the drawn shades, revealing the curved back of a wing chair by a brick hearth. A dying fire rasped and whispered as the tired flames licked a remaining log tumbling in on itself. Casting a faint shadow through the far corner of the room.

Yes, she was alone. She'd almost expected to find him seated in the corner, watching over her while she slept. The image of him remained, engraved in her mind, his face above hers, and the tenderness in his eyes…or maybe she'd imagined it. She'd been half-asleep and dreaming before her eyes had closed.

Her shoes were on the hearth. Her coat and scarf draped over the chair back to dry. She remembered Hennessey's hands, his touch. Was he near?

Why did she keep thinking about him? His voice rumbled through her mind like the bold edge of midnight, dark and all encompassing.

She tried lifting her head. Weakness left her breathing hard, a ragged sound in the peaceful room, so she sank into the pillows. Her head was spinning. She felt strangely thirsty. A dull ache low in her abdomen intensified, sending streaking pains down the center of her legs.

No. She rolled her face into the pillow, biting back tears of anger and frustration. She needed to rest. Then she'd be all right. She had to be all right.

Was that his footstep in the hall? She froze, her heart waiting to beat as the glass knob turned slowly, carefully, and the door whispered open. Dillon eased through the door frame, his wide-shouldered stance made larger by the wooden tray he carried in both broad hands.

Chicken soup scented the air and the faint jangle of stoneware accompanied his hushed step. He lowered the tray to the small round table near the hearth, and the weak flames flickered a respectful glow across his feet.

He knelt with sure, masculine grace. He could have been a knight of old genuflecting in an ancient church. As he added wood, the dwindling fire snapped in appreciation. The light changed from orange to gold, haloing him like heaven's touch, caressing his strong profile and the steeled length of his back, shadowing his warrior's face.

As if he felt her gaze, he pivoted toward her. The corner of his mouth edged into a slow, lopsided grin. "Good morning. Or should I say, good afternoon?"

She pulled the quilt to her chin. Should she mention how inappropriate it was to be alone in a room with him? While she was in bed? Her face heated, but Hennessey didn't seem aware of it as he added more wood to the fire with a steady competence, the way he did everything.

He concentrated on his task, handing one stick of pine after another into the flames, unconcerned by the heat as the fire licked higher and higher.

When his job was done, he unfolded his big masculine frame and pinned his attention on her. "How are you, pretty lady? You look whiter than those pillow slips."

"I'm simply tired, is all." At least that's what she hoped.

"Seems like it's more than that to me." His boots issued a warning as he dared to approach the bed.

"Truly, I am fine." She had to be all right. To prove her point, she pushed up from the mattress. She felt a sudden warm rush as dizziness swirled through her head, stealing the light and the room from her sight.

"Here, lie back now. That's it." His hands on her shoulders pressed her into the pillows. His words were a comfort as she waited for the spinning blackness in her head to cease. It hurt too much to think. She could only endure the wave of pain as it crashed through her.

Her vision cleared to see the man bowing before her, like a knight before royalty, his shoulders strong and broad enough to manage any burden. The long column of his neck, where his black hair was gathered back with a single leather band, made him appear strangely vulnerable at the same time.

The room righted itself and the light returned. It was no knight of old kneeling before her, but Hennessey, his wide fingers folded around hers, his touch like an anchor keeping her safe.

"A little more than tired, are you?" One brow quirked on his stony face. There was tenderness written there in the corners of his mouth and the pinch of his eyes. "Just close your eyes, angel, and rest."

"But—"

"Hush. The last thing you need right now is to be troubled by a packful of worries." His callused fingers could have been harsh, but when he squeezed, the power in them was comforting. "I'll take care of anything you need. You say the word, and I'll do it. How's that?"

Tears welled up, filling her throat and her eyes. He was kind. Kind, when she was helpless and he so strong.

"I brought up a full tray from the kitchen. Figured you might be hungry. I was. Ate the diner out of their entire stock of eggs and bacon, I'd bet money on it. That was some storm we came through, wasn't it?"

She nodded, the scrape of her hair on the pillows all the effort she could manage. Her vision blurred so that he was streaks of gray and black, backlit by the cheerful glow of the fire.

"It wasn't luck we made it here by nightfall. My horses have traveled in a lot of blizzards."

He moved away, the heat of his hand leaving hers. She rubbed the wetness from her eyes as he ambled through the half light in the room, his step a comforting knell on the wood floor, his drawl luring her attention away from the pain she was feeling.

"They're used to traveling, just like me. We've been over most of the West. That gelding and me have been through flash floods in New Mexico, an avalanche in Colorado, prairie fires in Texas. We've borrowed rides on the railroads from here to Mexico." There was a scrape of ironware and the sound of water pouring.

"Here." He knelt beside her, a cup cradled in his hands.

Her hands shook. The ironware cup was full nearly to the brim. She'd spill it for certain, but as if he could read her thoughts, Hennessey guided it to her mouth and held the cup steady while she sipped. The cool water tasted delicious across her dry tongue.

"Want to try some of that soup I brought?"

Her chest began hurting, too, at his kindness. She managed to nod. What manner of man was he? She didn't know, but she wasn't afraid to be alone with him. The sounds of his movement in the room and the rise and fall of his voice comforted her.

Ironware rattled, flatware scraped and he returned. The rim of the bowl brushed her bottom lip and the fragrant broth steamed her face. Not too hot, just right as she sipped slowly, letting the soup glide all the way to her stomach, warming her up. Soothing. Comforting.

There was that word again. She didn't want to be comforted by a man.

She couldn't seem to turn away as he held the bowl steady. She watched him over the curve of the rim.

"It's good to be back. I was raised here. It's the reason I took the job on your father's ranch. Figured it would do me some good to be close to home for a change. I could ride over and stay at my place now and again."

Her stomach began coiling up. She didn't feel right. She didn't feel good.

"You're looking more pale, if that's possible. I reckon it's a good thing I asked the doc to stop by." The callused pad of Hennessey's thumb traced away wetness at the corner of her eye.

"I can't pay a doctor." When she spoke, her words came rough and raw, and so quiet he had to lean forward to hear her. "I just need rest. No doctor."

She wasn't only tired, Dillon figured. She was weak. She was in pain. Her gold hair fanned along the crisp pillow slips that were shockingly white against her gray pallor. Fear wedged in his chest as he lowered the bowl.

"Katelyn? You rest. That's right. Sleep all you need to." He intended to make damn sure the doctor took good care of her. Where was that man? He should be here by now. If he didn't hurry up, Dillon vowed to march through the snowdrifts and haul him back by the collar.

She'll be all right. I'll see to it.

Her eyelids drifted closed, fluttering half moons against her cheeks. Dark circles bruised the delicate skin beneath her eyes. Exhaustion dug deep furrows into her soft brow and bracketed her lush mouth.

Maybe he'd been wrong to help her. If he'd known her health was this frail, he would have hauled her back to that house, and no amount of pleas and empathy for her would have changed his mind.

She was more important than anything, a good kind woman like her. Why would anyone cast her aside?

His fingertips drifted to her brow. He knew it was wrong to touch her like this, as if he had the right. He couldn't stop his thumb from trying to rub out the worry deep in her brow. He hated that she was ill. Hated that she was worrying even as her breathing changed to a slower, deeper rhythm.

I'll take care of you. He watched sleep claim her, his chest swelling, his entire being filling with a strange, powerful emotion. All he knew was that he would lay down his life for her.

Right here, right now, until his last breath, he would watch over her. Keep her safe.

A light knock rattled the door. The doc ambled in, set down his black bag and shrugged out of his coat.

"'Afternoon, Hennessey."

"Hi there, Haskins. Appreciate you coming over."

Dillon stood, jarring the bed, and Katelyn heard his easy gait ringing on the wood floor. Pain washed over her. She really wasn't feeling well. She tried to open her eyes and through the curl of her heavy eyelids she saw a man about Hennessey's age, competent looking as he unbuttoned both sleeves and began rolling them up his forearms.

"Are you responsible for this woman?" the doctor asked.

"Yes, she's mine." Hennessey's rumbling baritone was nearly a whisper, but the impact of his words shouted through her.

That was the reason he'd been caring this morning.

Noble, as he knelt at her side. Dependable, as he'd held the cup to her lips.

Mine, he'd said. She squeezed her eyes shut, turning her face into the pillows, but the image of him standing before the door remained. The image of Hennessey watching her, hat in his hand, heart on his sleeve.

Chapter Eight

Hell, yes, she was his. Saying it was different than hoping for it. Saying it gave a man reason to hope.

What was taking the doc so damn long? Dillon tossed the hat onto the sofa cushion next to him and took up pacing the short length of the inn's lobby. Her color hadn't been right. First pale, then gray. That couldn't be good.

The doc'll know what to do. The thought comforted him, but he still couldn't calm down. Couldn't make himself sit on that narrow dainty sofa and wait for the doc to come down those stairs.

"You must have marched a good mile since I've been standing here," Mrs. Miller commented from behind the front desk. "Sit down, you're making me nervous."

"Sorry, ma'am." He blushed.

The cushions were too small and too hard. Dillon tried sitting there without fidgeting. His worries kept shooting right back to her. It sure had been something to be near her. He couldn't say why he felt the way he did about Katelyn Green.

He only knew that every time she was near, his gaze riveted to her like a rock rolling off a cliff's edge, falling fast and far, helpless, to the ground below. There wasn't one thing to stop it.

He could only hope the impact wouldn't tear him apart.

A pair of women, dressed in traveling clothes, descended into the lobby, giving Mrs. Miller orders for a ride to the train station.

That got him to thinking, and he popped to his feet again. Was Katelyn planning to head out on a train? Was there any chance he could convince her to stay? How much time did he have? Was she going to be all right? What if the long day traveling had harmed her?

"Hennessey?"

Doc's voice broke through his worries. Dillon made a beeline across the lobby, toward a man with concern surrounding him like a cloud. "Is she all right?"

"She should be."

Relief shook him to the marrow of his bones. Left him weak. Left him dizzy. Left him feeling a far sight too vulnerable. All that mattered to him was her well-being.

"It's a good thing I stopped by." The doc went on. "She's not well, I won't lie about it. She had a hard time of it, if I can figure out the truth in all she wouldn't tell me. Her health is fragile, and we have to be careful. She's not recovering the way she should."

"Hell, Doc. You said she was going to be all

right.'' His chest exploded as if a bullet had ripped through his flesh and bone, leaving him in agony.

''She is, but she needs care. She needs rest.''

''Then that's what she will have.'' He was still hurting. He felt as if the wound remained, that his chest was ripped wide open and raw. ''I'll take care of her.''

He'd keep her here for a few weeks if he had to until he could move her to his house, where she'd be warm and snug.

''I'll be back to check on her. In the meanwhile, she's to be kept in bed.''

Dillon thanked the man for his time and expertise. He was sure grateful to him, and determined, he snatched his hat from the sofa and took the stairs two at a time.

He opened the door a crack to peek in, see if she was sleeping. The shade was drawn and the curtains closed to block out the stubborn cold draft.

A small pool of lamplight spilled over Katelyn's still form lying beneath the quilts. Her knees were propped up with pillows beneath them, raising her legs higher than her head.

She didn't move. Was she sleeping? He couldn't tell if she was even breathing.

He dared to step in and close the door slowly so the hinges wouldn't rasp, and he turned the knob carefully so the click wouldn't disturb her.

Oh, she was something. An angel sent to save him from his loneliness. Or, so he hoped.

Could he be that lucky?

The train whistle called through the town, a sharp series that announced its intentions to leave soon. As

Dillon towered over her, staring down at the perfect line of her nose and her lush mouth made softer in sleep, he wondered. If he tried his best, if he risked everything he had, could he keep her?

Or, if he gave her every piece of his heart, would she leave on that train anyway, as soon as she was able?

How did a man risk everything, the very core of him, knowing he could lose?

He sank to his knees, overwhelmed. She slept, unaware of his torment, unaware of the emotion hot and tender and aching all at the same time, filling up his chest like the first flow of water into a new well. Bubbling upward, unstoppable.

This frail female, so delicate he could see the blue veins beneath her porcelain skin. So fine, she felt like rich silk when he brushed a fingertip down the back of her hand. So dear, her heart-shaped face made him hurt just to look at her. What could make her want him? Could she ever?

He had no notion. And that made him afraid for the first time in his life. He drew up the chair and watched over her while she slept.

Hurting, just to look at her.

Katelyn battled her way through the watery weight of the drug the doc had given her to the surface where a faint, distant light flickered in the dark room. Her vision cleared and she drew a deep breath, exhausted simply from waking up.

Hennessey. He was the first thing she saw. The only. A hard, shadowed man dwarfing the chair, the hearth at his stocking feet, where the flames leaped and danced as if happy to have the privilege of giving him light and warmth. This man silhouetted by the fire, his head slightly bent, a book held open like a Bible in his big hands.

"Oh, dear, you're awake." A lady's voice, maternal and soothing, sounded from the darkness. There was a shuffle, and a matronly woman, her soft face framed by short brown curls, settled on the edge of the mattress.

"Your color's improved. What a blessing." Friendly, the woman held a cup and offered her a folded paper with white powder in the center. "Let's get this medicine down you. It's just the thing you need to be feeling better."

Katelyn remembered the doctor's visit. He'd been speaking about her physical recovery, of course. She understood that. There was no consolation. Not even the bitter-tasting powder and the warm, honey-sweetened tea could take away what truly hurt.

She accepted that. She knew this sorrow in her heart would always remain.

"Hey, pretty lady." Hennessey, the book shut in his hand, strolled over to the foot of her bed. "It's good to see you looking better. Can I get you anything? Do you need anything?"

"No." She couldn't meet his eyes.

"Mrs. Miller has been here. She says it's not appropriate for me to be here alone with you."

"She's right."

"See, Mr. Hennessey?" Mrs. Miller piped in from the corner, where there was a chink of porcelain and a rush of pouring water. "I told you so. You have to pardon him, ma'am. Some men have lived too long on the range to recognize decent, civilized behavior.''

''I admit it.'' He looked invincible and not apologetic for his social shortcomings. ''I made you a promise I intend to keep.''

Katelyn closed her eyes. Hennessey was a problem, and she was not strong enough to find a solution to him. Maybe she'd been wrong to run as she had, knowing she was not well enough for an arduous journey in a blizzard. She could not panic again and make the situation worse.

She would regain her strength, and then she would handle him. What could he do in the meantime? Nothing. She was not a horse to be bartered. She was not property to own. She was her own woman, and she did not need him.

I can make it on my own. Alone.

A warm, wet cloth bathed her brow in an awkward dab and pat that told her it wasn't motherly Mrs. Miller holding the cloth. Hennessey. It was him, a man with his own agenda. But what did he want?

She peeked at him through her eyelashes. She had a brief flash of his face, gentle and strong, before her eyelids fluttered shut. The dark stubble of a day's growth shadowed the steely line of his jaw. How long had he been here, watching over her? How long would he stay?

The pain didn't disappear, but she felt oddly weightless as she lay on the soft cotton sheets. So tired. Endlessly tired. The pain was a fist in her low abdomen. She knew if she let go, let sleep claim her, she would no longer be aware of what hurt her.

She opened her eyes, one last time, as the cloth

edged along her jaw and circled her chin. He took the cloth away. He did not speak as their gazes locked. Like thunder crashing through the sky, vibrating the ground at her feet, that's how it felt. Awareness bolted through her like lightning and every inch of her skin tingled as he moved away.

She's mine, he'd said. It felt as if he was saying it now, again, without words. His stare was intense, possessive. The air crackled, the flames leaped, a pop in the fireplace couldn't stop the way he bent over her. Or the heat of his kiss to her brow. Heartfelt. Tender. True.

A brand on her flesh that remained as he opened his book with a creak of the leather binding and found his page with a rustle of pages.

A shank of dark hair tumbled over his high, intelligent brow as he leaned over the book, intent on the words printed there. Her chest tightened, and not from exhaustion or pain or from the medicine that pulled her down into sleep. Listening to his baritone rise and fall as he read, Dillon Hennessey made her ache the way a winter's night longed for the dawn.

Only one man in her life had read to her while she was ill in bed. One other man, who'd stood as tall as the sky, and forthright as a warrior of old, just and right and stronger for the gentleness he'd shown her.

Katelyn wondered, although she could not dare to hope. Was Dillon Hennessey such a man as her father had been?

"You should go now, Mr. Hennessey." Mrs. Miller set her knitting aside and rose from her place by the fire. "It's nearly midnight. You need your rest as well."

"That's a polite way of saying a man shouldn't be in a lady's room. I'm not fooled." He closed the book, set it safely on the edge of the night table. It was time to stretch his legs but not to leave.

"It's only proper."

"I don't give a damn about proper. Only her."

"Think of her reputation, then." Mrs. Miller narrowed her eyes at him, crossed her arms around her middle and planted her feet, as if prepared for battle.

She'd best prepare to lose, because he refused to leave.

He unfolded from his position on the small, uncomfortable chair. His left ankle cracked and his right knee popped. His low back pinched tight in protest. It was hell being thirty, and he figured this was only the start of things to come. He'd broken more bones than he cared to admit over the years. Training other men's horses meant dealing with troubled horses. Even the best horseman wound up ass down on the ground now and again.

Which brought his thoughts right around to Katelyn.

Maybe it was time for a change. He'd always been a determined man, independent, finding his own way through life. It was tough knowing his future wasn't entirely up to him anymore. Would she have him?

He doubted it. But it was a hope that lingered, that gave him the fortitude to pour a glass of water from the pitcher Mrs. Miller had brought up fresh an hour ago. Gave him resolve as he turned up the wick as the night deepened, ignored the innkeeper's caustic comments and reclaimed the narrow, wicked chair that made his back hurt.

Bending over the book, he thumbed through the pages and found his place. Took a sip of cool water, let it ease the scratchiness of his throat before he continued reading.

The windowpanes rattled with the sudden force of a mean wind. The lamplight flickered, sputtering out. A new blizzard howled along the edges of the eaves and the corners of the room. Dillon lit a match and held it to the wick until the flame caught. A new storm had arrived, but it didn't trouble him.

He had everything that mattered.

The wind was howling. A lonely, weeping sound that made her feel as if she wasn't alone in her misery. The wedding ring flashed in the faceted light from the crystal chandelier. Brett was angry again; she could hear the clank of the decanter. He mumbled to himself, his words indistinct from the butler's pantry in the back hallway, but his tone was unmistakable.

She'd failed him again. There was nothing she could do but brace herself, wrap her arms around her swollen stomach and try to figure what to say to calm him.

There was no calming him tonight. His face, red with anger, flashed in front of her. He was standing in the parlor now, throwing his empty snifter. Angry. So angry.

She told him how sorry she was. She hadn't considered how it would look, going out on the boardwalk in her condition. She would not do it again.

His face twisted. She'd said the wrong thing. What

else did he want from her? What would cool his tem-
per? The flat of his palm connected with the right side
of her jaw, knocking her over the arm of the chair.

It wasn't decent, going out like that. His fist shot
out. Pain exploded in her cheekbone. Angry words.
More blows. Until she was on her side, curled around
the child she carried, feeling the blood rushing out of
her body. Her baby! The first clench of a contraction
made her scream.

"Katelyn." Big hands curled around her forearms,
holding her up, holding her.

Trapping her? The wind howled in agony, and a
fire snapped and crackled as her scream faded. A huge
man towered over her, his grip sustaining not impris-
oning.

"It's the laudanum. You had a nightmare, that's
all. You're safe."

Her vision cleared. Dillon Hennessey, his face
craggy and lined with exhaustion, helped her back
onto the pillows. His eyes glowed with a strange fire,
and a muscle bunched and jumped along his clenched
jaw.

The emotion of the dream lingered, and something
dropped onto her hand. Something wet and warm. Her
tears.

"The poor dear," came Mrs. Miller's voice, sounding distant from the far side of the room. "Is she all
right?"

"A dream, go back to sleep. I'm taking care of
her." Most men would have sounded controlling with
that authoritative, booming voice, but he sounded in
charge.

As if she could place her trust in him.

She didn't want to trust him. Not any man. Ever again.

"I reckon you might want a cup of tea? I think it's still warm."

"No, thank you." She couldn't say what she needed.

As if he understood, he eased onto the bed beside her. The mattress dipped with his weight and the bed ropes creaked in complaint. His solid thigh settled against her ribs.

The contact was oddly comforting. It was wrong, she knew. She didn't want to need him, but she hurt so much in so many ways. Wanting to be comforted, just a little, wasn't wrong. Was it?

The bed jostled as he leaned to retrieve his book from the floor where it must have fallen. She felt pain when the mattress moved again as he straightened, the volume safe in his wide-knuckled hand. Such capable hands.

"Do you want me to read to you?"

Her throat ached, and she shook her head.

"Okay, then. What do you want? Name it. I'll get it."

She closed her eyes, afraid to reach out. What did she want? It burned in her soul, a need she didn't understand. Her fingers crept toward his.

Suddenly he lifted her hand, settled it on his knee and twined his fingers through hers. He held her the way an anchor secured a boat at sea, unshakable.

"Go to sleep, Katelyn. It's all right. I'll be here."

When she awoke, hours later, the dawn was dark

as the night while the blizzard raged. Hennessey drowsed, sitting up, his fingers tight around hers. Holding her. Holding on.

She was holding on, too.

Chapter Nine

Dillon woke with a start. The doorknob clicked shut and he blinked, looking around. Jeez, he'd fallen asleep. He raked a hand through his hair, and the movement made him notice the kinks in his back.

Katelyn was worth it. His chest warmed with a tender fierceness. She looked better this morning. Still pale as the sheets, but better. It was something to feel good about. It didn't matter what the doctor had said—Dillon had still worried. He stayed the urge to touch her. To run his fingertips along the curve of her cheekbone. To kiss the soft tip of her nose.

One day. Soon. He wanted the right to kiss her. To claim her soft rosy lips with his. To hold her while she slept, safe against his chest. To feel the soft comfort of her body against his.

His blood burned in his veins, and he stopped his thoughts right there. This woman was his, and he intended to honor her. To respect her. To treat her so well she would love only him.

The faint bruise on her cheek was a shadow, nearly gone, but every time he looked at it rage kicked through him. She'd been badly hurt. Her dream last night… Hell, it had to have been horrible for her.

He swiped his hand over his face. He'd better never see that fancy judge who'd married her. Who had thrown her away like garbage in the street. He knew the type. Had worked on too many rich men's ranches not to know there was ugliness in the hearts of rich men as well as poor. The rich covered it better with their money and varnish. Only a weak coward struck a woman. Only the lowest sort of man left a woman because she hadn't borne him a son.

I'd be happy with a dozen daughters, he wished he could tell her. The thought of having a family with this woman, why, that choked him up. Seized his throat. Made his eyes burn. A family. Now, wouldn't that be something?

And best of all would be having Katelyn as his wife. He'd cherish her. No doubt about that. He would love her so well and hard that she'd forget any other man.

Her eyelids fluttered and she moaned, struggling against the laudanum. Or was it another bad dream? The thought of her being afraid made him desperate. Should he wake her? Or comfort her?

She moaned again, a low, despairing sound in her throat. He laid the length of his hand to her jaw, cupping her face tenderly.

No more bad dreams. He willed the words from his heart to hers. *You are safe now and forever. I swear it.*

She stopped moaning and pressed her cheek into his hand, snuggling closer.

His heart cracked wide open. Love for her spilled in, filling him up.

Her eyes opened. She saw him and sighed in what sounded like relief.

The love in his heart began to hurt. A keen, tightening ache. He'd comforted her. And she liked it.

"Good morning," he greeted her, because it was the best morning of his life. "How are you feeling? Can I get you anything? Tea? Water?"

She glanced past him to study the room. "Where's Mrs. Miller?"

"Must have gone downstairs. What do you need? I'll fetch it."

"I, uh, need Mrs. Miller." She bit her bottom lip and stared at the colorful pattern on the quilt.

"Why, I'd help you out—*oh.*" Realization hit him. "Sure, I'll, uh, get the innkeeper. You wait right here."

Embarrassed, Dillon couldn't look at her as he smacked the door shut behind him. Offering to help her—jeez.

He found the innkeeper in the kitchen, stirring eggs over a red-hot stove. Breakfast for the few other guests. He convinced her to let him take over, he'd been taking care of himself for thirteen years and knew how to handle a fry pan. Katelyn needed her, and that was more important than cooking breakfast for strangers, anyhow. Mrs. Miller called him an impertinent fellow, which wasn't the worst thing he'd been called in his life, and handed over the spatula.

A man didn't know how to cook, huh? He found a second pan, melted butter and set the grated potatoes to browning. Cooking over a stove was a luxury. How many nights had he fried up supper over a campfire?

Too many. The open range of Texas under a sky

clear and bright. Or high on a Colorado plateau. On the endless plains with the coyotes howling. It had been a lonely life.

Maybe that loneliness was about to change.

He'd do his damnedest to make sure of it.

"Feeling better this morning, are you?" Mrs. Miller asked in her pleasant way as she left a cup of bracing tea on the edge of the small night table. "Goodness, you had that Mr. Hennessey worried. He stayed the whole night, as improper as that was. I couldn't get him to budge."

"I know you stayed, too. Thank you."

"Doctor's orders. And they are still in effect, missy. You lay back. The doc was most clear in his orders. You've been through a very serious thing. Lost a child myself I did. My first. It is a heartache to this day." Sadness welled in the woman's eyes. "Although it has been thirty years."

"I'm sorry." Katelyn tamped down the wave of grief threatening to rise up and bury her.

"I am, too. It's hard to lay to rest that sorrow, but time has helped. You'll have more children one day, as I did, and that will help fill the emptiness. It's my guess your Mr. Hennessey would help you with that. A bachelor his age, he's serious. He's looking for a wife."

The pain left her reeling, and Katelyn struggled to dull that, too. The innkeeper had no way of knowing there would be no more children. No family to fill Katelyn's emptiness. The future stretched out before her like a void.

Alone.

"A man that age, he'll make a good husband. Mark

my words.'' Mrs. Miller swept through the room straightening pillows and knickknacks and folding a crocheted afghan. ''He's been around. Got all the temptation out of him. He's done everything he's wanted to do by this time, is my guess, and he'll make a steady husband. I've seen it before. Trust me—you live long enough, you see the pattern of things. Your Mr. Hennessey is devoted to you. Are you hoping he'll be offering you a ring soon?''

''I'm hoping that I can get out of this bed in a few days.'' She didn't want to think about Hennessey. ''I can't pay what I owe you. I wish I could, but perhaps I can find work here. I'll be good for the debt.''

''Goodness, you fret too much.'' Mrs. Miller halted by the bedside and patted Katelyn's hand with maternal kindness. ''You get well first and worry about that later, when you're stronger. Besides, you're not alone. That's what I've been trying to tell you. When a man like your Mr. Hennessey courts you, he means it. He's paying for your stay here. And the doctor, too, as I understand it.''

He's not my Mr. Hennessey, she wanted to say, annoyed and frustrated and irritable because she wasn't feeling well. Instead, she inhaled deeply and started counting. By the time she hit fourteen, her temper began to wane.

It was good, too, because there he was, striding through the doorway as if he owned the rights to her. Hennessey looked pleased with himself, confident and bold, and he dominated the room with his presence.

She ought to hate him for it. For making her pulse surge and the memories return. His voice reading her to sleep. His touch of comfort against her face, and how she gave in to it, pressing her cheek into his warm palm. She was ashamed of how she'd needed him, and she knew it.

She didn't need him now.

"I know the doc said broth and tea, but I figured you might be hungry." Only then did she notice the plate he held, heaped with scrambled eggs with a melted topping of cheese, thick slices of crispy salt pork and golden-brown, butter-fried potatoes.

Mrs. Miller's hand flew to her throat. "Why, you *can* cook! I can't believe my eyes. I thought I was in peril of scaring my guests away if I left you alone in that kitchen."

"I'm a man of my word." He winked, making light of it, but his truth rang true and undeniable.

Truth Katelyn didn't dare believe in.

"I left the plates in the warmer. I didn't know what rooms have guests."

"I'd best go see to it, then." Mrs. Miller scurried by, pausing to study the plate of food he held, shook her head in disbelief and, beaming happiness, bustled into the hall.

"Am I right? Are you hungry?" He approached the bed, his plate an offering he held out to her.

"What about you? Where's yours?"

"Don't tell anyone. I sampled the food in the kitchen. Ate enough to get me by." He drew up the hard-backed chair and eased his big frame into it. "I suppose you're used to food prepared better than I can make it, but at least it's hot and edible."

"It smells wonderful." Her mouth was watering, and she supposed it couldn't hurt to accept the food. She did need to regain her strength. "I didn't know men could cook."

"I grew up in a house of six brothers and no

mother. My father cooked until I was ten, and then I took over." He grabbed an extra pillow and tucked it behind her when she sat up.

He was so close she could feel his body's heat, a strange radiation of warmth and man that curled through her. He smelled good, too, masculine and woodsy.

"Is that comfortable?" His gaze met hers, a connection more jarring than if they'd touched.

A connection that chased the air from her lungs and turned her mind into a muddled confusion. She managed to nod, since she couldn't seem to find any words to speak with.

"Good." Satisfied, he whipped a tray from where it rested against the nightstand, stowed, she guessed, from last night's tea. He set it on her lap to serve as a bed tray.

"Your breakfast, ma'am. Cooked special just for you."

"What about the other guests?" she asked as he slid the plate in front of her. "Didn't you cook for them at the same time?"

"You're confusing a courting man. I've heard, in some social circles, that isn't polite behavior." A slight flush crept across his high, proud cheekbones. "I expected more of you, Katelyn."

"A courting man? I thought you expected to own me outright. Just as my stepfather promised." She set her chin, braced and ready.

One dark brow shot up in a face that didn't look cruel or angry. No, not Hennessey with his penetrating stare and his capable hands that could lure a wild stallion on a starlit night. His touch could lure her, too, as the weight of his palm settled on her shoulder, right in the curve of her neck. His thumb stroked a daring circle in the hollow of her throat.

It was a possessive touch. She wanted to hate it. Wanted to tell him to leave her be. But it wasn't only possessive.

"This may be a free country, but it is a man's country." He looked about as understanding as steel. "Don't worry. I'm not about to force you into marrying me. I'm not that kind of man. But it's my hope you might consider it."

"Are you proposing to me again?"

"No. I'm courting you. Proposing would put the cart before the horse. I've learned that never works well."

"But my stepfather's offer—" She couldn't say the words. She couldn't admit that she was a woman no man would want. Besides, she didn't have to say it. Everyone at the ranch knew her situation, surely the horseman did, too. Why was she even wondering? She didn't want to be courted.

"Willman's offer was a cruel one. I helped you out of that house because the truth is, I've never seen such a fine woman as you. I'm not much, but remember I've got my own piece of the Montana prairie, I work hard and I'll be better to you than any man in this country."

"You'd want to dominate me as you do those horses you break." She wasn't fooled, although the allure of his voice, the strength in him, hooked her like a fish in water, pulling her toward him when she wanted to escape.

His thumb traced up the line of her throat. Caressed the curve of her chin. Mesmerizing. Brett had never

touched her the way Hennessey did. As if he wanted
to comfort her. And the pleasure of it...

She squeezed her eyes shut, her entire being shut,
against the need for it.

"I don't break horses." He leaned close until his
words were a whisper against her ear. "I show them
they can trust me."

"Trust? I've seen how horses are broken to ride."

"You haven't seen the way I've done it." He knew
she hadn't watched him through the window, the way
he'd watched her. Or she would know he did not
wound a horse's spirit. He did not use spurs. He did
not use a whip.

He used touch and language. Would it work on a
woman? He was ignorant on such matters. Not one
thing in his life had ever been as important as this
moment. As this woman.

"My father was a horseman." Affection changed
her, took down her defenses, and the tension vanished
beneath his fingers.

"Was he? The ranch was his, then."

"Long ago. I was six when he died. Just old
enough to really remember him. To understand the
void in my life when he passed."

"Was it an accident?" Plenty of men died breaking
horses. It was common in his profession.

"He fell ill in the spring and was gone by midsum-
mer." The sadness lingered.

Dillon could feel it in her as if it were his own.
She'd loved her father. And he knew how it must
have gone. A widow alone with a ranch to run, land
and horses worth a small fortune, and the ruthless
banker who loved money more than anything. Yep,
that pretty much explained the situation he'd wit-

nessed on Katelyn's family ranch. And the stepdaughter who'd been married off to improve the family's standing.

She hadn't married because of love.

That was important to know. Dillon kept that in the back of his mind. A woman wanted to be loved, no different than a man did. Wanted to find the missing piece of her heart.

Just like he did.

He traced the cup of his palm down the round of her shoulder and the length of her arm. Watching as she eased into his touch. It was a subtle thing, the way she moved into his caress like a cat wanting to be stroked. She didn't appear to move at all. But he felt it, a slight lifting, or maybe it was a wish for affection.

It was the first step in this perilous wish of his.

"Eat up before the food gets cold." He released her, breaking the contact but not the connection.

She lifted her fork and took a tentative bite. After the taste of the cheesy eggs registered on her tongue, her eyes lit up. "It's very good. Thank you."

Another step. Small but sure. Pleasure filled him to the brim. "You're surely welcome."

Her shy smile was all the encouragement he needed. Casually, as if he had nothing to lose, he dragged a book from the shelf on the night table. A book he'd dug from the bottom of one of his saddlebags.

"Do you like Dickens?" he asked.

She shone a little brighter. "I love him."

More certain now, Dillon opened to the first page to the start of Pip's adventure. It was a good thing he'd read the book more times than he could count, or he'd be stumbling over his tongue. How did a man concentrate on anything when his hands were damp and sweat was breaking out on his brow?

This must be the reason why he'd never courted before. The worry of it was likely to kill a less hardy man.

He read, while she ate, doing his best to concentrate on the story when she was right there in front of him, setting him on fire, making him feel as if his chest was wide open again and she could look right in and see everything he was.

And everything he wasn't.

What would it take for her to want him? What would it take for a man like him to earn her love?

He was about to find out.

It's my hope you might consider it, he'd said. Consider marrying him.

She tried to put that thought out of her mind. Every time she looked at him, it returned. Over and over until she had to face it. Her stepfather had given her to Hennessey. And he was trying to court her in his fumbling, unskilled manner.

While she knew the story nearly by heart, he was ruining Dickens's narrative. Stumbling and losing his place and pretending he wasn't.

Brett had courted her with all the right words and all the right gifts. He'd been perfect and charming and in control, making her feel as if he could take care of anything.

"Whew, I need a drink of water." He cleared his throat and set the thick volume on the edge of the bed. "Can I get you something? Tea? Water?

"No, I'm fine."

"Anything you want from the kitchen? Mrs. Miller has coffee. And apple juice, I think. I sure wouldn't object to fetching you some."

"No, thank you."

"Are you sure?" He lifted the pitcher and poured. "The stores are opening up this time of day. I could run down the boardwalk and get you anything you want."

"You're awfully helpful for a man."

"That might be because I'm trying to make a good impression." He grinned at her over the rim of the glass. "Is it working?"

"It depends on the impression you're trying to make."

"Why, showing you the kind of husband I'd be to you." He drank, swallowing all the water in the small glass without stopping. "Useful. Considerate. I hear the ability to fetch things is a good trait in a husband."

"No, that's in a dog," she teased.

"Right." He laughed at himself and put the glass down, shaking his head in disbelief. "I've been making myself look like a fool, have I?"

She shrugged, unable to agree. He wasn't a man practiced in courting, but he was sincere. He had taken care of her more in the short time she'd known him than her own mother had in her entire lifetime. Than had her husband, who'd sworn in a church before God and one hundred witnesses to love and cherish her always.

The horseman had cared for her with his strapping outdoorsman attitudes and appearances. He had made her dream again with a single touch of his big, rugged, working-man's hands. She didn't want it to be that way.

"That's why you said what you did. About the kind of impression I was trying to make." He winced. "I must not be doing a very good job."

"I haven't seen worse, it's true."

"I'm a horseman. I know horses, not how to charm women."

"Oh, that's what you're doing? Trying to charm me?"

"I'm failing. It's obvious you're not charmed." He looked sheepish, but there was an amazing quality in him. One that drew her attention to him so that she was aware only of him as he eased onto the bed, sitting beside her when it was far from proper.

Maybe she didn't want proper. Her pulse skipped as she hoped he would touch her again.

No, she wasn't charmed. She was more.

"It was worth a try." He didn't look diminished. He appeared as noble as ever, spine straight, shoulders set. He looked stalwart, able to defeat any foe who crossed him. But something in his eyes... Had she hurt him?

He retrieved the book and studied it, as if debating. "Do you want me to keep reading to help you pass the time? Or was that a shameful attempt, too?"

This was her chance to send him away. Why was her hand reaching out? Why was there a pulse of hope in her soul as she laid her hand on his much larger one. "I loved the reading."

"Yeah?" He tilted his head, cocked one brow, studying her hard as if reading her sincerity. And then reaching deeper, as if trying to see into her heart.

She drew the blanket around her chest, shielding

herself, keeping him away. *I ought to send him away. For now. For good.* Letting him stay, allowing him to think she'd consider marrying again and so soon, permitting him to continue courting her, was wrong.

"Then I'll keep on reading until you tell me to stop."

He's going to kiss me. She knew it as surely as if he'd told her. His eyes went black, focusing on her mouth. His lips parted slightly, as if in preparation. Slowly, as her lips tingled with both dread and want, he leaned closer.

The room faded, the light dimmed, the fire silenced and his mouth covered hers in a brush of heat and brilliance. Its radiance dwarfed any other kiss. Firm and yielding at the same time, and the pleasure of it radiated through her like a bolt of sunlight.

His hands settled on her cheeks, framing her face as he held her to him like a new blossom to the sun, kissing her with his whole heart. The beauty of it forced her to answer with hers.

He drew back, leaving her dazed and dazzled, irrevocably changed. How could a kiss be so much? How could it dip into her heart like that, past the sorrow gathered there? How could he make her *feel?*

He had. More than the sorrow of her loss, more than the betrayal of her husband's false vows, Dillon Hennessey had made her feel new. He made her feel alive. Quietly, wholly, achingly alive, and, again, she was a woman with desires and needs.

He opened the book with care and began to read as if nothing out of the ordinary had happened. His deep baritone, as mellow as twilight shadows, wrapped around her like a wool blanket, warming her, sheltering her. It wasn't Dickens's story she heard, but Hennessey. The man he was, steady and kind and proud on the outside.

What type of man was he, deep down, on the inside? Why did she want him to kiss her again? Ashamed of how she needed him, she closed her eyes. Tried to hold back a tide of feelings she didn't understand. Didn't want. Refused to act on.

If she wanted a second kiss, all she had to do was to sit up and she knew he'd take her into his strong arms. And give her, for a moment, the chance to be alive again.

A knock sounded on the door, and Dillon snapped the book shut.

"It's the doc." He lifted her hand and pressed a kiss to her palm. A hot caress that made her dream.

Dream that a woman like her could be loved. Even just a little.

"I'll be waiting outside." He laid her hand on her stomach with care, with authority.

She couldn't look at him as he walked away. Hated that the ring of his boots permeated her senses and made her aware of him. Only of him. Of his low mumble to the doctor and the squeak of a board beneath his foot. Of the creak of the door he closed. She could feel him in the hallway, like an unseen source of heat radiating only to her.

She faced the doctor with a weak smile. Answered his questions. Endured his examination. Listened to his advice.

"The weakness will continue for a while." The doctor drew up a chair. He was a kind man, meek but not weak. He pushed his spectacles back into place and studied her somberly. "That's to be expected from so much blood loss. From the birth."

She nodded. She knew that. "I know it will take time to regain my strength. But how much longer?"

"You've had a setback, traveling as you did. It will take a long time to heal from such trauma. But my worries are your emotional recovery. The loss you've suffered is the worst a woman can face, I believe."

Tears abraded the backs of her eyes. Tears she refused to let fall. "I am managing."

"You need time for that as well."

The compassion in the doctor's voice was meant to be kind, she knew, but somehow it made her hurt more. "You didn't answer my question. I have a mounting hotel bill to worry about and your fees. I need to be able to work."

"You need to heal. I told you. At least two more weeks, is my guess. You have no fever, no other complications to worry about. I'll come back in a few days to check on you. Let me know if your condition worsens."

He rose to leave. Katelyn steeled her hopes, protected them, even as she asked the question, "Is it your opinion, too, that I cannot bear another child?"

The doctor froze. His face saddened. "It is certain there will be no more children. I'm sorry."

"Thank you."

She waited until the door closed before she let the first tear fall. It was the emptiness of it, the finality. The knowing she'd never hold her own baby in her arms. She'd never be a mother. Never have a family. She'd lost her only chance.

What was she doing wanting another man's kiss? She buried her face in the pillows, hiding from him when the door opened again, and it was Hennessey's gait rolling toward her. Hennessey's touch to her back.

His comfort she did not acknowledge as the blizzard howled outside. Her heart cooled and her hopes froze until both were as glacial as the relentless north wind.

She'd let him kiss her. Dillon couldn't think of anything else as he watched her sleep. As the hours ticked by and she lay on her stomach, her face turned toward the wall, buried in her pillows.

Just seeing the fall of her luxurious hair down the fragile column of her neck and the glimpse of creamy skin at the flannel collar of her borrowed nightgown made him weak. Like a blow to his knees. Like having the wind knocked right out of him.

She sure is special. How a man could have set her aside, he couldn't figure. Couldn't imagine it. She was beautiful and smart and kind. She had a heart of gold and an invisible halo crowning her head. He was sure of it, for when they kissed, the instant his lips had met hers, the desire he kept banked roared like an inferno feeding on kerosene.

What more could a man ask for?

There was no single woman on this earth as special as her. And she might be his. There was a good chance she would say yes when he proposed. Be at his side, as his wife and lover—

The thought of climbing into her bed nearly tore him to pieces. What would it be like to claim her completely? To loose the ties at her throat and pleasure her breasts and thrust deep inside her sweet woman's body? To make her completely and everlastingly his?

The doc had said she would be strong enough to be up and around some tomorrow. In a week, maybe two, she'd be strong enough to buy a passenger ticket and leave him forever on the afternoon train. He had to work fast. He'd kissed her and she'd accepted it. She'd kissed him in return.

That meant he kept moving forward with his plan to make her fall in love with him. To show her the man he was, heart and soul. He might not be an educated, rich man, but he was decent and he'd love her better than any man could. If he showed her that, would it matter to her?

Or, if he gave her his heart, showed her his soul, would she leave anyway?

On the other hand, how did a man hold back when everything he ever wanted was right in front of him? So amazing and precious, he'd spend the rest of his days mourning her loss?

Chapter Ten

"**G**ood morning." Dillon's thundering baritone boomed over the crackle of the brown-wrapped packages in his arms. He dropped at least a dozen of them on the foot of her bed.

Katelyn's hand stilled, and her grip tightened around the wooden handle of the hairbrush. She simply stared. Eight days had passed and she was stronger. But she wasn't ready for this. The way he stood so proudly over her and the steady, measuring way he studied her made her stomach ball into one huge knot. "What is this?"

"Necessities for you, ma'am. Mrs. Miller had a hand in that. She told the seamstress what you would be needing." Bits of snow clung to his dark hair, turning to ice and then translucent as they melted.

One thing was for certain. She would not melt. She could not relent. "You are a thoughtful man. But it wouldn't be right for me to accept gifts from you."

"And why the hell not?" He quirked one brow, not angry but determined to know. "You need clothes, it's that simple."

"Then I can worry about procuring them."

"The doc wouldn't want you to be up and around shopping for hours. He said you're to stay indoors. I thought I could help make it more enjoyable for you."

"You took that burden upon yourself, huh?" She frowned, as if trying to figure out what he wanted from her.

That's one worry you don't need to have, angel. His chest filled with the certainty, the responsibility of it. He would not hurt her or use her. She didn't believe it now, but she would. "I don't mind taking up the reins and seeing a task gets done. You needed more clothes, since you didn't have the foresight to pack a bigger bag."

"I didn't think I was strong enough to carry one."

"Did you think you were strong enough to walk to town in a snowstorm?"

"Yes, if I wasn't weighed down by heavy baggage. Besides, there is nothing I want from that house. It's my past, and it's behind me." Her chin shot up, all fight. There was no self-pity, but strength and unwavering determination.

He liked her spirit. "Ready to start a new life? Maybe you'd be willing to accept a helping hand with that."

"And you're willing to help me, is that it?"

"I am. I'm the right man for the job, and I intend to convince you of that. You'll see."

He sure looked like the right man. In every possible way. Katelyn felt a sudden, expanding sensation in her chest. A sensation she refused to name. Refused to feel. She did *not* find the horseman attractive. Truly, she didn't.

To make a liar of her, her body warmed. Her senses filled with him. Her hand ached to lie at the base of his strong neck, where his shoulder and back met, and feel the heat of him against her skin. Her mouth tingled, remembering and yearning for the taste of his kiss and the power of it. She ached deep inside for him.

It wasn't what she wanted. She didn't want another man dominating her. Controlling her life. Withholding affection because he had the power to.

"Unwrap these, go on." He nudged a half-dozen packages toward her. The largest he set in the corner. "We'll keep this one for last. Go on. I'll be right back."

What she ought to be was wary. Guarded. Hadn't Hennessey admitted to trying to earn her affections? She had to put a halt to this. She had to make him understand she was a woman strong enough to stand on her own feet. That she'd been married once. And never again.

She didn't need gifts from a man. What she needed was to be strong enough to find work. She shouldn't be wondering what was in these packages, what the horseman, who'd stood so proud and pleased, had bought for her.

It doesn't matter. Leave the packages alone, Katelyn. It was the right thing to do, but she *wanted* to open them.

It was weak of her, she supposed.

A clatter in the hallway tore her away from her thoughts. Was that Hennessey? What was he up to?

The metallic clanging came closer until a big steel tub filled the threshold, hefted by the brawny, capable horseman. His sleeves were rolled back to display the ropes of muscle cording beneath his brown skin.

He placed the tub on end in front of the fire, leaving it balanced against the wall while he moved the wing chair out of the way.

She watched him work. How could she not? He was a sight to behold, the magnificence of him, the elemental maleness of him as he worked. His intensity of concentration, the care he took with his task, the masculine grace as he moved and bent and tugged to fit the big tub into a narrow space. The fall of hair over his brow, the curve of his neck as he knelt, the line of his back so wide and strong.

She wanted to put her hand there, between his shoulder blades, and run her fingers down the deep furrow of his spine. To feel the heat of his skin. To kiss him there and taste his salty male heat.

It wasn't what she wanted, not rationally. But the woman in her craved something that did not exist. Or was so rare, it might as well be nonexistent.

He simply looked wonderful. Of course her basic humors would respond to this example of male perfection. What woman wouldn't want to be held safe in his arms? What woman wouldn't want to believe there was comfort and love and tenderness to be found snuggling against his impressive chest?

"You're not opening your packages." He tossed her an infectious grin—he had to know how charming he was—and disappeared through the doorway and into the hall, his steps fading away into silence.

Stop trying to see a man as good as Papa in him.

Her father had been a rare individual. Protective and strong and gentle with her, and the memories made dim and fuzzy from time remained powerful enough to still the pain inside her. A brief remembrance of a man who had spoken softly, acted deliberately and hurt no one.

There were good men in this world, but how scarce they were.

Hennessey burst into the room carrying two steaming ten-gallon buckets as if they weighed nothing at all. "Hope you like your bathwater hot."

"I can't believe you're doing this. I could manage to make it to the necessary room *downstairs*. Where the bathtub belongs."

"Sure, but then I can't be your hero by bringing a hot, soothing bath to you."

"I can arrange my own bath."

"Sure, but then I wouldn't be here to help you." He emptied the heavy buckets handily.

Had she heard him right? "I don't need help getting a bath ready."

He strode from the room as if he hadn't heard her.

As if she couldn't have gone downstairs and asked Mrs. Miller to heat bathwater. Katelyn rescued her hairbrush from the folds in the quilt and brushed her hair until it crackled, and tried not to watch Hennessey every time he entered the room. Every time he hefted the buckets with ease and rippling muscles and quiet competence. A competence her spirit admired, even as she set her mind against it.

"You'll need this." He ripped open a brown-wrapped bundle and a snowy white robe tumbled to the covers. So soft and luxurious looking that it made her fingers itch to touch the fabric.

"Let me help you." He lifted the brush from her hand and set it aside. His pupils grew huge until there was a tiny ring of brown around the black as his knuckles grazed her chin. There was a tug and a yank and the top button at her throat released.

"I can do this myself."

"I know." He loosened the next button and the next until the flannel placket fell forward, gaping, offering him a view of the top slopes of her breasts.

His gaze pinned hers as he continued unbuttoning. The pad of his thumb pressed into the inner curve of her right breast. She shuddered deep inside.

"This is wrong. You need to leave." She couldn't seem to summon up enough strength to make the words sound forceful.

"I suppose that would be the proper thing to do." Hennessey released the last button and the fabric fell free.

Air danced across her exposed nipples. They pebbled, tellingly, and heat crept up her face. She was strangely aroused. Liquid, spreading heat curled deep in her abdomen. Her breathing quickened. Her skin felt alive and craving his touch.

She'd never felt this way before. What she ought to do was send him from the room.

Slowly, as if destined, he lifted her hair away from the side of her neck and pressed his kiss there, hot and thrilling, beneath her earlobe.

Want flickered through her like fire.

She knew what he wanted. She'd been married. The quiet horseman might have little experience with women, but she didn't doubt he had experience of a different sort.

Here she was, alone with him, half-undressed on the bed. If she allowed it, he would have her out of her drawers, too, and naked beneath him spread out on the mattress.

Her stomach turned, remembering what that was like. The lovely heat in her midsection cooled into a faint disappointment.

"I can't." She couldn't look at him.

"Do you think I'd try to take advantage of you?" His hand curled around her neck, so much strength and latent force, but his touch felt soothing and heavenly. "Damn that sorry excuse of a man for what he did to you. But you're with me now. You're about to find out what a real man is like."

"A real man? Are there any of those left in this world?"

"A few of us sainted souls still roam the earth." He winked, acting cocky, trying to make her smile.

It almost worked. The sudden tension in her eased a little. The hard knot she didn't know was in her stomach loosened a bit.

He changed, softening the way a rugged granite mountain range softened with the dawn, and leaned his forehead to hers. Close. Intimate. As if he were suddenly a part of her flesh and bone.

"You're with me now, Katelyn." A promise, as sure as the earth and sky. As dependable as the floor at her feet. "Trust me, all right? If you do, you'll see how a man treats a woman."

His hand sneaked beneath her hair and cradled her head in his palm as his lips slanted over hers. A tender, heartrending brush of steel and heat and desire. A man's loving kiss that left her stunned, her senses spinning. Her entire body quivered with awareness.

"Come with me." He took her hand, so small in his, and helped her to her feet.

She was too dazed to argue. He drew her forward and she moved. She felt the heat from the water and the heat from him and burned, wholly, deeply.

He smoothed the nightgown from the curves of her shoulders and the fabric fell in a whisper down her arms, over her hips to pool on the nubby carpet beneath her feet. He moved behind her, his fingertips digging into the curve of her hip, holding her as he fit against her, his kiss to her nape, his hand in her hair. As if he belonged there.

He doesn't belong with me. She willed the words into her mind, but they were not strong enough to stop the power of his touch. It sifted through her like snow from a benevolent sky, fragile and stunning and unstoppable and so peaceful she closed her eyes and wished it would never end.

His fingertips scraped down her ribs, skimmed lower and caught the cotton waist of her drawers. His breath fanned her nape as he tugged the bow loose and the fabric hung at her hips, ready to fall at any moment.

Naked, exposed, vulnerable, she shivered, but not from fear. Hennessey's kiss traveled from her nape to her earlobe. The tug of his lips on sensitive skin felt like paradise. His palms caught her hipbones and his fingers interlocked over the curve of her stomach, trapping her against his steeled chest and the hard, impressive manhood jutting against the small of her back.

"I have never seen such beauty." His confession was a low caress against the sensitized shell of her ear.

She broke then, like snow from the face of mountain, crumbling apart, unable to stop. Inevitable, fated, she closed her eyes and leaned into his strength. She allowed his arms to hold her up as her heart tumbled. What was he doing to her?

"The bath is waiting for you." His words skimmed the curve of her earlobe. "I'll just turn around while you, uh, take off the rest of your things."

Was that shyness she heard in his voice? she wondered as she let the cotton slip to the floor. She laid one hand on the back of his shoulder as she dipped one foot into the steaming water. The lap and caress of the hot water melted her very bones. She brought her other foot into the tub and eased all the way in.

Heaven. She rested her head against the hard rim and closed her eyes. When was the last time she'd felt this good? She couldn't remember. The delicious water comforted her soreness. Her worries drifted away on the rising steam to evaporate into nothing.

"Does it feel good?"

"Hmm." She couldn't speak. That's how good it was. She was like a hunk of butter melting on a stove. Grateful tears ached in her throat.

Dillon had done this for her. She couldn't remember anyone doing so much for her in what felt like a lifetime. She had to think of something to do for him in return.

She heard the hush of fabric and the crinkle of

paper. Hennessey's step moved closer. Fabric whispered to a rest on the chair cushion, within reach. She summoned up enough strength to open one eye a slit. He'd brought her the new robe.

"And for you. I hope you haven't read it." He laid a volume and a towel next to the robe.

A book? He'd bought her a book? She sat up. Water crashed against the rim of the tub and splashed over. Dillon knelt and handed her the towel to dry her hands.

A more disciplined man would say it was water droplets glistening in the lamplight on her bare, silken skin that aroused him. Or the graceful sweep of her slim hands as she took the towel and dried the dampness from her sensitive fingertips. A better man than him wouldn't sneak a quick peek at her generous, rose-tipped breasts and creamy thighs.

He wasn't a saint. He looked at her, blood stampeding through his veins. His ears buzzed. His vision blurred. He panted for air in short, fast gasps. He was instantly throbbing hard.

It was all he could do not to reach through that sheen of glittering water and fill his hands with her soft breasts. So big, they'd fit his hands with some to spare. If only he had the right to touch her like that. Love her like that. He'd make sure to take care of her. To give her pleasure. To make her want him.

"Oh, Charles Dickens." Even her voice aroused him more. Soft as a caress on bare skin.

She's not yours yet, Hennessey. He fought for control as he handed her the thick book. She was talking, but her words came from so far away and he couldn't hear them over the drum of his pulse in his ears. A beat that pounded through his entire body. How he wanted her. Needed her.

This is for her, remember that. As much as he wanted to haul her wet and naked into his arms, he turned his back and grabbed the pitcher from the nightstand to fill Katelyn's tin cup. The cold water and the cool cup felt like ice in his hand. He heard the tinkle of water as Katelyn settled back to read her book.

Just give her the cup. And don't stare. Don't scare her.

"Dillon, how can I ever thank you enough?" Her face was flushed from the heat. A healthy glow. Her eyes sparkled with pleasure.

"This is only the beginning, ma'am." He set the cup within reach and kept his attention on her face. She was lovely. He ached with the need to touch her. If only to run one fingertip down the inviting curve of her face.

"So, this is how a real man treats a lady? He pours her a bath and watches her?"

"Sorry. Guess I shouldn't be sitting here." His face burned, but he stayed right where he was. "But a real man doesn't leave a job half-finished."

"What job?"

"Why, ma'am, I brought up the tub and the water, but there's more work to be done. It goes against my conscience to be a lazybones and leave you to do all the work."

"What work?"

"Why, that's a complicated question. The first answer would be this. It's my duty to help you feel better. After what you've been through and how you were treated, it's my sworn duty to show you not all men are jackasses.''

''Sworn duty?'' Over the top of *A Tale of Two Cities,* the humor vanished from her face. Wariness crept in.

Just how much had that bastard hurt her? A slow burning rage tasted bitter on his tongue as he eased around to the back of the tub. Slow. Easy. He wasn't about to frighten her. ''That's right, ma'am. Relax, it's all right. Keep reading.''

She turned with a swish of water to watch him. ''What are you doing?''

''Me? I'm simply following the rules.''

''What rules?''

''Real men's rules. They're like commandments. A decent man always follows them.''

''Decent? You call gazing down at a bathing woman decent?'' Some of the wariness was easing.

He kept his voice low and easy and warm, as he did when he talked to horses. ''Just mind your business, ma'am, and read your book. Leave the rest up to me.''

''Dillon.'' She tensed. Her jaw tightened. Her eyes pinched. The wariness crept back. ''I thought you would leave. I know what my stepfather said, but you can't— I'm not—''

Sure she was worried and expected the worst. She'd been hurt and hurt badly. Didn't know if men did anything else. Just like the horses he worked with. And he knew exactly what to do. Exactly what she needed.

''I know. Believe me, I would never hurt you.'' He

gathered her long hair and slipped it over her shoulder, baring her neck.

He touched her before she could leap up and bolt for safety, before her nervousness could escalate into panic. He drew up the warmth from his heart, the way his grandfather taught him, so she could feel him. Feel that he meant her no harm.

He felt her intake of breath. Yeah, she felt him all right. His hands stroked up the length of her neck, from shoulder line to her hairline and on up past to the crown of her head. A light, soft, slow touch. "Like that?"

"Oh." She breathed the word. "Yes."

"See? It's a job to serve a pretty lady."

"You're just trying to convince me to m-marry you. You said so." She stiffened and shuddered.

He could feel the hurt move through her and into him. "That I did. I'm just being honest. That's the best course between a man and a woman, don't you think?"

She nodded, her beautiful face pinched. Yeah, it was as he thought. So much pain.

It's okay, my sweet angel. It's all right now. He stroked his fingertips up her spine again. He could feel the rounds of her vertebrae, the heated satin of her skin, the gossamer softness of her hair.

His trousers became more uncomfortable as he grew unbelievably harder. There was no denying the desire that pulsed through him. Hard like a hammer's blow. But this wasn't about his needs. His desires.

He wove his thumbs up her neck, digging in between those small vertebrae.

''Oh, that's nice.'' She leaned into his touch, just a bit.

That's right. It feels good, doesn't it, honey? As if in answer, she sighed in a long, slow release. A contented sound. Yeah, she liked it. She liked his touch. *I'm gonna make you feel better, see?*

He cradled his left hand at the base of her skull. She didn't rest her head, she didn't trust him yet. Fine, he'd show her that she could. He stroked along her hairline, behind her right ear and lingered when he heard the tiny moan low in her throat. He ran his hand across her brow. Over the top of her head in slow easy circles.

She rested the weight of her head in his palm.

That's right, angel. He wanted to hop up and dance a jig. Throw open the window and shout his triumph to the wind. Instead he caressed the length of his hand down her neck and into the dip of her right shoulder.

''Oh.'' She sighed.

He kept going along her shoulder and down her arm and back again. *I'm going to treat you good and gentle. I'm going to make it all better. I can do that for you. Yes I can, sweet lady. See?*

As if in answer, she relaxed even more. Sank lower into the steaming water. He held her head steady. Caught the book as it began to tip out of her hands.

''I'll just put that over here.'' He had to smile. Her eyes drifted shut, her face as soft as if she were sleeping, as trouble free.

He'd done that for her. It made him feel good, manly, satisfied. She was his now, whether she admitted it or not. But she'd already decided it. He could feel it in her surrender.

He pressed a kiss to the top of her head. Affection began to grow in his lonely heart. *I'll take care of you. I'll never hurt you like that. Never.*

"Here's your book." He retrieved it for her, found the page she'd been reading and placed it into her hands.

"That was wonderful."

"Just doing my job, ma'am." His clothes rustled and a knee joint cracked as he straightened to his full height.

She felt his gaze as strongly as if he'd reached into the water and grabbed hold of her breasts. Why wasn't she upset about that? She pulsed at the thought. She glowed all over. Every inch of her.

From his touch.

"It's your job to gape at my naked form?"

"It sure is." A blush crept up from his collar to his chin and stained his cheeks. Bashful, but he didn't look away. "Since I mean to marry you, I might as well see what I'll be getting."

"That was indecent." She tossed the washcloth at him.

He caught it in midair before it could hit him in the face. "Yeah, but you liked it. Want more?"

"More?" Oh, heavens, yes. The thought of his touch, like rapture along her skin, like bliss to her soul, made her want. Made desire swell low in her abdomen. She'd never felt like this before.

She knew the marriage act was cold duty. And it was nothing like Hennessey's touch. Nothing like the kiss he'd given her. Nothing like the liquid pleasure pooling within her.

He knelt beside her. His eyes had gone black. She

could see his chest rise and fall in quick, sharp breaths. The intensity of him, the desire for her naked on his face. His hand splayed along her throat, drawing her into his kiss. It was more than a kiss.

Soft touching, the way the first snowfall of winter finds the earth. Tentative, following its destiny. Snow could no more fall upward than she could break away from Dillon's kiss. Soft, tender, and then harder. Hungrier. A storm that came from him and swept through her. Carrying her away, making her forget all that had come before. The pain. The unhappiness. The loneliness of being with another man.

This man healed her. With his kiss, with the sweep of his tongue, with the brand of his mouth to hers, there was no pain. No unhappiness. No loneliness. Just the singular pleasure of being wanted. Cherished.

He broke away, breathless, looking into her eyes as if he could see the frozen ice around her heart. He leaned his forehead to hers, and she swore she could feel him. His feelings. A warm bright glow that she'd never felt anywhere.

She wanted him to hold her. To kiss her again. To shelter her in his strong arms and let her feel that light in him. That soft comforting brightness of his affection.

But he moved away.

"Enjoy your bath, beautiful. I'll be close by if you need me. Just holler."

He closed the door behind him, leaving her alone.

Leaving her wanting. Sharp-edged barbs of need that did not ease as she tried to read. She couldn't. The words were merely letters and she couldn't concentrate on the story. All she thought of was the horseman. His touch. His tender kiss. The warmth that he'd set to glowing, like ashes breathed back to life, and it hurt.

It hurt.

What was this feeling? And why did this man have so much power over her?

Not a bad power, she conceded. Closing her eyes, she could bring him back. The memory of his callused fingertips at the base of her neck. Of his leather and winter scent. Of the vibrating rumble of his voice as he spoke, and it moved through her. His touch, his kiss, his soft comfort.

She thought of nothing else until the water grew cool. She washed quickly, dressed and hurried to bed. She pretended to be asleep when Hennessey returned to check on her. Water sloshed as he worked quietly so as not to wake her. He carried away the water bucket by bucket and then the tub.

Before he left her alone, he approached the bed. He bent over her and brushed away damp curls from her face. His kiss to her cheek was feather soft.

He whispered into her hair, "Sleep well, angel. I love you. I do."

She kept perfectly still. Like a bud drawn tight during a freezing night. She waited until the door creaked shut and the knob clicked. Until his retreating step faded into silence before she crawled out of bed.

He loved her? That couldn't be true. He didn't know her. And of the men who had known her well enough, they had found her wanting.

Except for one man. He'd been a horseman, too.

Katelyn's chest tightened, and not from exhaustion

or pain. It was her conscience. Her heart. Aching the way a long cold night ached for the dawn.

She pulled back the curtains to watch the street below. There he was, a dark form on the endless prairie, a lone rider growing smaller and smaller until the shadows stole him from her sight.

Chapter Eleven

Dillon had to stop thinking about Katelyn. It sounded pretty damn easy. He figured he could just start concentrating on other things. Things like seeing his brother again. Checking on his land. Seeing if any wild varmints had decided to hole up in his cabin. And what about the stallion? That had to be a priority.

The trouble was, when he thought about the stallion, it took his mind right back to her. How she'd looked asleep, framed by pillows and lace, an angel too fine for the likes of him.

Was there a chance? She'd surrendered to his touch. She'd wanted more of it. It was a start on a long, uncertain road. Liking having him rub her neck was a far cry from loving him, heart and soul.

His mustang stumbled as a section of hard-packed snow gave way, snapping Dillon's attention back to the task ahead of him. He had to get the cabin cleaned up and ready if he was going to bring Katelyn home.

Would she come? He could make her. She was a woman alone, without family or friends who would help her. She had no place to go. A home with him was better than being destitute and homeless, and in her weakened condition, too.

It was one way to rope her. To put a ring on her finger and make her his. But it wasn't the right way. It wasn't the way he wanted to do it.

Should he give her a choice? That would mean he'd risk losing her, and the thought of that ripped a hole in the middle of him. *I want her so much.*

But not at any cost.

As the miles passed, the clouds overhead broke, giving way to a reluctant glimpse of an ambivalent sun. White curtains of light rained from heaven to earth and, in celebration, the snow winked like fine-cut diamonds.

Like the kind of diamond Katelyn would deserve on her wedding ring.

Would he see his ring on her hand? He tried to imagine it. A slim gold band on her slender fourth finger. His brand marking her as his wife. Wife. Wouldn't that be something? He'd be able to love her.

The image of her in her bath, smooth lean thighs made to wrap around a man. He'd love her. He'd show her what a man could do for her. He'd make her moan low in her throat, groan in pleasure and then sigh, contented.

Damn, she kept filling his thoughts. It was certain to drive him mad. He'd never been like this over a woman. Never wanted to be like this again. If Katelyn didn't want him, if she didn't come to love him, then there would be no other woman.

She'd wanted him, a little. He remembered the way she'd moaned. The way she'd leaned into his touch.

The cabin looked lonely and forgotten with the

windows closed tight and the snow drifted over one corner of the small porch. His brother must not have had a chance to come over and check on things. A season's first snow always meant unforeseen work. Dillon dismounted, led the mustang into the stable and forked some fresh hay into the trough.

A faint whistle carried on the wind. The late-afternoon train.

Along the northern horizon, a bank of clouds was coming in from the northwest. It looked like more snow. Not a blizzard, but an inch or more on its way. This year winter had come hard and early to the plains.

If Katelyn didn't stay, maybe he'd head south. Escape the long winter. He'd had a couple job offers come in from Arizona.

He sensed the rider before he saw him. Small brown sparrows stopped in the middle of their song, scattering low along the frozen sheen of ice and snow. A gopher dove into his burrow with protest, his snow-clearing task interrupted.

Dillon had the fire hot and the coffee boiling by the time his brother stabled his cayuse and stomped the snow off his boots on the back porch.

"I didn't expect to see you here." Dakota hung his hat on the peg by the door. "Did that job finish early?"

"Something like that. Come in. Get warm." Dillon poured two cups. "Hell, it's good to see you, brother."

"I could say the same. You look like hell."

"Yeah? I guess a woman will do that to a man."

"What woman?" Dakota held his hands up to the

stove. "Don't tell me you have got yourself a woman? I don't see any signs of one."

"She's at the hotel in town. It's a long story. When you've warmed up, runt, I'll tell you all about her over a cup of coffee."

"Who are you calling 'runt'?" Dakota was every bit as big, but wider. Brawnier.

"Yeah, but I'm tougher." Dillon pulled up a chair, considered the significant layer of dust on the seat, and sat on it anyway. "Have you ever considered getting married?"

"Sure, but I was drunk under the table, an unfortunate decision in my youth, and after a bottle of whiskey I thought marriage sounded like a good notion. Then I sobered up."

"You're no help." Dillon studied the log house. The solid walls. The good chinking job. A sturdy roof that had never leaked. The thick walls kept the cold winter winds out, and the fire's warmth in.

It wasn't a rich man's fancy house. He couldn't imagine Katelyn here. Or could he? Did she know how to cook? She'd probably had hired servants in her former husband's house. He tried to envision her frying his breakfast eggs at the stove. It just didn't fit.

He had to be prepared to let her go. He had to be ready to lose his heart.

"Here's a pot of tea, love." Mrs. Miller shuffled into the predawn shadows balancing a loaded tray, a lace scarf covering her silvered hair. "Nothing heals what ails you better than sweet tea. I brought up some honey and a sourdough biscuit straight out of the oven. Eat up, now. Breakfast is served at six prompt. I'm making pancakes.''

''Thank you.'' Katelyn took the tray, the cup and saucer rattling as she lowered it to the small table beside the wing chair where she sat. ''Can you tell me if Mr. Hennessey will return this morning?''

''He didn't say.'' Mrs. Miller straightened her full-length calico apron before retreating into the hall. ''I expect Mr. Hennessey will be here before long. He lives just south of town. Such a fine man. He sure was concerned about you, dear. At least you have a little color in your cheeks.''

Katelyn thanked the innkeeper and, as soon as she was alone, her thoughts returned to Hennessey. She'd dreamed of him that night. Of being enfolded in his arms, snug against his chest and breathing in his night and winter scent.

When she'd awakened alone in her room in the lonely dark before dawn, her first thought was of him. As every thought had been since.

Was that him? She could *feel* his nearness like a change in the air. Or, maybe, the change was within her. She was not surprised when she heard the first strike of his boot down the hall. It was his unhurried gait in the corridor. It was his rapid-fire knock on her door.

''Come in.'' The words felt trapped in her throat, but he must have heard her.

The door creaked open and there he was, his face as expressionless as stone, his silence as impressive as a snowcapped mountain. ''How are you feeling this fine day?''

''Better. Stronger.'' She drew the afghan around

her lap. Even though she was dressed, she felt exposed. "Would you like some tea?"

"No. Here, let me." His broad hand closed over the dainty china pot, dwarfing it as he poured a cup. The delicate handle was too small for his fingers, and he looked awkward as he handed her the brimming cup. "Anything else I can get you?"

"I'm fine." She bit her lip. He was doing it again. Being overly accommodating.

"Do you want breakfast? I can head downstairs and dish you up a plate from the kitchen. Or do you want pastry? I could run over to the bakery. Pick you up some of those fancy treats they have."

"No, thank you." She sipped delicately, her fingers dainty on the tiny handle, and set the cup on the table with a clink. So perfect and proper.

While he was an inept suitor. He felt big and awkward and stupid. There was one silver lining in all this heartache, for if Katelyn rejected him this time, then he would never need to court another woman again.

It was tough enough to make a real man cry.

All right, ask her again, Hennessey. Try not to look like a fool. Just set out her choices and let her decide. It was as simple as that.

Not so simple. She was radiant this morning. The rest had helped, and surely, so had escaping the tension and worry she felt in her stepfather's house. Her skin was creamy, no longer ashen. The circles beneath her eyes were fading.

She was luminous, like a bright star shining in a perfect night sky. His angel. No, she was more than an angel. She was a seraphim, the highest order of angels, who stood closest to God.

When she spoke, her soft resonant alto could have belonged in paradise. "I've been enjoying the book."

The book? He blinked, and suddenly his mind started functioning again. She was talking about the Dickens novel he'd bought her. Why wasn't she wearing one of the dresses he'd bought her? He glanced around the small room and it was easy to see why. He didn't need to ask. The presents were still wrapped in brown paper. "You didn't open them."

"It's not that I don't appreciate them."

Did she have to be so good? Kind? Dillon would bet there wasn't a cherub in heaven that could reject a man more gently. "I had to try to win your fancy. It isn't often a woman like you comes into a man's life. Especially a man like me."

"Like you?"

Was she going to make him say it? "I'm a common man. I work with my hands and my back and my heart. I don't wear ties and I don't spend my day in a building being polite and proper. I'm not the kind of man you probably want for a husband, but I'm stubborn and I'm persistent. That's what makes me good at what I do. So here."

He didn't look at her as he opened his billfold and dropped one greenback after another on the small table in front of her, next to the teapot.

"Don't worry about the hotel or the doctor bill. I'll take care of them." He dropped the last greenback in his wallet on the small stack and folded the leather with pronounced concentration. "This ought to get you anywhere you need to go. And this—"

He reached into his shirt pocket and laid a slim gold band with a single square-cut diamond on top of the money. "This is my way of asking you to choose."

"Choose? Between marrying you or accepting your money?"

"No, between leaving and going where you want or accepting me. Heaven knows I want to marry you. I'll do my best by you. I've already told you that. But I don't want you to marry me because you have no other choice. I won't be someone you settle for. If you marry me, know that I'm the best husband you are ever going to get. And if not, then good luck and goodbye, Katelyn Green. The best to you."

He nodded in her direction, his movements quick and jerky, his hard body as tense as steel as he marched to the door and out of her life.

Five hundred-dollar bills stared up at her, creased in thirds from his worn leather wallet. That was a small fortune for a workingman. More than a year's wages.

She was nearly penniless. He could have pressured her. He could have used her situation to persuade her to marry him. And he hadn't.

"Wait! Dillon, please, don't go."

He stopped in the hallway. Splayed a sun-browned hand on the door frame. In his eyes she saw pain.

"You could live a long time on five hundred dollars, if you were careful." He winced, and pain shot across his face before his eyes shuttered completely, hiding all his light. "I suppose that isn't a lot of money to you."

"It will see me a long way. It's just what I need to start a new life. I was going to take the teacher's examinations come spring and see if I could get a school."

"You'd make a fine teacher."

How dark he looked.

How intimidating. So much pain emanated from him, she could feel it all the way across the room like a tug of emotion in her chest. In her heart.

He'd given her the means to be on her own. And he didn't need to do that. She could recover, find a job and pay her own debts. But she knew, if she did that, she would always wonder. Always regret that she had never found out what this was she felt in her heart for this man.

The timing was all wrong. Her emotions were still scarred, and her grief… Her chest fisted tight with a killing pain. No, she did not dare think about that.

She only knew she could not let him go. "Do you know the reason I didn't open your gifts? Because I don't want you to think I'm saying yes because of what you've bought me. I'll marry you because of how you've treated me."

"What did you say?"

"This ring could be just what I need to start a new life, too. *If* you are a man of your word."

"If? Angel, I'm that and more." Dillon couldn't believe his ears. He crossed the room in three strides and dropped to his knees in front of her. "You know what I am. I'm a horseman, not a judge."

"I noticed."

"I've got a log house, not a fine mansion on a tree-lined street. You know that, right? I'm not wealthy. There won't be servants and maids and a cook.''

''I wasn't expecting any.''

If she married him, he wanted her to know what was in store for her. The last thing he wanted to do was disappoint her. ''I'm not a lot of things that you're used to. Polished and civilized and educated. I am what I am.''

Were her eyes twinkling at him? Was she trying not to laugh at him? What was he doing wrong now? A shaft of pain bored through his left temple. He was glad this courting nonsense was over. He couldn't survive much more of it. ''Am I amusing you?''

''Yes. There's something you should know before you keep going on about how humble you are.''

''Now you're mocking me.''

''You don't have to worry, Dillon. My father was a horseman, too.''

His hands framed her face with tenderness and his mouth found hers in a kiss that lifted the soles of her feet from the floor.

Overwhelmed, she pulled away, chuckling, catching her breath. She hadn't expected this reaction. She hadn't even known what she would choose until she saw him walk through that door.

Marrying him was a practical decision. That was all. She was still weak, and being on her own, even with money in her pocket, would not be her best choice.

But marriage was permanent. Panic licked at her like a greedy fire at a log, and she couldn't deny she could be making a mistake. *If you marry me, know that I'm the best husband you are ever going to get.*

Look how happy he was. Surely that was a good sign. That meant he *was* going to treat her well.

Marriage was a practical, legal arrangement in her social circle more often than not. That was what had motivated her mother to marry. As it had been Katelyn's duty to wed her stepfather's good friend, a man who had brought many benefits to the family. She didn't see that kind of alliance had ever brought anyone happiness. Certainly her marriage had been sad and lonely and miserable.

Maybe that was simply the experience of matrimony. But surely being bound to a man who cared for her was a far better option than living alone for the rest of her days.

Perhaps, her life with the horseman would be pleasant. Peaceful enough so she could pretend not to feel her grief. She might find it easier to breathe in and out. To face each day and muddle through it. For what life could she ever have without her heart?

"When do you want to get married?" His touch to her face turned reverent. "Wait. Maybe it's best to get breakfast first. And the doctor, he's going to have to see if you're strong enough to ride in a sleigh. I don't want you tired out."

"Wait, Dillon, I—"

"I'll ask the town minister when he has time to perform a ceremony. Marry me now, and I'll take you home today. I'll take care of you."

Maybe I've made the wrong decision. She took his big hand in hers, workingman's hands. Callused from holding leather reins and training leads. Hands that were brown from the sun and rough from the wind.

Dependable, capable hands that had made her feel alive.

She hadn't thought what he would want from her in a marriage. This man, whose heart showed in his honest excitement and his affectionate touch.

Should she change her mind? Now, while she had the chance? And how could she? He cared for her so much.

"I'll go fetch your breakfast. That's the first thing."

He is a good man. A hard pain twisted in her chest. The pain of starting to care for someone again. Coming up through the grief in her heart like a seedling through snow.

"Open your gifts. Go on." He handed her a package from the corner of the bed. "I'll be back. Want anything special from the kitchen?"

"No." She set the afghan aside and stood. "I need to talk to you about something. You seem to have the wrong impression."

"I do?"

"You said that honesty is the best course between a man and a woman."

"I sure did." He took one look at her furrowed brow and his happiness withered. He gripped the lip of the wooden mantel for support. Was she going to change her mind?

"I don't know what you are expecting of me as your wife." She might be a petite woman who looked as delicate as the china cup she'd been drinking from, but she had backbone. Standing up to him. Looking him in the eye.

He liked it. She'd never been more attractive to

him. He should have known she wasn't about to go back on her word. "I guess I'm expecting the usual. Fidelity. Honesty. A happy home."

"Fine, but I mean, from me. The wedding night? Do you expect—"

"No." He hated seeing fear shiver through her. What had that bastard done to her? He hid his fury, schooling it from his voice, because he didn't want to frighten her.

He'd never want to do that. "I know getting used to me is going to be an adjustment. I'm not going to rush you on certain, er, uh, intimacies. It's not a duty, and I don't want you thinking you have to submit to me, all right?"

Her fisted hands relaxed. Relief erased some of the furrows from her crinkled brow. "Thank you for understanding."

"Why thank me? It's only natural that you'll need time. In the meanwhile, I'll draw baths for you and tuck you in at night. Is that a deal?"

What a man he is. There was no way he could know what his understanding meant to her. She pushed aside memories of Brett's impatience on their wedding night. And the act of marriage that she dreaded.

Dillon's touch had been tender and thrilling. Caring. As had his whispered confession when he'd thought she slept. *I love you. I do.*

No one in her adult life had said they loved her. The power of those words gave her courage now. She never wanted to hurt this man who stood as tough as a mountain and hid a gallant soul.

Just tell him, Katelyn. She took a breath while he

waited. "I know how you feel, but you need to know that I don't love you."

"Yet."

"I'm sorry. I want to be honest with you."

"I already know that, angel." His eyes looked pinched, but he stood as unshakable as ever.

"And you still want to marry me?"

"Darlin', I'd do anything for the privilege of having you for my wife." He stole the ring from the table, cradled her left hand in his and slipped the band of gold on her finger.

"No matter what happens in our life together, I will never abandon you. I'll never cast you aside. This is for always, Katelyn. I'll forever stand by you."

How could he know what his words meant to her?

He kissed her cheek, a tender brush of his lips. In her view, he stood taller and greater than he ever had before.

Chapter Twelve

"Do you take this woman to be your lawful wedded wife?" The minister's question hit Dillon like a sucker punch.

Although he had two weeks to get used to the idea that she'd said yes, it still left him reeling and gasping for air. You'd think a man who'd done nothing but wish for Katelyn's hand in marriage since he'd spotted her on that first moonlight night wouldn't be quaking in his boots when he was getting exactly what he wanted. But he was. It wasn't getting married that was scaring him.

His bride kept glancing toward the door.

Did she want to escape? Was she going to dash off down the empty aisle in the middle of her vows? Or was she simply going to say she'd rather crawl on her hands and knees over the Rocky Mountains in winter than marry a workingman like him?

Worrying about whether she'd bolt or not was going to give him an apoplexy.

Don't let me down, angel. Since he was in a church, he hoped the heavens would hear his request.

"Repeat after me," the minister instructed. "I, Dillon Michael Hennessey..."

He did his best to concentrate. He didn't want to make a mistake. He meant these words with all he was. Heart, body and soul. "...to honor and cherish, in sickness and in health," he vowed. He felt as tall as the sky. In a few more moments, she would be his wife.

His wife. He couldn't believe it. He felt near to bursting with pride.

"I, Katherine Lyn Green," she spoke, her words vibrating like a harp's string, she sounded so nervous.

You have nothing to fear, he wanted to tell her. He'd never let anything hurt her. He'd protect her with his life, love her with his heart.

She was beautiful in one of the dresses he'd bought for her. In fact, everything she wore had been from him. It was thoughtful of her, since the clothes she'd brought with her in her little satchel were much fancier.

But in the green-and-tan calico she looked more like a horseman's wife. Her hair was up in a knot, and a few unruly curls had tumbled over her brow and into her eyes. Such a beautiful woman, and she was his. All his.

The ceremony was almost over. She hadn't run yet. She'd repeated her vows perfectly. Her palms against his were damp and he could feel her fear the same way he could feel the flutter of her pulse at his fingertips.

"If there is any reason..." the minister called out in the empty church.

Words Katelyn could not listen to. They reminded

her of another wedding, of feeling as if she'd been handed a jail sentence with a man she didn't love.

What was she doing marrying another man she didn't love?

Dillon is different. He's kind. He's good. I care about him. But she didn't love him. Her mind swirled with doubt. What if this marriage turned out no better than the last?

No, Dillon was different. Better.

"I now pronounce you man and wife." The minister's words drew her from her thoughts and into the small church as her husband took her face in his hands, gazed down at her as if he cherished her only and utterly and covered her lips with his.

His kiss was like moonlight on the prairie. Stunning. Silvery. So beautiful it hurt. Tears gathered in her eyes. Hope took seed in her soul.

What about this man? He broke the kiss and in the reverent silence that followed, he folded her against him, his arms closed around her. Her cheek rested against his chest. She fit against him as if she'd been made to. Something happened inside her. Something changed. His hand settled into the small of her neck. His lips brushed her brow once and again.

How did he do it? How could he reach inside her like that with a kiss? Why could he stir her in places long dead and buried? Like frozen ground beneath a winter's snow? It hurt, this quiet affection finding life inside her.

His hand stroked her face, lifted her chin to meet his eyes, and when he smiled, the ice cracked. Like winter into spring, she felt as if she were breaking inside and renewing. She didn't know what the feeling was in her chest, growing and spreading and hurting all at once. It was more than caring. More than affection.

Was it love?

"C'mon, Mrs. Hennessey." He grinned at her and kissed the tip of her nose. "Let me take you home."

With him. She took a step down the aisle, through the echoing church. The pews were empty. Already her life was different. When she'd married Brett, it had been in a crowded church with her mother fussing about how everything had to look and her stepfather furious about last-minute expenses.

It will be different this time. This time, there was only her and Dillon. There was no expensive wedding dress, just the crisp new calico she wore. The marriage would be different, too, because the man was.

He held the door for her, and a bright sun warmed them.

Nearly two weeks had passed since she'd accepted Dillon's proposal and the weather had turned again. Melting snow plopped off the edge of the roof as she followed Dillon down the front steps and into the churchyard. A mild wind blew over her face as Dillon took her hand and helped her into his small wagon's high board seat.

He climbed in beside her. "Thank you for marrying me. I thought you were going to jilt me a few times. You kept looking at the door."

"I was nervous," she confessed. "I thought I was going to faint."

"Am I that terrifying?" He sobered, his brow drawing down, and he looked strangely vulnerable. This man so mighty.

"No. But I am scared."

"You're with me now. You're as safe as can be."

"I know." That made him relax, and when he smiled, she could see his love for her gleaming like a brand-new promise. One that had not yet been broken.

How did she tell him it wasn't that kind of scared? He could let her down. He could fail her. Because she cared for him so much. Was he truly the man she'd come to know? She was gambling her heart that he was.

How risky was that? She had grown up in a house where appearances were perfect, but beneath was a different story. Her marriage to Brett had been no different. He had been polished and well-spoken and had immense respect in the community. And once he'd gotten her back home after the wedding dinner at the town's best hotel...

Dillon's not like that. She knew that. But as his hands gripped the reins and he called out to the horses, the power of them was unmistakable. The truth was, she was gambling her future on a man she did not know well. And all because she had the chance to be loved.

The *chance*. Not the certainty.

Dillon waited until the bustling traffic and the noise of town was behind them and they were jostling along the open prairie. "Did I ever tell you about the real man's rules?"

"No, but you did mention them the night you drew my bath."

"Yes, I believe I gave you a good introduction."

"Introduction? You just want to see me without clothes on."

"True, I won't lie to you. I figured I was going to marry you anyway, and you were unwell. You needed help into that tub."

"And I suppose you didn't want to trouble Mrs. Miller to come help me, since she had an inn to run."

"See, you understand. I was only interested in bringing pleasure to you." He settled the reins in one hand so he could hold hers.

She loved the thrill of his fingertips grazing across her bared skin. How would he touch her tonight? Maybe he would rub his way from the base of her spine to the top of her head in those slow, deep circles she'd liked.

Desire welled up through her, like champagne newly opened bubbling up and over, spilling everywhere. He would be loving to her, right?

"These commandments come from my grandfather's teachings."

"Teachings? Was he a scholar?"

"He was a very wise man. He could talk with horses. A rare gift."

"You talk to them. I've seen you."

"I've been known to hold a conversation or two with my four-legged friends."

Dillon liked the way her fingers fit between his, how her entire hand could fit into his palm. He traced his thumb over the diamond sparkling on the gold band. The ring that made her his wife.

He was so committed. He was the man who would take care of her. Stand by her. Love her. She would never have to worry like that again.

The way she was now, delicate lines of worry crinkled between her brows and around her mouth. *Don't you worry, my love. I'll treat you right. I'll show you the man I am.* It would take some time but she would trust him. He'd make damn sure of that.

He still couldn't believe she was really his wife. His to love. Forever. It was too good to be true. But she was here, with him, of her own free will. He thought of his home waiting for her. Of their future together. All he had to do was get her to love him.

It sounded like a big task, but the hard part was over. That courting sure was hard work. After that, how hard could a marriage be?

"Did you live with your grandfather? Is that how he taught you?"

Yep, she was interested. "He was my mother's father. A Nez Percé warrior of great courage and goodness. I was honored to have known him."

"You loved him. It was his native tongue I heard you speaking."

"Guilty. My grandfather taught me a great many things. Talking to horses was one of them."

The image of him speaking to the wild stallion was etched into her memory. The lull of his voice, deep and strong and musical. The silvered moonlight, the pearled shadows on the snow-blanketed prairie and the lone man with his hand outstretched, a legend in the night.

And he is yours. The new ring felt strange on her fourth finger, a reminder of the choice she'd made. She listened to the wagon wheels splash in the melting slush and chunks of snow. Felt the temperate breeze on her face. Let her body relax into his.

Dillon affected her like the warm south wind, trying to melt away the shadowed places within her. Persistent and constant, and she was weakening. What would happen if she did?

"My grandfather has been gone nearly five years. He lived with me."

That surprised her. "Here? Not on the reservation?"

"In the house I built. He wasn't well toward the end, and I cared for him all day, every day until he passed. It was a heartbreak. I miss him still. That's the reason I began traveling. I couldn't stand to be alone in the house anymore. The sadness of losing him was part of it. The sadness of not having my own family was another."

"I lost my father when I was little. Whenever I'm in the ranch house, I remember him. He was so tall I had to tip my head all the way back to see his face. He was a giant to me. In all ways."

"He was a horseman?"

"Yes."

"We horsemen are good men."

When she smiled, a slow curve of her rosebud lips, Dillon swore he saw paradise. He wanted to kiss that amazing mouth more than anything. Ever.

She shivered, and he realized he'd been staring at her.

When the last rise of the prairie lifted them up on a field of brown, dead grasses and mud and white patches of melting snow, he had to admit it. He couldn't pretend even to himself that he wasn't nervous.

Nervous? Ha. That was a lie. He was terrified. He

loved his house. His brother and grandfather had helped him build it because he'd always hoped he'd find the wherewithal to court a woman and marry her. To raise a family there. Sons and daughters who would run and play in the pristine meadows and splash in the nearby creek.

So much depended on this woman he'd made his bride. Every bit of his future. His happiness. Hell, even his children. He wanted her to be happy. It wasn't much, but the structure shaded by a grove of cottonwoods to the north and framed by the giant Rockies to the west and hugged by wild prairie was his home. All he had in the world.

Would it be good enough?

He braced himself for her disappointment. Figured he'd done all he could to prepare her. He'd told her outright before he'd placed the ring on her finger how it was going to be. She'd made her choice. But what if she regretted it?

Please, Katelyn, please like the house. He drew in a shaky breath and steeled himself for what was to come as the horses crested the last rise.

"That's our place," he told her when the prairie rose up before them. "Welcome home."

She didn't say anything. That couldn't be a good sign, could it?

He tried not to let it trouble him. He had told her she wouldn't be living in a fancy house. He was a man of humble means. He hadn't pretended to be something he wasn't.

At his low command, the horses stopped the wagon near the front steps. He tried to understand her disappointment. Maybe she'd come to like the place in time. The cabin was cozy and snug. She was a good woman. She'd come to see that was a far sight better than a lot of people had.

"*This* is your home?"

She didn't sound unhappy. Not at all. When he dared to look at her, she shone.

"When you said you lived in a cabin, I imagined something much smaller. You know, like the ones we drove past on the way here."

"You mean the claim shanties." The ten-by-sixteen shacks that dotted the prairie in quarter section patches. "You're not disappointed because you were expecting worse?"

"Stop this. I didn't always live in a big house. Before my father built the ranch house, we lived in a claim shanty. I was probably four years old, but my best memories are from that time. From living in that shanty."

The reins slipped from his fingers. He wouldn't have guessed that about her. Her lack of arrogance and the affection that warmed her like summer on the plains. It warmed him, too.

He hopped down and circled around to help her down.

"Come in. I've got a fire going and I'll put some tea water on. You can look around and get used to the place. See if it's something you can make a few more good memories in."

"Maybe."

When she laid her palm on his, his heart rolled right over in his chest. When her foot tapped against the ground, her long skirts swished around her ankles.

The rustling sounds of her movements skidded along his skin.

It was amazing how she affected him. As if there was nothing and nobody in the world but her. Only her.

She left her hand in his, her step matching his as they climbed the few stairs onto the porch. She was here, on his porch, about to become a permanent part of his life. He had to be dreaming this. How else could he ever have an angel like her? What good had he done?

Nothing nearly good enough, but he wasn't about to argue. She was his, and he was determined to take care of her. "You still look tired. There are circles under your eyes. Let's get you sitting down to rest."

"Oh, yes, I know. I'm not at my best." She bowed her head, self-conscious.

Maybe he hadn't said that the right way. He unlocked the door, cursing himself a few times. "You look beautiful, did I tell you that? I feel proud to be seen with you."

"Dillon, you don't have to compliment me."

"How else are you going to fall in love with me? Unless you want me to start saying ugly things?"

"You know I don't. You are in a good humor today, aren't you?"

"Darlin', this is my best day ever."

He brushed a warm kiss across her brow, a brief stroke of heat against her skin. She inhaled his salty, musky scent, so pleasant.

He pushed open the door and stood aside. "What do you think?"

"It's home." Her home. Katelyn stepped through

the threshold into a parlor as perfect as a painting, constructed with an artist's touch.

Wide smiling windows framed the river-stone fireplace, topped by the carved wood brim of a mantel. Neatly chinked log walls shone honey-gold in the sunlight, like an invitation.

Like a place to belong.

"Do you like it then?" He stood on the porch, looking in, hands fisted, frowning.

He was a worrier, wasn't he? "I do. The workmanship is stunning. Did you carve this?" She ran a fingertip over the intricate mantel where swimming salmon struggled upstream in a wooden river.

"One of my brothers." He gestured past the fireplace to the arched doorway in the center of the house. His big hand caught hers.

His touch blazed through her as dazzling as sunlight. She held on, letting him warm her clear through. How good it felt, this bright love of his.

Would it last? Is any man's love true? Dillon had her in his home as his wife. How would he treat her now?

The memories of another man crowded in, like shadows in a night room when a candle burned low.

She screwed her mind shut against the memories that crowded out, even as she fought them. The hope in her heart, the chance to be loved, it was all the same. Finally having a home where a wonderful man would love her.

And he had grabbed her roughly by one arm and had frightened her—

Don't remember. She bit her lip, trapped the pain in her throat. She didn't make a sound as Dillon's touch, sustaining and true, brought her back to where she was. In his cozy home about to enter another room. The bedroom?

Panic clawed at her. No, he wouldn't do that to her. He'd given her his word. She would find out today exactly how well Dillon Hennessey kept his promises.

"Do you want coffee or tea?" he asked, leading her not into a bedroom but a sparse kitchen where two big corner windows shed light on a small round table.

That's your answer, Katelyn. See? Dillon was keeping his word. *At least at this particular moment.* The prospect of tonight loomed ahead of her, a dark, threatening cloud she couldn't seem to escape.

"Tea would be wonderful."

"Pull up a chair and rest. I'll bring it to you." There was a clang of metal as he set water to heat, working with the ease of a man used to taking care of himself.

It was odd to see a man at a stove. He dwarfed the small cooking range with his width and breadth. He swore when he dropped a spoon on the floor, picked it up, wiped it on his shirt and stuck it in the sugar bowl.

He glanced at her through dark veiled lashes, bashful when he must have realized she was watching him. "Oops. Guess I should have got a clean one out of the drawer."

"At least you wiped it off first." Katelyn bit her lip so she wouldn't laugh. "The question is, if I would have dropped the spoon on the floor, what would you have done?"

"Probably used it. I'm not too finicky." He switched the fallen spoon for a clean one. "I suspect the sugar doesn't have any dirt in it. I just cleaned the floor."

"I see."

She tried to imagine her first husband being so unconcerned, and she couldn't. How could she tell him what it meant? To take in the soft light from the window, to feel the peace in the room, to know that she wouldn't be broken by a yelling man losing his temper over every small thing.

He isn't going to hurt me. I know it. So why was her stomach cramped into a tight hard ball?

Because knowing something wasn't the same as seeing that it isn't true.

"What do you think of the kitchen? Think you'll like cooking in here?"

Did she tell him that she couldn't cook? "I think I'll find it very interesting."

"Good. Darlin', you're getting pale. Sit down so I can stop fretting about you." He tossed her a grin that made pleasure glide in a slow fall all the way to her toes.

The room was proof that a bachelor lived here and not often. Dust clung to the tops of the cabinets and in the corners along the puncheon floor. The cookstove looked brand-new, as if it wasn't often used, and still bore its first coat of black polish from the factory.

And the furniture, heavens, she'd never seen the like. Mismatched set of chairs, one that looked as old as the Revolution and the other that sat hidden behind the hand-carved oak table.

Such workmanship. She ran her fingertips along the

maple-leaf-and-acorn pattern carved into the rim of the rounded tabletop. She left behind a thin trail through the dust.

She'd have to figure out how to clean house, too. It would be a fine thing, to take pride and pleasure in her own home. To keep everything polished and spar-kling. An act of love, she figured. And a much better way of spending time than going to social events.

I could be happy here, with this man. Would she be? She didn't know. But anything was worth the chance. She craved the bright enveloping warmth of his love more than air, more than water, more than food.

''Your tea, ma'am.''

She sat in the closest chair and spooned sugar into the chipped cup he'd set before her. This giant of a man was her life now. And how she would live and how she was treated was up to him. Only him.

The knock at the door stirred Katelyn from her book. Dillon had gone out to put up the horses, leav-ing her to her tea and the sunny warmth of the kitchen.

Before she could rise, she heard the faint muffle of Dillon's voice outside. Whoever it was, he was taking care of it. He did seem like a man who could take care of anything. Made of steel and nothing could bend him.

She drained a comforting swallow of the tea from the cup. It was cooling some, and only then did she realize there was a haze of rosy light glowing through the window behind her. Sunset. She turned in the chair, rested her chin on the wooden crown of the ladder-back and couldn't believe her eyes.

Peace filled her at the sight of the streaks of purple and crimson and magenta painted on the underbelly of the clouds and the proud snowcapped mountains. The jagged lavender-tinted peaks dominated the horizon. Some things you could count on to last. To never change.

Was Dillon Hennessey such a man?

Horses grazed in the distant pastures. Why was she surprised to see them? Many of them bore the markings of the mustangs native to this country. Pintos with large patches of browns and blacks over their rumps and along their sides. Appaloosas with their showy blanket of white spots as if a hundred snowflakes had landed and decided to stay on those velvet coats of black or brown or gray.

She remembered the stallion, the one her stepfather had placed a reward on. Dillon said he'd captured him. Was the stallion here?

She felt Dillon even before the door opened on the far side of the house. The rustle of his clothes, the whisper of his movements and the snap of his approaching step rolled through her like a wave on a lakeshore, lapping lightly, inevitably, over and over again. Touching her in a way she couldn't see or describe but could feel deep inside.

"Supper." He burst through the threshold, stirring the serenity of the room, making every hair on her arms and the back of her neck stand up and tingle.

He carried a large wicker basket that he set on the table with a thud. Wonderful fragrances lifted from it when he opened the lid—roast beef and gravy and roasted garlic and fresh-baked bread. "I paid one of the neighbor ladies to cook up a feast for us, since I figured with the ceremony and whatnot I wouldn't have time to cook for you."

"I thought I was supposed to cook. I was going to try and figure out what I could make."

"Not on our wedding night, darlin'. You sit there and rest. Want more tea?"

"I do." She watched in amazement as he filled her cup with a steady hand.

Twilight crept into the room, and he lit the lantern on the table before he sat down to dish up the meal. As the evening passed, all she did was worry about the coming night. She couldn't concentrate on her reading while Dillon read across from her in the parlor, his newspaper crinkling as he turned the page.

When the regulator clock on the kitchen wall gently bonged eight times, Katelyn closed her book, said good-night and headed up the flight of stairs and into the dark second story.

Moonlight spilling through an open window led her to the bedroom. A carved four-poster bed dominated the inside wall. There were two plump goose-down pillows at the head of the bed. She sat down on the feather tick and sank just right. The soft down felt like paradise.

Was that a footstep on the stairs? She listened, heart thumping. Yes, it was Dillon. Coming closer. Step by step. Slow and deliberate.

Dillon will keep his word. She was sure of it.

But a ripple of uncertainty launched her from the bed. She waited, her palms damp and her pulse thudding in her ears.

"Have you found what you need?" He pushed into the room as if he belonged here. "There are clean sheets on the bed. A couple of quilts in the trunk at the foot of the bed, if you get cold. I put your satchel in the wardrobe over here."

Did he realize he was blocking the doorway? Probably not. It was making her nervous, but she wasn't in any danger. Stay calm. "I believe I have everything I could want."

"Good. Glad to hear it." He looked bashful as he focused on the bed. "The necessary room is through the door."

"I figured it was."

"Is there anything I can get you? Tooth powder? More water? How about I fetch some wash water for you?"

"Don't go to the trouble."

"It's no trouble. Do you need fresh towels? I could get you some." For all his eagerness, he was about as soft looking as the Rocky Mountain range. He was still blocking the door.

"I have everything I need. Good night, Dillon." Would he leave? A keen, slow quiver rocked through her. The bed stood between them. What would Dillon do next?

"Sleep well, my wife. Call me if you need anything. Agreed?"

She nodded, angry with herself because she was so afraid. Because she expected the worst of him. It was because she'd seen some of the worst a civilized man had to offer. She wrapped her arms around her middle and breathed.

Simply breathed. She doubted Dillon even knew

how he'd frightened her. What had he ever done to deserve her suspicion? He'd helped her, paid for her hotel and a doctor, taken care of her the way no one had since she was a very small child. And what had she expected of him?

I'll try harder, she vowed. The wounds in her heart couldn't remain forever, could they?

She brushed her teeth and washed her face. She changed into the nightgown Dillon had given her. A soft blue flannel dotted with sunny-faced daisies, and it was so comfortable she knew she'd sleep well wearing it.

She read another thirty or so minutes, in the light of a small battered lantern that looked as if it used to be brass. She listened to Dillon moving downstairs. To add wood to the fire. To fetch a cup of tea.

Hours passed while he read downstairs and she lay in the dark upstairs in his bed.

When the clock struck ten times, she heard the clang of a fireplace poker as Dillon banked the coals for the night. She listened to his slow gait echo faintly through the house as he walked from the parlor to the kitchen rattling the doorknob to check that it was locked.

The faint light creeping up the stairs from below was extinguished, leaving her in complete darkness.

Alone.

There was a faint rustling downstairs, as if Dillon shifted on the sofa, and there was only silence.

She finally slept, alone in her marriage bed. Her first night spent as the horseman's bride. Safe, as he'd promised.

Chapter Thirteen

There. That was one thing done right. The oven door clattered as loud as a gunshot in the silent predawn kitchen. Katelyn straightened, brushed the bark from the wood she'd carried in off her sleeves, and caught sight of Dillon through the window.

Talking to his horses. Simply from watching him, her senses stilled until the rugged mountains behind him and the wild meadows around him faded into nothing. Until there was only Dillon, his Stetson sitting high on his head, his movements easy as he approached a half-dozen horses. Hands out in a show of friendship.

She could feel his voice as if it whispered inside her, rumbling and magical and sure. She watched as dawn broke around him. The shadows ebbed as first light flowed into the world and the man was no longer a shadow as the horses gathered close to nip treats from his hand.

Dawn's brightness slanted into her windows, spearing the first shafts of golden light over the edge of the table and onto her. Emotion quickened in her chest and, like the day's first light, glowed graciously, quietly. Changing everything.

Why do I want him so much? Her whole being ached for him. She couldn't explain it. She'd never felt this way before about any man. She'd slept deep and sound last night, better than she could ever remember sleeping. Because of him.

The man bathed in the morning light blessed each horse with his touch, then climbed through the wooden planks of the fence and hefted the two ten-gallon buckets he carried. She watched until the draw of the prairie stole him away.

Maybe she ought to try to stop mooning after him and get to work. She chose a big fry pan from the variety hung on hooks in the back of a cupboard. A battered one, with a thin coat of oil to keep the metal from rusting, and a wooden handle worn smooth and cracked on one side from heavy use. Dillon's favorite pan?

There she was, thinking of him again. Looking forward to his sure, quiet presence in the kitchen.

How did Effie do this? Katelyn had spent half her childhood in the kitchen seeking shelter from her stepfather's disapproval. She'd even helped now and then. But helping wasn't bearing the responsibility for the entire meal. What did Effie do? The bacon first? Yes, that's right. Now, where does Dillon keep the bacon?

There were no doors that led to a well-stocked food pantry. Finally she spotted a ring in the floor near the far wall. She pulled and a section of the floor lifted up to reveal wooden steps descending into darkness. Hmm. A food cellar?

Yes. The shelves were bare except for a few dust-covered jars of jam and a stack of recent supplies stacked in no particular order on the closest shelf to the ladder. Katelyn found a wrapped package of what had to be bacon, a basket of fresh eggs and a brick of good cheddar cheese. A sack of potatoes was piled in the corner so she took several of those as well.

It was awkward climbing up into the kitchen with her arms full, but it was kind of fun, too. To think she was going to prepare Dillon's breakfast. She wanted to do her best, even though she had no cooking experience. She imagined a perfect breakfast, with eggs sunny-side up and crisp fried bacon, a wonderful meal for the good man she'd married.

"What do you think you're doing?"

Katelyn gasped. The potatoes were the first to go, rolling out of her hand to thud to the floor. The cheese slid off her arm and then the bacon. Adrenaline speared through her, swift and sharp.

"I couldn't find you, I started to panic."

Concern. Not anger. Katelyn tried to calm down, tried to stop the shaking that rattled through her like an autumn wind.

Dillon's grin was sheepish as he knelt to catch a rolling potato. "I thought you may have changed your mind and taken off on me."

"Did you honestly think that?"

"Yep." His hand shook as he reached for another potato. "I figured you'd gotten an eyeful of how it was going to be living with me and gone back to your family."

"You are my family now."

"Yeah?" He rose, dropped the food on the counter. "I suppose I am, being your husband."

Not a sophisticated answer, but it was the best he could do considering his state of mind. The panic of not finding her in the house was giving way to a tight knot in his chest. He wanted to grab her close and hold on to her forever.

But she was staring at him with those wide angel's eyes of hers, and her unspoken fear tore at him.

No, he was never going to hurt her. But he had to show her that. Trust was something a man earned.

"What were you doing down in that pantry?" Dillon gentled his voice, spoke with the same cadence he used with the horses. "I thought you were supposed to be taking it easy. Doctor's orders. Or am I wrong?"

"No, you're right. But I thought— I just wanted to do something for you. After all you've done for me. This dress, for instance."

She brushed at the delicate white-and-pink calico he'd picked from a shelf at the seamstress's shop. Satisfaction filled him. It did look fine on her. Made the little color she had in her cheeks rosier. The fabric hugged her just right, too, over the curve of her fine breasts to the dip of her waist.

Why, it made a man want to run his hands along the shape of her, peel off that dress and...

His blood turned so hot he was ready to melt. *One day soon.* He'd wait until she was ready.

She was *that* precious to him.

"I'd like to do something for you, even if it is breakfast."

She shyly pushed a lock of gold behind her ear,

escaped from the braid that trailed down her back. The diamond and gold sparkled on her finger, bright and new.

His ring. He loved that. He did. She was his now, his to take care of. She gazed up at him, watching him carefully.

She didn't know how he was going to react next, he figured. Like the horses he came across who had good reason not to trust one more man. A wounded heart was a wounded heart, and he knew just what to do. How he was going to treat her, his wife.

His wife. That filled him up. Slow and easy, so she could see there was nothing to worry about, he set the potatoes on the table and approached her. She stiffened a little. It was best to start talking, let her hear in his voice how he meant to treat her. "I figure we can fix breakfast together. What do you say?"

"Together?" She took a little intake of breath as he leaned close. "All right."

"Good. It's settled then. And if you get tired, why, all you have to do is sit down and I'll take over. Agreed?"

She nodded, wary as he lifted the packages out of her arms. He was close enough to tilt his head and he'd be able to brush a kiss against her temple, to breathe in the female and flowery fragrance of her hair.

He waited, wanting to kiss her more than anything, to brush his lips over hers. To fit her body against his, to show her there wasn't one thing she ought to be afraid of. Because he was going to love her good and hard and completely...

Her mouth parted, as if she wanted it, too. He could

see her pulse fluttering in the hollow of her throat. He'd scared her and that fear lingered. He pressed his forehead to hers, not a kiss, but a connection. He swore that he could feel love rise up from his chest and pour into her.

As if she felt it, too, she rose, somehow taller against him. The tension holding her so tight eased, and there was less wariness in her eyes when he stepped away.

"Guess we'd best get started with the bacon." He kept his voice steady, calm. To let her know everything was just fine. "I see you found my favorite fry pan. It goes everywhere I go. I've cooked a lot of good meals in that pan. And a whole lot of bad ones."

She quirked one brow at him and didn't say a thing.

In truth, his favorite pan wasn't the best topic of conversation. He was no parlor-room conversationalist. On a sigh, he wrestled the bacon from the thick paper and took a knife to it. Cutting through the meat gave him something to do so he wouldn't have to say anything to embarrass himself further.

Just think before you speak, man.

"What about the stallion?" She shouldered close and peeled a thick slice of meat from the cutting board. "Something bad happened to him and you didn't want to tell me. Or you forgot about him."

"If that's the kind of horseman you think I am, then I've got to change your opinion." His chest tightened, and he put down the knife. "I haven't said anything because I wanted it to be a surprise."

"A good surprise?"

He felt her hope, tentative and fragile like a young seedling in a March rain, easily drowned. He chose his words with care. "The one thing you need to learn, beautiful, is that the only surprises in this house will be good ones."

She smiled, that tentative hope strengthening, and he felt as tall as the sky.

Katelyn peered over the top of her book through the front window to see if she could spot Dillon riding in from the far fields. After making most of the breakfast—she paid careful note so she would know how to do all the cooking tomorrow morning—Dillon had banished her to the couch for the rest of the day.

Not cruelly or by barking orders as Brett would have done. No, the horseman had used his kindness to his advantage. He'd simply taken her hand in his, told her how good it was to see his ring there, kissed the palm of her hand and asked her to do something for him. To lie down and rest, because he worried about her.

How was she so lucky? That night when she'd watched Dillon for the first time trying to lure the wild stallion closer, how could she have known she would end up here in his house as his wife? That he would be the one? The man she didn't believe existed because he was too good to be true.

She still thought that when he rode into sight through the fallow meadow, sitting straight and proud and mythical on a white spotted horse. He used no saddle or bridle, not even a lead rope snapped to a halter. The proud Appaloosa and rider moved as one being, one entity, cantering across the plains.

If she squinted, blurring the modern clothing of Levi's and his heavy winter jacket and imagined away the Stetson covering his dark locks, he could have been a native warrior on his Indian pony, hunting the plains for his tribe. Or on a spirit quest. He was regal and noble to the very core.

Something she had never seen in any man before.

She put aside her book and folded the wool blanket he'd covered her with. The one he'd slept beneath last night, she knew, because it smelled faintly of winter wind and leather and him.

"Did you take a nap?" Dillon asked the instant he walked through the door.

"I rested." She swung her feet off the couch and he was there, his hand taking hers to help her stand. "You're spoiling me."

"Good. You may as well get used to it. This is forever, just like I vowed." His kiss feathered across her brow.

Making her quiver deep down. He almost made her believe as he led her to the door, grabbed her coat and escorted her into the stunning day.

The wind was cool and smelled of snow, although the clouds were moving high and fast. The wind ruffled her coat hem and chilled her face as Dillon tucked her hand into his and led her down the steps and along the fence where a dozen horses gathered. Not mustangs and cayuses, but fine-blooded animals.

"Where did you get these animals?" Katelyn rubbed the nose of a big black Arabian who nudged her mitten.

"Got them in trade, mostly, whenever someone couldn't find the cash to pay me for my work." He reached into his pocket. "Hold out your hand flat."

She did, and he dropped a broken length from a

peppermint stick onto her palm. Before she could blink, the black mare lipped the treat from her hand. The others crowded around.

"In trade?" She accepted a piece of candy for each hand and held them out to two of the other mares. "You sometimes choose the horses instead of the ranch owner's daughter?"

"There was only one woman I ever wanted bad enough that I'd try to talk to her. And that's you."

"Try to talk to? What does that mean? You used smoke signals? Wrote notes on a slate?"

"I'm thirty years old and until yesterday, I was a confirmed, lifelong bachelor. And the reasons why? Because I'm too shy to get up my courage to talk to a woman. Courting is one daunting experience. I don't see how most men live long enough to stand before the altar."

"You've never courted anyone?"

"Just you." Over the velvet nose of the sorrel mare, Dillon blushed. A slow heat crept up his face from his chin to his hairline.

How did he do that? Make her feel special to him with two simple words?

"This one here, the little gray mare, she's a delicate thing. See how she stands off? She's never sure about strangers. I was riding through Omaha of all places, just passing through on my way south to Tucson, and the street was jammed. People riding up onto the boardwalk just to get around. Tempers flaring. It was summer and hot as Hades.

"When I got up to where the problem was, there she was, on her knees with her sister—that mare right there, the white—and this teamster was whipping her.

She couldn't get up. He'd ruined her. Pushed her too far. She couldn't move and no amount of fear or pain would get her to.''

''You saved her?''

''I gave him everything I had on me for the two of them, unhitched her. I stayed with her until she could move. Brought her water and food. Convinced her there was a reason for living. A nice cool meadow right here where she'd never feel the sting of a whip again.''

Katelyn closed her eyes, willing away the image he'd created in her mind. So, he made a habit of collecting the unwanted and the wounded. And brought them here to heal.

The gray mare nudged Dillon's arm for attention. When he stroked his big hand down her nose, she leaned into his touch, trusting.

Was that what Dillon saw in her? Katelyn wondered. Someone to pity? Or to save? ''You must be gone a lot with your work. Does your brother look after your herd?''

''It keeps him out of trouble. I'll have to have him over for supper one night soon.'' He took her hand. ''The stallion is over here. Since he can leap six-foot fences without much trouble, I put him behind eight feet of board so he stays put.''

''It's sad to pen him up when he's used to running free.''

''True, but this country isn't wild, as it used to be. And there's a price on his head.''

''Cal Willman lives far from here.''

''A day's journey. A wild mustang and his herd will roam twice that distance. There he is.'' Dillon nodded toward the paddock in the shade of the log stable. "He gets two meals a day and he doesn't need to fight off predators. Hello there, boy."

The stallion paced the far end of the paddock, constant motion, his mane flying, tail up, ears laid back.

"He doesn't look happy."

"No, but he's better. That wound to his shoulder had begun to fester, so I treated it. He seems to be recovering."

"I'm glad." Seeing the majestic creature penned up made her sad.

Dillon climbed through the boards, talking in a low gentle murmur she didn't realize was a different language, it lulled her so. Tranquil sounding. The horse must have thought so as well because he stopped pacing.

"A few days ago, my brother and I rode out and wrestled him home between the two of us. He broke our best rope. Even injured, he was a tough one to bring in."

Such an impressive animal. Big for a mustang, brawny but not stocky. A perfect head as black as night with a blaze streaking down the center of his nose. His spots were a flecked blanket draping his shoulders and back and rump. Strong legs, built both for speed and endurance, were rooted in the earth as the stallion waited, ready to flee.

Katelyn held her skirts and climbed through the space in the boards. Before she could straighten, Dillon was there, holding her steady, then guiding her to his side where they faced the nervous stallion together.

"He's huge." Being so close to him made her feel

small, easily crushed. The stallion's power radiated from him like heat from a stove, like light from the sun. A wild power that was as unstoppable as the wind. As rare as a new star in the sky.

"It's a shame to break him."

"Then we'll gentle him. There's a difference, you'll see." Dillon dug a peppermint out of his pocket. "Want to feed him?"

"No." She took one look at the horse, so big now that she was closer. Raw power. Strong muscles rippled beneath his perfect black-and-white coat as he pivoted and ran, pivoted again.

She took another look at the horse as he shot around the rim of the fence. Hooves cutting into the hard-packed earth propelled him forward in a blur of black and white and flying mane. The beat of his step vibrated the earth, moving up through her, through them, leaving her spellbound.

"Watch." Dillon spoke in that musical, gentle language and the running horse began to calm. The hard line of his elegant neck became softer, arching as the stallion swiveled his big head, keeping one eye and both ears on Dillon as he circled the paddock.

"Hold out your hand."

She did as he asked and he dropped another candy into her palm. Dillon's arm slipped around her back to rest on the space between her shoulder blades. His closeness a comfort, warming her like a summer's wind, from the outside in, as the magnificent stallion slowed, swiveling his ears, considering the softly speaking man and the enticing scent of peppermint. His intelligent eyes studied both humans, as if considering.

What was Dillon saying? She'd love to know. She didn't want to interrupt the magic to ask as the stallion reached forward with his big head, stretching his neck long, nostrils flaring. He was at the far end of the paddock, distant but considering.

Dillon kept talking conversationally and if Katelyn made her heart still, she could understand what he was saying. Dillon was telling the animal that he was safe, that he wouldn't be hurt, that they would be friends.

She didn't know one word of his grandfather's language, but she could *feel* Dillon like the emotions inside her. She was mad to think she could feel his heart with hers. She'd never heard of such a thing, but then how could she explain it? Maybe because she'd heard him say those same words in English, and yet there was something of the heart in that unfamiliar cadence.

Something she could sense, and it was Dillon. It was *his* infinite respect for the stallion, *his* honorable sincerity and *his* affection. A caring that reached as deep as the earth and as high the stars and as boundless as heaven. It was a brilliance that filled her as Dillon's kiss brushed her brow.

A spark like a shock in the air flashed from his kiss to the depths of her.

"Look at that." Dillon's whisper was like a tide that moved through her. "He's decided he wants the treat. Stand real still now."

The tide crested inside her, swelling like the top curl of the wave rolling in to break on the shore of her heart. As if myth, the spotted stallion approached, noble and regal and so big he blocked the veiled rays of daylight from the sky. But he was not what moved her, what changed her.

Dillon's whisper swept through her again, a sweeping current washing through her until she felt submerged in it. Drowning in it. His love. His commitment. His tender words as he spoke to the stallion. Or was it to her?

Still he spoke, drawing the stallion closer. Drawing her closer. Her heart felt as if it were lifting, opening as the tide of his heart swept against hers. A warm, sweet surge that eroded the hard, icy protection and laid open the deepest part of her, leaving her too vulnerable, too open. She tried to step back, but Dillon's hand stopped her. His touch reassured her.

The stallion was quick. She felt the whisper of his satin lips against her palm and the tickle of his delicate whiskers and then he was gone, retreating to a safe distance to crunch the treat. His attention remained on Dillon, watching him, assessing him.

"He's a smart one, but what a spirit he has." Dillon's touch grazed up her spine to nestle against her nape. "It's going to be a pleasure to get to know him, don't you think?"

"I do."

"Do you want to help me gentle him?"

"I don't know anything about training a horse."

"I do." His confidence was as reassuring as the wind on her shoulders. As his touch was as loving on her neck. "I've tamed a few cayuses over the years."

Katelyn remembered the pintos and Appaloosas in the back field. She knew why wild horses came to love him, why they clamored close to him, and not only for the peppermint he offered. How could anyone not come to believe in him?

"C'mon, let's get you inside. I've got supper to put in the oven and you've got a nap to take."

"You're too good to me, Dillon."

"Sweet lady, I'm not nearly good enough." He offered her his arm, gallant as a knight in flawless shining armor.

She slipped her arm in his and they walked to their house together.

Tiny, perfect snowflakes filled the air, as crisp and as light as spun sugar. Sifting like grace over the land, over Dillon.

Over her.

Chapter Fourteen

"Did you get enough to eat?" Dillon asked as he grabbed the tea tray, leaving the full cup of sweetened tea on the bedside table. She'd eaten all but a few crumbs of the snack he'd brought up with a pot of chamomile tea. "I can run down and get you another slice of cake. Or some tea. I'll brew up a pot for you."

"No, I'm fine." Katelyn smiled at him from the bed, where a pile of plump feather pillows braced her as she sat up, her book open in her lap. A colorful afghan covered her and kept her warm.

"Do you need something else before you settle down for the night? Are you hungry? I could make you a sandwich."

"Really, I'm fine." Her eyes danced at him. She was trying not to laugh at him again.

He didn't blame her. He was new at being a husband. It was harder than he'd thought. It would take some learning, that was for sure.

He found refuge in the hallway out of her sight. He took the steps two at a time, the ring of his boots echoing all around him, but the house didn't feel empty with her here. He didn't mind the dark corners and shadows where no light reached in the parlor and the kitchen where the table waited in darkness.

There was a peace in the house now, because of her, the mercy she'd brought with her in her smile, with her presence, with the way she smelled like springtime and everything good in the world. Everything beautiful.

You're a lucky man, Hennessey. She'd chosen him, not because she had no choice but because she wanted to be with him. Right here, in a humble log cabin with horses, with him, just the way he was.

He might not be a fine enough man for her, able to offer her a luxurious life. But he'd give her something more. He would give her everything he had, everything he was, everything he would be.

He would treat her well, with all his good intentions. He'd never hurt her, never make her sad or unhappy. He'd take the sadness from her heart and chase away the shadows from her eyes, from her soul. As he'd done in the paddock today, when the wild stallion had eaten from the palm of her hand. She'd seemed lighter, as if she'd let go of something that had been weighing her down.

Maybe she was beginning to heal. That was a good thing.

He heard the squeak of a loose board and the pad of her step in the necessary room overhead. Brushing her teeth, he figured, getting ready for the night ahead. He thought only of her as he rinsed the tea things and set them in the wash basin for morning. He climbed the stairs, following the faint glow of her bedside lamp that grew brighter and brighter, drawing him close until he was passing through the threshold.

She sure improved the room by being in it. He swore that he would forever remember her like this, with the subdued golden lamplight burnishing her with a celestial glow, like an angel on high.

He burned into his memory the way she turned the page at the upper corner with a graceful turn of her wrist, her brow furrowed, her concentration sharp as she read. The soft movement of her mouth as she sipped at her tea. The way her hand cupped the mug as if to draw in all its warmth.

He loved how she lit up from the inside when she saw him.

"Enjoying your book?"

"I'm riveted." Katelyn's left hand rested against the page, holding her place, but her attention, all of it, was on him. "I should be asleep by now. I'm exhausted. I just can't seem to stop reading."

"Me, either. I've got my book downstairs. I'll pick it up tonight, meaning only to read a chapter, and the next time I'll look up, it'll be midnight. You watch. That happens to me all the time."

"Me, too." She tried to stifle a yawn, but she couldn't. Her hand flew to her mouth. Tears brimmed her eyes, and she chuckled. "I'm not sleepy. Really. I can read one more chapter."

"Darlin', you can say it, but that doesn't mean it will be true."

"I know." She set her cup aside.

He watched, spellbound, as she raised both arms. The fleecy soft flannel nightgown she wore strained over the generous curve of her breasts.

She plucked the hairpins from the knot in the back of her head and his blood thundered in his veins. Lustrous locks of her hair tumbled down like a shower of rare, perfect gold and nearly dropped him to his knees.

He could still see her in the tub, with the water pearled on her skin, bare and enticing. He fisted his hands when he wanted to reach out and touch her. Strip the flannel from her breasts and caress her the way the light did. Reverently and thoroughly until she wanted him, wanted more. Until she opened up to him like a flower to sun and, oh, the pleasure he'd give her—

If you follow that thought to its natural conclusion, your heart's going to explode, man. Like a keg of gunpowder. Dillon pulled back on the reins. He wanted her with a force that would put a tornado to shame and outblow every blizzard that had ever hit the Montana plains.

But he was a patient man. He believed in self-control. "Let me help you with that."

"Oh?" She looked surprised, even startled, and it was something, when he thought about it, how little she expected. As if she wasn't used to anyone caring for her.

I care for you. A wave of tenderness left him speechless. He took the brush from her fingers settled beside her on the bed. The ropes groaned with his weight, and it was different being alone in the bedroom with her this time.

This was *his* bed she was sitting in. The bed where he'd always slept alone and never thought there would be a woman to sleep beside. And never such a lovely, gentle-hearted woman to hold in his arms. To cherish forever.

He filled up with the significance of it. A love like this came along once in a man's lifetime, if he were lucky.

He'd never brushed a woman's hair before, and he didn't know if he was doing it right. Too hard? Too light? The bristles disappeared into those radiant locks and as he stroked downward she drew in a satisfied mew. She liked this, did she?

The bristles reached the long, curled ends of her hair and the strands crackled. The scent of wild roses filled his nose and sparked his blood.

He rested the bristles at the crown of her head and stroked downward, listening to the crackle of her hair. He breathed in the woman and floral scent of her, and desire thudded through every inch of him. Every hard inch.

I want you so much, my love. He ran the brush through her hair again, and she lifted up imperceptibly, as if she were enjoying it.

"Do you like this? Does it feel good?" he murmured against the soft pink shell of her ear.

He felt pleasure move through her, traveling down her spine in a luxurious, tingling thrill. He knew her answer before she nodded, felt the truth of her feelings for him, so new and tender.

"You have beautiful hair. Hmm." He raked his fingers through fine threads of gold silk and breathed in. Crushed them in his hand, so soft.

He relaxed his hand, and the curls sprang free, cascading down her slim neck and over her shoulders. *Amazing.* Love for her glided through him, like a bird on a hard wind, lifting him higher and higher until he felt tall with it, great with it. This love he had for her had no end, no boundary, no measure.

One day soon, *she* was going to want him. *She* was going to long for the pleasure of his touch. *She* would be the one to step into his arms and give him her kiss. She would pull back the covers and invite him into their bed. She would let him unbutton those buttons again and this time run his hand down the creamy valley between her perfect breasts over the soft curve of her belly where their child might take root and grow, and open her thighs to welcome him into her.

One day soon.

"I've got to make a trip into town in the morning." It was hard to hide his desire for her, but he did it. Veiled it behind talk of the everyday and the ordinary.

"I'll be gone early and back after noon. It might be too long a trip for you. Give me a list and I'll buy whatever you want."

"What are you going to do?"

"I have feed to pick up. I've got winter supplies to put up for the horses. Molasses, grain, see about getting more hay and straw delivered. It's going to be a hard winter by the looks of things."

"The early snow?"

"That and the wildlife. Prairie dogs and beaver and waterfowl have all dug in or built thicker nests this year. They have a way of knowing things."

"Did you learn that from your grandfather?"

"Yes. I learned many things. He was a great man."

"You mourn him still."

"Always." The brush stilled in mid-stroke.

Katelyn wondered what it would have been like to

have family ties, the kind that sheltered and endured, that made you stronger instead of tearing you down. And then she realized she *did* know.

It had been her father's steadfast affection, protective and decent, that had been everything to her once. And the knowledge of it, although the relationship had been a different one, made her believe now. Made her believe in the man seated beside her, with a fierce passionate love blazing in his eyes, trembling through him.

Dillon set aside the brush and caressed the line of her jaw with his knuckle. "You're sad."

"I'm thinking of my father." Even though his touch was an unbreakable promise of love, it was hard to open up her heart like a room and let someone in. To trust someone, even a man like Dillon, with all of her, all of who she was.

She *should.* She should just give in, let go, let the tide of emotion carry her away from shore, and trust Dillon to hold her up, keep her safe, never let her down.

"Are you ready for bed?" he asked in an intimate drawl.

She nodded, unable to speak, feeling the tide of emotion well up inside her again, from him to her, lifting her up, threatening to carry her away.

Without a word, he lifted the afghan from her lap, leaving her in the nightgown he'd bought for her. She felt oddly naked, as if the soft fleece was no covering, no protection from his eyes, which had already seen her without clothes. He folded down the thick blankets and the top sheet, arranged the pillows as she slipped her feet under the covers and relaxed.

He rose up over her, his arms enfolded her and his kiss was perfection. The warm velvet brand of his lips against hers made her arms lift and her hands curl around his solid shoulders. The sweep of his tongue was a deeper, intimate caress that made her want to surrender. Made the defenses covering her heart, like water on snow, break apart in slow, painful eddies.

"Sleep well, my wife." He touched his forehead to hers. Tender love flowed from him, a powerful, unseen current that touched her deep inside.

He drew the covers to her chin, turned down the lamp and as the flame died on the wick, the last image on his face remained. Like a bronzed statue of a man as tough as the earth, as loyal as the sun, and as tender as morning. His love was a steady glow that did not fade in the dark as he closed the door behind him. His step faded in the stairwell and was no more.

Alone, in the darkness and silence, she was comforted. Loved. Her body achingly alive, thrummed with want for only one exceptional man.

How could she be so fortunate? What could she ever have done to deserve Dillon? The darkness gave no answer. Nor did the night as she crawled out of bed and sat by the window. Snow fell like shining crystal in the faint light of a dwindling moon. Storm clouds battled and won, hiding the moon, leaving only snow and wind and midnight bleakness.

She remembered all the nights she'd sat alone at the window, as a judge's wife, full of hope as the babe within her grew. And later, at her stepfather's ranch, watching the night and feeling as if she'd been the one to die. And now this, this strange awakening to love and happiness.

When she had given up all hope, when she had lost everything that mattered, fate had smiled on her. Why had she been given the chance to love this incredible man? How rare, to have any man love her, a barren woman, who could never birth a son. And rarer still to have a man so exceptional to love and hold close for the rest of her days.

It was too good to be true. Far too good. Would this happiness with Dillon last? Could it grow into a lifelong gift?

How could she be that lucky? Afraid to hold on, and afraid not to, she watched the snow fall and the storm end and slept only when the promise of dawn came to the plains.

Was that Dillon? Katelyn heard the clop of steel horseshoes echoing faintly, muffled by the thick log walls, and put aside her knitting. She'd missed him. His presence, his lopsided, bashful grin and the ring of his gait through the house.

She was halfway to the door when she saw the bay mare and the woman holding the reins beneath the shelter of a fringed surrey. A neighbor, maybe? Or someone Dillon had sent from town? He'd mentioned hiring the laundry out.

But the woman who stepped down from the expensive surrey didn't look like a laundry woman. She was dressed in a simple calico, but there was a noble air about her, not arrogant, but good.

The woman's smile was direct and friendly the moment their gazes met. "Hello, Mrs. Hennessey."

Goodness, that was the first time she'd been called by her new married name and it felt right, like a key into the lock it was made to turn. She was now Kate-lyn Hennessey, the horseman's wife.

The slim, light-haired woman lifted a large basket off the floorboards, where it had been safe from wind and cold and in danger of sliding out of the vehicle.

There was something about that basket. There was a glimpse of blue flannel as she hefted it carefully into her arms. "I'm Mariah Gray. I live on the neigh-boring ranch. Our husbands are friends. I was the one who brought the supper basket by the other night. Congratulations on your marriage."

"Thank you. It's nice to meet you. Please, come in." The wind was cold, but the fire snapped merrily in the stone hearth, and Katelyn felt proud of this home, finely made but not fancy. "I'm—"

A small whimper sounded from inside the basket. Mrs. Gray eased back the flannel and looked lovingly down at the small round face cradled there, puckering up in preparation of a good hard cry.

The baby was so small it couldn't be more than a month old. Maybe two. A beautiful blue-eyed little boy who raised his fists swathed in flannel to keep them warm and cried again.

"This is Jeremy, who apparently is unhappy that I didn't introduce him first." Mrs. Gray gave an apol-ogetic shrug before she rocked the basket gently to settle the infant.

"Riding in the surrey usually puts him right to sleep, and he stays that way, but no, not today when I was hoping he'd sleep for a good long spell, so I could get to know you." The woman's good-natured words were filled with love for her child.

Katelyn held the door wide, holding her emotions

very still, sternly keeping all memories locked away. "Please, come in where it's warm. I'm so glad you came. I wanted to thank you for the delicious meal you made for us. And the chocolate cake was the best I've ever tasted."

"Why, thank you, I'd be happy to share the recipe."

"Would you like to stay? I'll make tea."

"I'd like that."

Katelyn hung her visitor's wraps by the mantel to warm them and then led the way to the kitchen, where the teakettle gave a low-noted whistle while it simmered.

Don't look at the baby. She kept busy finding the ironware teapot, plain but serviceable, and measuring out just the right amount of tea. She ignored the sounds of the cooing baby, happy now that he was the center of attention.

Mariah Gray had set the sturdy basket next to the table, a safe distance from the stove. She unwrapped the baby's blankets and peeled the mittens from his tiny hands, chatting sweetly to him while she worked.

As Katelyn carried the sugar and creamer to the table, she caught sight of two tiny fists waving in the air. So tiny.

Do not think of it. She refused to think about the baby she'd buried. The little girl she had never held and never murmured loving words to.

The sugar bowl tumbled from her fingers, falling onto the table. The lid toppled and the jar rolled and brown sugar avalanched everywhere.

"I do that at least once a day," Mariah confessed

as she folded her baby's things. "Something is always spilling."

It was a kind attempt to make her feel less awkward, but it wasn't shyness that troubled her. It was that baby, so small and helpless. So precious. Pain sliced through her like an ax stroke to her soul. Did Mariah know how lucky she was?

Katelyn swept up the fallen sugar, wiped down the table and set out spoons, cups and saucers. By the time she'd filled the teapot, Mariah had taken a chair by the window and was rocking the baby's basket with her foot. A soothing, gentle rhythm that had the little one quieting. Those tiny fists stilled. His perfect, button face relaxed. Dark curly lashes fluttered shut.

"He's so sweet," she managed to say past the emotion wadded unwanted and unspent in her throat.

"Thank you. I never thought I would have a baby of my own. I married later than most women do. He is a blessing." A true mother's love gleamed in her eyes.

Katelyn had to stare hard at her empty cup. Empty, like she was. There would be no baby for her.

That Dillon could love her, a barren woman, gave her strength. It was the reason she could pour the steeped tea without spilling. The reason she could leave the memory of her daughter in a closed-off room inside her and keep the door tightly shut.

She had Dillon, a good man who loved her. The thought of his touch eased some of the tightness in her throat, some of the pain from her chest so she could breathe.

"Do you sew?" Mariah asked as she reached for the sugar bowl. "I'd like to ask you to my house this

Friday noon for our weekly sewing circle. There are three of us who meet, and we would surely like for you to join us. So we can get to know you.''

''I've never belonged to a sewing circle before, but I'd love to come.'' This was a chance to settle in and make friends with Dillon's neighbors, and now hers. ''What should I bring?''

''Just yourself and your sewing basket. The girls will be so pleased to meet you.'' The baby squalled again in mild protest. ''Oh, and Jeremy would like to see you again, too. He likes to be the center of attention.''

Mariah lifted the infant from his snug nest and into her arms. The little guy waved his fists and rubbed his face.

She would *not* remember another little baby. Another little round face.

''Would you like to hold him?''

Katelyn shook her head at her new friend's kind offer. She poured too much milk into her tea before she set the creamer aside. ''No, thank you. He looks content where he is. He's starting to fall asleep.''

''He's a good baby. Tell me about you. What part of Montana are you from? All Dillon would say was that he fell in love with you at first sight and he married you before you could change your mind.''

Katelyn struggled to understand Mariah's words. Her gaze would not lift from the baby. From the tiny rosebud lips and the dimple in the middle of his cute little chin—

Don't think of her. Katelyn locked the door to that part of her heart and turned the key. She *would not* remember. Or she would shatter into a million irretrievable pieces.

"Afternoon, Mariah." Dillon shrank the kitchen with his presence as he lowered a crate to the worktable, the wooden box overflowing with staples for the kitchen. A molasses tin and tea and a small bag of white sugar were a few of the items she recognized.

Dillon swept off his Stetson and dropped it onto the worktable, too. "What did you bring with you today, ma'am? Someone downright precious, I'd say."

"That he is."

"Howdy there, little fella." Dillon lifted the tiny babe with his big, strong arms and cradled him in one arm, safe against his chest. With experience and confidence, the way he did everything. A mighty man stronger for his gentleness.

He'd make a good father. Katelyn ached with sorrow as she watched him. Ached for what could never be.

Dillon's gaze met hers with longing. With sheer, unveiled desire. Yes, he wanted to be a father. Very much. He didn't bother to hide his desire from her. What man didn't want a son in his image?

And Dillon, it was obvious as the smile on his face and the shine of want in his eyes. He wanted a baby boy of his own to hold and love and dream over.

And yet he'd chosen her and courted her and married her. Why? Did that mean as much as he wanted a child that he wanted her more?

"Well, little man, it's been good seeing you. You come by any time to visit and bring your ma with you. Mariah, thank you kindly for coming by." He laid the infant in Mariah's welcoming arms, pressed a tender kiss to Katelyn's brow and grabbed his hat on the way to the door.

"He sure is in love with you." Mariah's eyes sparkled. "My, what a lucky woman you are. It is everything, isn't it, to be loved wholly and true, and to have the chance to love the same way in return. To love more than you ever thought possible."

Katelyn nodded, overwhelmed. The door to that small room of her heart was breaking, as if a tornado were hammering at it, splintering it grain by grain, sliver by sliver. "I am very fortunate."

"Yes, to love someone so completely you would give your life for them." She pressed a kiss to her son's brow. "Look at what can come from that kind of love."

Not for Dillon and me. Katelyn couldn't help it. As Mariah's visit concluded, when the tea was gone and they had run out of polite conversation, she sneaked a glance at the child. At how the knit cap snuggled over his round, baldish head. At the fuss he made, shaking his fists and squalling when Mariah slipped his gloves on his soft pink hands.

Mariah rescued her wraps from the parlor and donned them. "I'll see you in a few days, then."

Katelyn watched the woman stow the infant safely in the surrey before climbing in. There was something so ordinary about that. She'd probably seen women make sure their babies were safe and snug in their wagons and buggies and sleighs her entire life.

It would never be something she would do. Not for the child she had never been able to hold. Not for the son she would never give Dillon.

The future stretched bleak before her, dim without the chance of her own child. Not the one she'd lost. Not the one she wished she could have, a round-faced, blue-eyed son for Dillon.

There would be no first birthday parties. No first steps. No first day of school. No graduation or wedding. No grandchildren to welcome and spoil and love.

Just an empty house that would never know the sound of a child laughing and at play. There would be days spent in neat order as she embroidered or cleaned or sewed. Evenings spent in front of the fire in the winter or on the front porch in summer, just her and Dillon.

Their lives would be orderly, content and calm. Not interrupted by footsteps pounding down the stairs or an argument between brothers in the yard, or the excitement of Christmas Eve, when the children could not sleep knowing Santa Claus was on his way.

It was so lonely. Her arms were so empty. Grief overwhelmed her, breaking apart the locked place inside her, rending her wide open until she was on her knees, her face in her hands. She willed back tears even as they fell, blurring her vision and wetting her cheeks and tapping to the wood floor.

She wanted her baby, the one she could never have.

"Katelyn?" The back door creaked when he opened it, and his voice echoed through the empty kitchen and dining room, as if to emphasize the loneliness of rooms. "Did you want to help me with the stallion?"

"Yes." She swiped the tears from her eyes with

the hem of her sleeve, but more trickled down before she could stop them. "I'm coming."

"I'll wait." So good-natured, he sounded. So loving. "I'd wait a lifetime for you, angel."

See how he loved her? What was wrong with her that she was crying instead of celebrating? The grief in her soul, like a February wind, held back the spring. Sorrow, like winter's selfish hand, would not let go.

Dillon could love her, and she was barren. He could hold another child and not wish for one of his own. Even now he was waiting patiently, and he'd spoken to her with love in his voice. Not contempt.

"Katelyn, honey, are you all right?" He was kneeling at her side, ever the gallant warrior, her champion who never let her down, never hurt her. Even now, when she couldn't explain why she was crying over a child she'd lost and at the same time the child she couldn't have and she felt so empty.

He filled her up. His love. His compassion. His endless integrity as he cradled her to his chest, where life beat through him and into her.

"I'm sorry," he murmured into her hair, his whiskers catching and tugging, his words vibrating through her like mercy. "I didn't stop to think seeing a baby would remind you. I don't blame you for grieving. For being sorry. That's a devastating loss, but, my darlin', you haven't lost everything. It just feels that way."

His words could have been trite and his sympathy shallow, but they weren't. Her pain echoed on his face in tiny lines and shadows. Her sadness saddened him. Her desolation became his.

She let him hold her until there were no tears. He wiped the tears from her face with the pads of his thumbs. Erased the memory of them with a trail of tender kisses that made her wish all the harder. This man loved her truly for who she was and what she was not.

That was the way she wanted to love him. All of him. To stroke him until he reached only for her. To love him wholly, flesh to flesh, and make him a part of her. To drive this pain away with the hope of a newer, greater love.

''You need to rest, angel.''

His kissed her brow, her champion. Her savior. He lifted her to her feet as he lifted her heart. Like a phoenix rising from its ashes, born anew.

Like a new flame, she glowed when he touched her. Laid his arm around her shoulder to guide her because she couldn't see, couldn't tell where she was going. All that mattered was Dillon. His touch, his presence, his love like radiance warming away the shadows inside her. Every grief. Every loss. Like a new spring come to the shaded places that felt sunlight for the first time.

Dillon's touch was the soft brush of a western wind against her grateful skin. She clung to him, to the bold heat of his kiss. Of the need they shared, the need to taste him, hold him, bind herself to this man she loved more than anything. *Anything.*

She wanted him with the sweetness of a new dawn, when the light was innocent and gentle. She wanted him with the bright passion of a burning sun, and melted when he sat her on the edge of the bed, splayed his hands on either side of her hips and asked the question without words.

Yes. She needed him. Like no man she'd ever needed before. She burned with it, was torn apart by it and made whole all at the same time as she loosened the button at her throat. His eyes went black. His chest rose quick and fast, and a flash of fear bolted through her like lightning in a clear sky. Brief. Lonely.

"You say the word, and I'll stop. You hear?" Like a caress to her soul, his words swept through her.

He was already laying her back, his hands tugging at her clothes with a steady competence, so that she burned like a midday sun, exposed and naked and a little afraid.

She hated that she was afraid. He tugged her laces free and the corset gave way, and with a sweep of his fingers to her hips she was naked before him. Vulnerable. Open. And wanting to cling to him. To be a part of him. To feel him in every part of her.

It would be like that, wouldn't it? Doubt crept in, even as he moved into the frame of sunlight from the window, burnished with gold and so awe inspiring as he stripped the shirt from his shoulders, her doubts frizzled. She craved the touch of his hand to her ribs.

On a sigh, as if she already knew how it would feel, his hand fit over her breast and stroked, squeezed, bringing a sharp, flawless pleasure.

"You are the love I've been waiting for all of my life," he murmured as he stretched out naked beside her. "When I first looked at you, I knew. I would love only you."

"I've never known a man like you." She realized

it was true. So good, so strong, everlasting. A real man she could trust with the deepest part of her.

"Angel, I am not finished yet."

His kiss was tender, his touch beautiful. He drew her against him and she explored the hardness of him and the differences. He was magnificent and touching him melted her within, the way her touch melted him. Forcing a new emotion to take root within, in those vulnerable shadowed places. She opened her arms and let him in.

He moved over her, as if he were made to be there. The push of his hard, thick shaft forced her open, not roughly but inexorably, and the feel of him filling her, completely wounding her anew in her heart. A wound of deep love that hurt as it healed, that burned as it shone.

She felt his overwhelming love, the force of it, the pulse of it as he cupped her hip and showed her how to move with him. Creating a rhythm that tightened her around him like a new bud, clenching tighter and tighter against the sun. She held him so tight, and his kiss grazed her brow, her face, her lips.

Reverent, that's what he felt. A love so huge nothing could extinguish it. Being with her like this, having her wrapped around him in every way, clinging to his shoulders, his hips, her satin heat gloving him as he pumped harder and harder, it was meant to be. Fated. He could feel it with his body, with his heart, with his soul.

Overcome, he touched her face. Oh, so beautiful. She was incredibly beautiful to him. What a lucky man he was to have her as his wife. To have her trust him and love him. His passionate, loving wife. He buried his face in her hair and moved beyond feeling when he felt her begin to break around him, the first tight pulse of her release like hot, wet silk fisting him. That she would trust him like this, surrender like this, carried him beyond words.

He drummed harder, faster, coming as she did, crying out as she did, spilling all he was into her, his love, his seed. She cherished him with kisses to his throat and the side of his face. Honored him with the graze of her fingertips across his back. Her tenderness changed him, made him better, stronger, renewed.

"I love you, Katelyn." Breathless, resting thick and heavy inside her, he kept her against him. Touched her face. Opened his soul. "To think that I'm here with you like this. I love you so very much."

"I love you, too."

She'd never known anything like the gentle bliss as the passion cooled in her blood and they rested together, joined, touching. He ran his forefinger down her nose, over the rise of her lips and into the dimple at her chin. Then lower to take her breasts and tease her nipple.

Pleasure rose through her like flames to the sky, higher and higher. His mouth closed over her nipple and she arched her back to offer him more. And felt his thickness inside her swell and harden.

She'd never dreamed love could be like this. She let him love her again, sweeter this time. Slower. A joining not only of bodies but, incredibly, of hearts.

Chapter Fifteen

The prairie looked crisp and new and the inch from last night's snowfall crunched beneath their shoes. Katelyn felt cherished as she walked beside Dillon, her fingers entwined with his. The closeness from their lovemaking lingered between them like a warm blanket nestling them both.

As they walked, horses rushed up to the fence line. Dillon stopped and offered pats to each mare and their peppermint rewards. He took the time to teach Katelyn their names. Beautiful, pedigreed names for the purebreds. Fitting, western ones for the pintos and Appaloosas. Finally they moved on.

Snow broke from the sky above, tiny, frosted flakes that fell straight from heaven. They clung to Katelyn's hair and eyelashes, and sneaked down the back of her collar to make her shiver.

Dillon drew her close to mumble in her ear. "I could always warm you up."

"Oh? And how would you do that?"

"By lifting those skirts of yours, my sweet, and making your blood burn." He nipped her earlobe, making pleasure skid along her nerve endings. "You just say the word, and I'll be happy to oblige you."

"Happy to? I suppose there's nothing you gain from the experience."

"Only the satisfaction of pleasuring you. I live to serve you, my love."

"Aren't you a true gentleman? Putting a lady's needs above your own."

"I sure hope so. You tell me."

"Well, I may need you to satisfy me again. Practice makes perfect."

"That's not true, because you are already perfection." He brushed a few flyaway curls from her eyes. She leaned into the affectionate stroke of his fingertips, loving his tender strength.

What a man. She floated with love for him. Were her feet touching the ground? She was certain they weren't, that he made her walk on air. Her body felt well loved, a new and wonderful sensation. Desire for him, to have him inside her, coiled within her.

How could she already want him? Yet her body was ready for him, wet and trembling and alive. The way only *he* could make her.

"Hey, pretty girl." Dillon welcomed the gray mare with his hands, holding her big, comely head against his chest as he stroked her cheeks and jaw.

The mare he'd rescued, who'd been beaten. Katelyn held out her hand and the Arabian shied, stepping back, skin flicking over her taut, powerful muscles.

"Easy, girl," Dillon said, switching to his grandfather's language, the lilting music speaking to the mare's soul and calming her.

Katelyn saw the harsh scars raked into the animal's

back and rump. At least three dozen of them, ugly and ragged. The poor thing. Those were made by the angry lash of a bullwhip, reminding her that all of these horses were unwanted or abused or homeless.

Was that why Dillon had chosen her? Doubt fluttered in her chest. Did he love her? Or was she someone to save? Someone who needed rescuing and sheltering? Like these mares.

Somehow that made his love for her less. Made her unsure as he released his hold on her to dig more peppermint from his jacket pockets.

"Hello there, Spirited One." Dillon held two treats, one in each hand. "He's angry because I've ignored him. I usually come see him several times throughout the morning. Today, I had to buy more peppermint. But going to town isn't the reason I'm late."

He tossed her a sideways glance and blushed. The memory of his lovemaking sizzled through her, making her hot when she ought to be freezing.

The stallion watched and waited, not pacing today, just watching. Quivering.

"He can't be happy with me. I brought him here. Caged him in."

"Doesn't he resent you for it?"

"Maybe a little." Honest, Dillon held out both hands, waiting. "He knows I'm helping him, and he's grateful, but he's not the kind of animal anyone can pen in for long."

The stallion lifted his head, his wide nostrils flaring, scenting the candy. Debating.

"You're going to lure him close with the peppermint and then rope him, aren't you?"

Dillon realized she wasn't only speaking of her fears for the stallion. "If I trick him, I teach him I'm not a man he can trust."

"But you need to break him. You'll have to trick him sometime."

"Never. I don't trick horses. *Ever.* Besides, I told you all I want to do is help this stallion. I swore that to you, remember?"

"I know."

"Did you think I'd forgotten?"

"No. That never crossed my mind."

"Good." He hauled her against his chest, turning her so he spooned her and protected her from the wind. All she had to do was lean against him and he sheltered her from the elements, held her up and kept her steady as the stallion ventured close, wary, enticed by the candy Dillon offered once again.

Snug in his arms, she waited with him. Watched, spellbound, as the stunning creature ambled forward. She noticed the gash on the animal's shoulder, where the bullet had grazed him, for the first time. A large scab marked his black coat. "Is that the bullet wound?"

"Yep. My brother and I had a hard time holding him to get the bullet out and lancing it." Dillon's chin rested on the crown of her head, light and affectionate, and nestled against him she felt wanted.

Loved. Valued. A month ago it had been unthinkable that any decent man would want her.

And this man, the most decent and honorable of them all, wanted her. Just her.

Dillon spoke in the magical language, as it sounded, of gentle words and sounds that eased the worry from her heart. Made bearable the wounds in her soul. She watched the stallion stand taller and the shadows ease from his eyes. It was the emotion behind the words, she realized, the steady affection that any creature wanted.

Especially her. Grateful, she kissed Dillon's jaw and he grinned at her, lopsided and handsome. So very handsome. How was it that he became more dear to her and more attractive with every day that passed?

Because I love him. It was true. The warm, bursting affection, the emotion that thrilled through her when they touched. She kissed him again.

"Be careful what you start, ma'am, because I'm the man who will finish the job." He was still erect, his hardness something she began to think about more and more. How treasured he'd made her feel. And he wanted her again. So soon.

Does he really want me that much? It seemed incredible, and she closed off the memory of another man, who had turned away from her touch. Who had come to her at night out of duty. Whose touch had not sparked a connection within her and whose kiss had not lit a fire of want and need.

Dillon was making her love him, the same way he charmed the horses with words and gentle touches, and she could not stop the current of feelings drowning her with need and caring. The stallion reached over the top fence rail, warily, but beginning to believe he would come to no harm, and stole the treats from Dillon's hand. Crunching greedily, he backed away.

"Good boy," Dillon praised in the magic voice that swept through her, knocking down every defense, and laid her bare. She was as vulnerable as the sand to the ocean tide, and he was sweeping her away.

"One day he's going to stay close and ask for another piece. We've got him interested. He'll start negotiating soon."

"Negotiating?"

"He wants something, and we want something. I've started with the peppermint. He likes it and wants it, and I want him to get used to coming to me when I show up. So it's mutual. That's how it starts, the partnership between him and us." Dillon pulled a wrapped disc from his pocket. "Want one?"

"Well, I do have a sweet tooth."

"Lucky me." He unwrapped the candy and focused on her mouth.

She parted her lips before he moved. The candy slid across her bottom lip and over the tops of her teeth. His fingertip followed, stroking craftily along the sensitive surface of her mouth.

"Good?" When she nodded, he blushed, growing bashful. "Why, thank you, ma'am. I'm glad you think so."

He kissed her with great care, so she could feel what sang in his heart.

It had been a wonderful day. Katelyn glowed with contentment as she looked over the top of her book and across the breadth of the hearth where Dillon was stretched out on the length of the couch. His brows frowned in concentration, the thick book standing on end in the center of his chest, lost in reading.

I love him. She felt like a bird caught on an uprising wind, lifting her frighteningly fast and far from the solid, reliable earth. Drawing her so far up, where she'd never flown before.

She loved a thousand things about him. He was handsome and gentle and as steadfast as the mountains. He was shy and confident, all at once. He was strong and smart and good-hearted. He made her content just to be in the same room with him. He made her feel with a part of her she didn't know existed. So new and fragile.

He turned the page with a rustle of paper that warred with the pleasant crackle of the fire. She looked around the room, sparse and in need of a woman's touch, but it was snug on this cold winter's eve. It was home.

How long has it been since I've felt safe and loved? Katelyn hugged the book to her chest, thumbing through all the years in her mind. The years of loneliness and unhappiness married to Brett. The bleak decade after her mother had married Cal Willman. The lean, desperate times after her father's death when her mother could not make ends meet and crumbled beneath the burden of it.

A long time.

The clock bonged the hour ten times from the emptiness of the dark kitchen, echoing through the house and stirring Dillon from his reading. He watched her over the top of his book.

"It's damn good to have you here in my parlor." He grinned, that bashful, self-conscious smile of his that made him appear both vulnerable and invincible. A tough western man with a tender soul.

"It's good to be here."

"Yeah?" One brow quirked, as if he were surprised. "Then you don't regret marrying me."

"This is the happiest I've ever been."

Her confession stunned him. Dillon marked his page and put the book aside, overwhelmed with the emotion flaring to life inside him. He'd seen it over and over again, and he didn't know how wealthy people could be so poor.

He could see it in Katelyn, the devastation of it, the wonder in her eyes whenever he held her, as if surprised he'd want to do that. As if it had never occurred to her that any man would desire and cherish her.

It made him furious how she'd been treated. He could see the wariness in her as he climbed to his feet and grabbed the poker from the iron hook. Wariness. She'd been hurt, and he hoped to high heaven that she didn't think he'd ever hurt her.

Maybe, he reasoned, hers was a deeper kind of distrust. That she wondered if he would be good to her for the long haul of a marriage, the day in and day out of it. The tough times that inevitably came along through the cycles of a lifetime.

I'll show you. I'll teach you that there are some things that can never be broken. His love for her was one of them. He broke apart the crumbly logs and watched the embers glow and brighten as air hit them.

That's what he needed to do. Break apart those dark places in her heart. Give them light and air. Let them glow until there was no more doubt, no more fear. He would show Katelyn what her husband was made of.

And she would come to believe it.

His ankle popped. His knee creaked. Being a horse-man was a demanding job. And now that he had Kate-lyn in his life, he wouldn't need to be on the road, traveling from job to job.

For the first time in a while, he had a real home. And the woman of his dreams to share it with.

There was just one problem. And it was an enor-mous one. He was a direct man, practical, who took life one step at a time. And so that's what he'd done with Katelyn. First he'd concentrated on helping her, making sure she got a chance to know him. Then he worked on getting her to marry him. And now that she was here, he wanted her to love him, genuine and true and forever. The way he loved her.

The trouble was, the thing he hadn't considered was that she needed him. He'd given her a choice in the hotel room—money to last her at least a year if she used it wisely or his wedding ring. She'd chosen him, and he was damn glad. Damn proud to have her in his life. That was for absolute certain.

But would she be happy here? Or would she grow discontent after the novelty of learning to cook and keep house wore off, like polish on a new shoe, and begin wishing for her old life with a cook and maids and a fancy lifestyle to amuse her?

She was like a priceless china figurine on a hand-made wooden shelf. She didn't belong here, even though she wore his ring on her hand. A symbol of the vows she'd made to him. A promise to love him forever.

Would it be possible? She might not even intend for it to happen. Feelings changed sometimes. They did, without explanation, without meaning for it to happen.

Time would tell, he figured. And in the meantime, he'd do what he could to bind her to him. To love her so hard and true, it might make her belong here. Belong to him rightfully and forever without question.

"Hey, ready to go up to bed?" He lifted the book out of her hands gently. If she protested, he'd give it back.

She sparkled, like the first star in a night sky, tentative but unable to hold back the light. "I suppose it is getting late."

Was that her roundabout way of saying she wanted this night to be different than the others? *Please.*

He'd been hard all evening. All he had to do was be alone with her. Showing her how to boil potatoes on the stove, cooking side by side and being able to touch her, just touch her, run his hand across her back as he reached around her for a hot pad to lift the kettle lid with. To stop and breathe in the scent of her hair and shampoo as he set the beef steaks to frying.

He was harder now and wanted her with a fierceness that he'd never felt. A hunger unparalleled. He set the book on the floor with a thud and held out his hand. She rose from the chair, a sensual womanly movement that stirred his desire. Her fingertips lightly stroked the center of his palm as she grabbed his hand that kindled his need for her.

And led him up the stairs. This night *would* be different. He was going to get to hold her all night long, her nakedness against his. Desire crackled through him, roaring hotter and higher.

He watched the sway of her fanny beneath that

pretty calico dress. And the curve of her neck and the subtle sway of her perfect breasts, which moved with her every step.

I'm a lucky man. Without a single doubt. She was like grace come into his life, a haven from the pain of loneliness. A balm to a deeper wound he hadn't been aware of until now.

The wound of not being loved. It was an unhappiness that was gone, and looking back, he could see how discontent he had been. It was why he moved from ranch to ranch, always traveling. To cover up the fear that no woman would ever think he was good enough to love.

Katelyn loved him. She'd said so, and he'd felt the truth of it. He was still afraid she might change her mind.

And now that he had a sample of what it was like to be loved by her, why, it was paradise. How could he go back to living without her?

He couldn't. It was as simple as that.

As Katelyn led him into their bedroom and searched through the dark for matches to light the lamp, he lifted her braid and kissed the sensitive spot just above her collar.

She drew in a surprised intake of breath, as if she hadn't expected this but liked it. She leaned against him, already surrendering, already wanting.

He drew her into his arms, her back to his chest and, chin on her head, began unfastening the buttons that kept her breasts from his touch.

He'd waited long enough. He'd not wait another second to bind her to him, make her a little more his. He brushed the dress from her shoulders and the garments beneath and led her to their bed. He laid her down and made love to her, his wife, his love.

He gave her all the pleasure he knew how to give. Gentle touches and hot kisses and slow deep thrusts that made her arch up to take him deeper. That made her fingers dig into his back as she surrendered. It was *his* name she called when she broke around him, his name she whispered as she kissed his face afterward.

She clung to him when, sated and full of his seed, sleep claimed her.

Even in her dreams, she held fast to *him*.

Chapter Sixteen

Wasn't it a beautiful day? Katelyn couldn't believe how light she felt. As weightless as those tiny snow-flakes floating in a crisp morning sky. It was because she'd awakened in the warmth of Dillon's arms, tucked against his chest as if he thought she was the most precious thing to him.

He's that precious to me. Love for him glowed like a noontime sun within her, warming her from the in-side out. Memories from last night rippled through her. The passionate taste of his kisses. The possessive gentleness of his caresses. The liquid glide of him inside her, the pleasure of it, the intimacy.

She'd never known that kind of pleasure existed. And that it could get better each time. As her affec-tions for him did. Each time he made love to her, the feelings inside her heart doubled. How could that be?

She strolled into the kitchen, warm and toasty. Dil-lon had lit the stove for her, on his early-morning trip to the stables. Wasn't that thoughtful?

A small bundle wrapped in brown paper and tied with a piece of twine sat precisely in the middle of the table. "To Katelyn, my love," was written in a bold script.

Dillon had gotten her a gift? What a thoughtful man. What a wonderful man. He'd gone to town yesterday, and he'd taken the time out of his busy errand running and supply buying to choose a little something for her. Should she open it now? Or wait?

As if in answer, the wall clock bonged six times. What she'd better do is get breakfast cooking, that's what! The gift would be all the better for the waiting.

She sliced bacon and set it on to fry. While the meat sizzled, she sliced potatoes and melted butter to fry them in. She kept stealing glances over her shoulder.

It was something small. Like a barrette for her hair. Or a pin for her lapel. Ooh, what could it be? She tried to imagine what Dillon would have selected. A bar of scented soap? A length of lace?

She ground the coffee beans the way Dillon had shown her and put the ground coffee on to boil. The kitchen smelled of sizzling bacon and buttery potatoes and coffee perking. Her stomach growled as she flipped the crisping slices of bacon. Good, she liked them crispy. It was almost time to put on the eggs.

"Who is this beautiful woman in my kitchen?" Dillon clomped across the kitchen in his boots, bringing with him the sting of a winter's breeze.

The cold clung to his clothes as he wrapped her in a big hug from behind, snuggling her against him, as wonderful as a dream. "Wait, I know who you are. You're my wife."

"Imagine that." She leaned against him, sinking against him. She could close her eyes, relax and stay right here forever. "That's what happens when you take a woman to the minister. She tends to come home with you and cook your breakfast."

"I'm just glad you're here." His fingers traced the ring on her left hand. His kiss against her brow. Tender. Heartfelt. True.

"Me, too." It was like a dream, being in his house, in his arms. She flipped the potatoes and he held her, held on. He was about as soft as iron, but his heart, why, it was as genuine as heaven's light.

It was like a fairy tale, like everything good in the world, and she was living it. Here, in an ordinary kitchen with an ordinary wedding ring on her finger.

And the man she'd married, why, legends could be written about him and still fall short of the truth.

When he kissed her brow, it was like soaring on a wind above mountains. When he tilted her head just enough so he could slant his lips over hers, it was like being lifted into the clouds, so fluffy and sweet.

When he pulled her around to face him, and clasped his strong hands at the small of her back, pulling her against his unyielding chest, it was like gliding in one fast, breathless flight to heaven.

"You didn't open your present," he murmured against her lips. "I hurried in just to see the look of delight on your face. Now you've disappointed me."

"I'm so sorry."

"I'm sure there's something you can do to make it up to me."

"What? Let me think. Oh, I could burn your breakfast."

"Ah, not what I had in mind." Chuckling, he released his hold on her just enough to let her turn but not let go.

He kept both hands on her hips and his chest to her back while she flipped and stirred the potatoes and turned the browning bacon strips.

"I've got to get the eggs on," she said, as if she expected him to move away from her.

No force on earth or in heaven was strong enough to make him. Dillon stayed right where he was. Breathed in her sweet female scent and treasured the silken tickle of her hair against his shaven jaw. Filled his fingers with the soft feel of her. Remembered how it had been last night, loving her, inside her, making her his.

His fingers crept across her stomach and cradled her low. He knew she'd had a tough pregnancy and miscarriage, but maybe one day their son would take root.

Their child. Tenderness left him weak.

Having Katelyn in his life... Overcome, he couldn't find the right words. It had changed everything. Already his life was completely new. Where once he'd been a lonely man with nothing to anchor him, now he had a loving wife and a happy home and a reason to risk building his dreams. For the son that might come along one day.

For the woman who held his heart in her hands.

She didn't appear to know it as she flipped the eggs with care, the way he'd shown her, to keep the yolks intact. "Today is the sewing circle gathering at Mariah Gray's house."

"Need a ride, do you?"

"I don't like that tone in your voice, sir. You sound mischievous."

"No, just call me a man who sees an opportunity. You need a ride, and I can hitch up the horse for you. The question is, what will you give me?"

"How about your breakfast served on a plate and not tossed at your head?"

She was laughing. He could feel it move through her, and it was good. She trusted him enough to be playful. "Hey, I'll behave. All right. I'll drive you anywhere you want to go, all you have to do is say. Just don't pelt me with fried food in my own kitchen."

"This is my kitchen now, too."

"And I thought marrying you would be a *good* idea." Chuckling, he pressed kisses into her hair. He loved her so much. And this was only the beginning. Right?

"Go open your present." He stole the spatula away from her. "I'll finish up."

"Hey, it's my kitchen. I'm in charge." She stole the spatula back.

"Whoa, there. I didn't know you were so bossy."

"That's what you deserve after the short courtship you gave me." Laughing, she flipped an egg with a splatter of grease.

"Short? I admit it. You are the first woman I ever courted. I had no notion of what I was doing. I'm pretty inexperienced as a married man, too."

"That's not true." She bit her lip to keep from laughing at him. "You seemed to know what you were doing last night."

Heat crept up his face. "I, uh, am not without, um, experience."

"I am a very fortunate woman to have such a skilled husband." She took delight in the way the pink staining his nose and cheeks changed to a bright, pure red. Even the tips of his ears were red.

Poor Dillon, all six feet of him, so mighty and invincible. And bashful. Then he lifted one shoulder in an uncertain shrug. "Am I skilled enough to make you want to stay?"

"What? Why would I leave?"

"You might regret your decision to stay." He stole a second spatula from the drawer, not looking at her, keeping his face averted. "This isn't a life you're used to. We've talked about this."

"I see." She tested a yolk, found it done, and flipped the eggs onto a plate. "So you think I'm the kind of shallow and insincere woman who would marry a man so he could take care of me, so I wouldn't have to work or some such nonsense. Is that what you think?"

"You know it isn't."

"No, I don't." She removed the pan from the heat, remembering to count before her temper got away from her. "I'm happy here. It would help if you had faith in me."

"Oh, darlin', I do." He snatched the egg-filled platter and carried it, along with his plate of crisp, golden potatoes, to the table. He didn't look at her. "It's me. I just want you to say you're here because you want to be."

Was that defensiveness? she wondered. How could

he not know? What was he trying to tell her? Was he having regrets?

"You haven't opened your gift." Cutting her off before she could speak, he shoved the small package across the smooth wood to her.

She didn't want to open the gift. What she wanted to know was if he were wishing he hadn't proposed. No, that couldn't be true, because he'd been so persistent. And last night... Pleasure thrilled through her at the memory of his touch, his kiss, his loving.

She tugged the string and the bow unraveled. She tore away the brown paper to the small wooden box beneath.

A carved box. "You did this?"

He nodded. "I made it a long time ago. I meant to make a cigar box, but it didn't turn out that way. I figured that maybe it was a sign that I would meet a woman to fall in love with one day. And when I did, I would give it to her."

"It's beautiful." She ran her fingertips over the etched layers of roses embedded in the lustrous cherry-wood grain.

"Look inside."

Dillon appeared intense, shoulders straight, back straight, his jaw clamped tight. Or was he worried?

She lifted the lid. Inside, on a snug bed of blue satin, winked a row of small diamonds strung on gold. The bracelet felt like a silken thread between her fingers.

"To replace the one you lost. The one your step-father tried to pay me with."

"How did you know it was mine?"

"It sure as hell wasn't his, and a small dainty thing

like that wouldn't fit your mother. That only left you.'' He curved his hand against the side of her face, bold and gentle in the same moment.

Uncertainty pinched the corners of his eyes, and he appeared so vulnerable, his heart wide open, this great warrior of a man. ''It's not as expensive and the diamonds aren't as big as the original, and I'm sorry for that, but I hope you like it anyhow.''

''I love it. Because it's from you.'' On tiptoe, she brought her lips to his. ''You don't need to buy me diamonds and gold to make me happy.''

''I do want you to be happy here.'' He drew her to him when she moved away, sealing her against his hips and chest, against his heart. ''I do love you.''

His kiss was like dawn. Shy and sweet, a gentle glow that warmed her and gave her hope.

''I married you,'' she confessed, ''because I had to know what this was. This feeling inside me.'' She clasped her fist between her breasts. ''What I feel for you, I've never known before.''

Relief left Dillon feeling as if he'd downed a good portion of a whiskey bottle. ''Me, too, darlin'.''

To hell with breakfast. He felt her melt against him, felt her need as if it were his own. A need not for a husband to provide a roof, food and safety.

But a need of the soul for its match. For completion.

He was *that* man.

With her new bracelet sparkling in the gray winter's light, Katelyn reined in the red gelding Dillon had hitched to his smallest sleigh. ''He's a tame fellow who will do what you want, not at all like me.''

She remembered how Dillon had winked, as if he knew darn well he wasn't always a tame kind of man.

Remembering their lovemaking in the kitchen, her pulse skipped through her veins. She'd driven less than a mile, and already she missed him. He'd be working with his horses right now, in one of the corrals with a lariat in hand. Or maybe he'd be riding today, putting the mares through their paces.

"Katelyn, welcome." Mariah swept down from the porch step. A shawl draped her shoulders to protect her and the baby she snuggled in her arms from the falling snow. "Just leave your horse and rig. My husband will be by to take care of them. I'm so glad you came. I hope you like chicken."

"I do. It's so good to be here." Katelyn tried not to look at the baby, snuggling close to his mother.

"Come in and take off those wraps." Mariah led the way into a spacious, warm kitchen that smelled like chocolate cake and coffee.

Two women sat at a large oak table in the corner. One had long curling dark hair and the other was fairer of hair and complexion. "Hello," the women greeted in friendly unison.

"We have all been friends together since public school," Mariah explained after laying the baby down in his cradle near her chair at the table. "You are the first woman we've invited to join us. Wait, no, not the first."

"Remember, we invited that woman from the farm down by the river," the dark-haired woman added. "But she was awful. She was a gossiping sort."

"We're given to gossip now and then," the blond woman chimed in. "But we only tell nice gossip."

"And she brought this horrible sauerkraut dish. Now, I like good sauerkraut." Mariah took Katelyn's wraps with efficiency, shook the snow out of them in front of the stove, and began hanging them up on wall pegs with the other coats and scarves. "But the woman put what had to be raw fish in that perfectly good dish."

"No, I don't think it was raw," the blond woman said with great consideration. "Just not terribly well cooked."

"How well cooked does a fish have to be? A few minutes on the stove and it's done. I'm *sure* it was raw. Sure of it." The dark-haired woman smiled and pointed to an empty chair. "Please, sit and join us. If you're not too afraid of us."

"I would be," the blond woman confessed.

"Rayna, what a thing to say!"

"Well, it's true. If I didn't know us, I'd think, who are these crazy women? Get me away from them as fast as greased lightning."

This wasn't the sort of social gathering Katelyn had been to in nearly a decade. What a waste, all those stuffy, proper dinners with Brett's somber friends. Years passed by, whether a person lived them or not.

Brett casting her out and severing all legal ties had been the best thing that had ever happened to her. He couldn't love her—well, that didn't mean much. He couldn't love anyone, save himself. And she'd been existing in shadows for too long.

She had a whole new life. She had a cozy house to take care of, a great man to love and who honestly cherished her, and now this chance for real friends, the kind she used to have long ago when she was young.

She set her sewing basket on the floor, took the offered chair and joined in the merriment.

Dillon noticed the small brown sparrows stopped in midsong to scatter in their hiding places in the deep white meadows. He drew the gray mare to a halt on a tight rein, reassuring her when she started to sidestep. Was someone coming? Or was it a wild predator? A cougar or a wolf come to cause trouble?

He quieted. Listened. A gopher dove into his burrow with a loud protest, his snow-clearing task interrupted. The road was clear. Katelyn wasn't back yet from her visiting. The mare was scenting something, lifting her well-shaped head to the east, nostrils flaring and ears pricked.

It sure as hell wasn't danger, or she wouldn't be so interested in the newcomer. He caught a flash of color in the dips and draws of the snowy meadows. Yep, it was Dakota, riding his white pinto bareback, the reins knotted and left to lie on the mare's neck.

"C'mon, girl." He reined the mare around, opened the gate and pushed her hard across the silent prairie.

"Brother." Dakota greeted with a nod. "I heard you made it official. You made her your bride. Is that wise?"

"I think so."

"You look like hell, but then your ugly mug always does." Dakota turned his pony toward the ranch, leading the way home. "Does she make you happy?"

Overjoyed. "Happy enough."

"That's all a man can expect from a woman."

Dakota's judgment of marriage had never been a good one. Dillon understood that. He'd seen a lot of unhappy marriages in his life. In his line of work. It was rare to find your match, he knew.

I'm so lucky to have her. Longing filled him in one slow sweep.

He knew she felt this, too, the indefinable connection between them. A bond that was deeper than emotion, more substantial than flesh and bone. That went so deep that his love for her was everything. Everything he was. Everything he wanted. Everything he would ever be.

For a man who never could get up the courage to court a woman before Katelyn, he was doing damn good. He'd do his best to keep going, to prove to her beyond a doubt that she could trust him. That she could give him the pieces of her heart she was holding back.

One day, the wariness and the shadows would be gone, and when she looked at him she would see the man she loved and trusted beyond anything. Without question. He simply had to keep doing his best.

"How's that new stud of yours doing?" Dakota signaled his pinto to the corral where the stallion watched.

When the Appaloosa spotted Dakota, he laid back his ears and showed his teeth.

"Guess he remembers you, brother." Dillon laughed as he told the stallion, "If you feel the urge to bite one of us, make sure it's him."

"Funny." Dakota slid off the mustang's rump and approached the fence. "I came over to see if you needed help lancing that wound a second time. But it looks like it's healing up clean. Is there any pus?''

''Nope. I've been keeping a good eye on it.'' Dillon's gift with animals was small compared to Dakota's. He watched while his brother spoke to the stallion, the language of their grandfather rolling off his tongue with ease.

''He's in less pain and he's starting to figure out he's stuck here.'' Dillon dismounted with a creak of leather. ''He's getting cranky.''

''He's not happy to be here.'' Dakota climbed on the fence and braced his forearms on the top rung. ''He's a Spirit Horse. You can't keep him here. You can't train him to saddle and bridle the way you did the others.''

''I know, brother.'' Dillon braced his elbows on the wood planks and studied the rare Appaloosa, as black as midnight from his nose to his hooves. Except for the perfect blanket of markings over his withers and rump.

''He can't be tamed.''

''He *shouldn't* be. There's a bounty on his head.''

''How will you keep him? Imprison him here when he's made to run free? Keep him penned like a trained pony?''

''I can't say it hasn't been troubling me.'' But it had been Katelyn who'd dominated his thoughts. Katelyn he'd been teaching to trust.

''I figure I'll worry about the stallion when he's well.'' Maybe by that time he would have earned her love and she would be his completely and forever. He'd never have to worry about her growing discontent or regretting her choice to come here.

"Hey, you're not listening, brother. You're thinking about her, aren't you?"

"Who?" Dillon shook his head. His thoughts *had* drifted away. He worried that he'd imprisoned her. Given her a future that she'd needed but, deep in her heart, didn't want.

And yet, her words came back to him, tentative but honest. *I love you.* She'd said those words to him and meant them. She'd do it. She'd come to trust him completely, he'd make damn sure of that.

Everything he did from this moment on, he would do for Katelyn.

"It's no sense talking to you." Dakota waved him away like a speck of dust and whistled to his pinto. "You stay there and moon over that woman of yours. I'm going to go take a look at that filly of yours that's hobbling. Is she still in the stable? Why do I bother to ask?"

Dakota stalked away in disgust.

One day, brother. You will feel this way, too. Dillon had never before been so close to a woman. Being married wasn't all that he thought it would be. He figured at the best it would be a companionship. A soft sweet presence at the end of his day, to walk into the house, tired from hard work, and she'd be a friend to talk to. A lover to take into his bed at night.

Katelyn was more. He couldn't define it any more than he could define the wind. He could feel it on his skin, watch it move through the grass and shake the cottonwood boughs and force the clouds across the sky.

But he couldn't hold it in his hand. And that was the nature of love, he realized.

He knew the moment she was approaching. The prairie could hide her in its swells and troughs, and still he could feel her like the wind on his face. Like the grasses in the fields, he was moved.

Sure enough, there was the faint ring of steeled shoes on hard-packed snow. The birds stilled. The gophers hid. The mare and stallion both swung to the north, watching as the familiar sorrel nosed into sight on the rise, drawing the sleigh he'd built himself.

Katelyn. She was a small dot of gray hat and coat, and he filled more and more as she came near. There was no other way to describe how he felt. He was whole when he was with her.

He loved watching her drive into the yard. She was smiling. She must have had a good visit at the neighbors'. Women needed time together, he'd observed, and he was glad she was making friends. Fitting into the fabric of things. *Please, be happy here. Please, never want to leave.*

He took her hand to help her from the sleigh. "Is that chicken I smell?"

"Yes. There were so many leftovers, Mariah handed out plates of food as we were leaving. This will save me from having to make supper."

"Oh? Maybe we can make something else instead." Embarrassed, he looked away.

He supposed he oughtn't to speak of his need for her outside the dark haven of their bedroom, but he couldn't help it. He had to let her know he desired her. Only her. For the rest of his days.

There would be no other woman for him. Ever.

He let his kiss tell her. Let his devotion well up

from his soul and flavor his kiss. He felt her respond with warm velvet kisses and tenderness.

Oh, yeah, she loved him. He kissed the tip of her nose. The dimple in her chin. *Now give me the rest of your heart, darlin'.* "If my brother wasn't here, I'd carry you upstairs and show you how much I love you."

"Your brother's here?" She honored him with one last tempting kiss. "If he wasn't here, I'd surely let you."

"Really?" His low rumble of satisfaction vibrated through her. She could feel his want and his love for her. "I'll be right back. I'm going to go chase my brother off so I can have you all to myself."

"You'll do no such thing! If your brother is here, then he's invited to supper. There's more than enough, and I can make the biscuit recipe Betsy gave me. Wait!" She squealed as he wrapped her in a bear hug, tenderly overpowering her and tossing her over his wide shoulder.

Their laughter drifted around them like the snow-flakes gently descending.

"It was a fine meal, Katelyn." Dakota thanked her with a polite nod before pushing his chair from the table. "I thank you for it."

"I'll pour the coffee, if you two men want to take it in the parlor." Before Katelyn could rise, Dillon was there, pulling back her chair, taking the opportunity to skim his fingertips along the back of her neck as if saying, *later.*

Desire flickered through her, flame hot and staggering. *If my brother wasn't here, I'd carry you up-*

stairs and show you how much I love you. His promise beat in her blood, growing bigger, brighter until it was all she could think of.

She wanted his touch. She wanted the callused pads of his fingertips grazing against her bare skin. The satin heat of his kiss, firm and demanding on her mouth, her throat, her breasts.

She melted, remembering. He'd made love to her this morning, right here, laying her over the table and she could feel his love, his heart, all he was as they moved toward release together.

She blushed, turning to the stove and pretending to search for a hot pad. As if he knew exactly what she was remembering, Dillon lifted the braid from the back of her neck and planted a hot, sucking kiss on the back of her neck.

She came alive, body and soul.

Dillon left the room, but his effect on her remained. The affection he felt for her was as tangible as the stove's heat on her skin.

She was home. For the rest of her life. The first thing, now that she was well, would be to make curtains for the windows. Her man apparently did not think of those kinds of necessities, so she'd be happy to do it for him.

Maybe a cheerful yellow gingham for the window behind the table. She tried to envision it as she set the full pot on the stovetop. Yes, it would do nicely, something soft and draping with full ruffles.

As for the parlor, something softer. Lace maybe. She could crochet it herself. She had some small talent with a crochet hook. And her grandmother's pattern for garden-leaf lace that would complement the log walls perfectly.

"...I don't know if I know you anymore, brother," Dakota was saying, his deep gruff baritone barely audible as she hesitated at the threshold.

Maybe she'd stay here and give the brothers time to talk. Her book was on the worktable. She turned around and heard the next snippet of conversation.

"...next thing I know, you'll have yourself a passel of children running around this place..."

Oh, Dillon's brother didn't know. Why would he? Being barren wasn't something a person advertised in the weekly edition of the town's newspaper. It was a private sorrow.

"That's my hope, brother." Dillon's answer, his words solid and sure.

He doesn't know? The blood rushed from her head, and the house tilted sharp and swift. She grabbed the wall for support, the light draining from her vision. She slid down the wall until she sat on the floor.

Breathe. If only she could breathe, she'd be fine.

She couldn't get air. Her chest clamped tight and she was drowning. Gasping, fighting to breathe. *Dillon didn't know. He didn't know.*

How had that happened? Surely the doctor had told him. Surely the gossips on her stepfather's ranch had told him. She couldn't remember if she had. She couldn't remember actually saying the words to him...

She hadn't. *It was true.* She'd never told him that by marrying her, he would be childless, too.

There would be no sons. No daughters. No babies to cuddle close on a cold winter's night. No children running around the yard, laughter like music in the air.

He had wed her believing they could have a normal life together. A family life and all the happiness and trials that came with it.

He *wanted* children. She'd heard the tone in his voice. The certainty of it. The desire.

No decent man will have her. Her stepfather's voice haunted her like a ghost in the corner, rising up with the shadows as the lamp sputtered on the table, dancing a slow writhing death.

You're useless to me. Brett's words. Brett's disdain. *If you can't give me a son, what good are you?*

Air squeaked into her throat and she coughed. *What if that is what Dillon would think, too?* Not again, no. She couldn't go through that again. She couldn't endure being shunned and put aside, not as good as other women who could bear their husbands a son.

Dillon wouldn't do that to her, would he? He wouldn't make her feel useless and worthless for something that wasn't her fault, would he? No, he wouldn't.

He wanted children. Sons and daughters. Their bedroom was not the only one in the house. There were empty rooms, echoing and lonely, waiting for children to play in them, laugh in them, sleep in them.

Dillon had built this house with his own hands. And in it, he'd kept his dreams. Dreams for a loving wife and their children together.

How did she tell him? How did she say the words that would destroy his hopes? That would change the radiant love that sparkled inside him—all that love, just for her. She couldn't watch that love fade and wither.

There were plenty of women who could give him what he wanted. Why would Dillon want her?

The lamp on the table gave one last sputter, and the one ray of light died silently, sadly, leaving only darkness.

Katelyn climbed to her feet, kept to the shadows and crept up the stairs. Dillon's laughter rumbled through the wood flooring. There was a faint clinking sound from the kitchen, as if he'd poured the coffee himself.

The coffee. She'd forgotten her promise to bring cups in to them in the living room, to enjoy with their cigars and conversation. It was a small oversight, but tonight it felt like the worst of failures.

Well, not the worst. She kicked off her shoes and climbed into bed. She swore her womb hurt from sorrow. Her heart, her soul, bled with it as she drew the covers over her head. There were no tears. Her grief was greater than that. There would be no end to this sadness.

No healing from this loss.

"Katelyn?" Dillon's step outside the door. His concern as he ambled into the room.

She didn't move. Maybe if she stayed very still, the truth would somehow change. Fate could not be this cruel, she decided, as to give her the perfect love, a rare and singular man to love, only to snatch it away.

And leave her more broken than before.

Yes, fate could. She felt her husband's hand stroke her forehead.

"Are you tired?" he asked. "Well, then you sleep, my precious wife."

His step was halting as he left. The door whispered nearly closed, then paused, open. There were no footsteps marching away. Was he watching her?

Then the knob clicked into place and she was alone.

As she was meant to be.

Chapter Seventeen

"Katelyn?" The hour was late, for the faint ring
from the downstairs clock had sounded once through
the floorboards while she'd tried to sleep and
couldn't. He smelled of cigar and wood smoke and a
faint hint of whiskey as he eased beneath the covers.
The ropes groaned as he leaned over her, watching
her.

His kiss on her brow was heaven.

I don't deserve you, Dillon. She squeezed her eyes
shut. Fisted her heart. Shuttered her soul. He was
faithful and loving. He was an incredible husband.
Never once had he treated her poorly, neglected her,
devalued her or in any way belittled her.

No, he'd been honorable and devoted and giving.
He loved her with his whole heart, as he had vowed
to do when he had placed his ring on her finger, when
he'd made her his wife. He was a man of his word.

But he hadn't known the truth when he'd made
those promises. When he'd said his wedding vows.

The sheets rustled as his hand curved over the

crown of her head and stroked, lightly, so he wouldn't wake her.

He believed she was asleep.

"I love you so very much, my angel."

I love you, too.

The plump feather pillows whispered as he laid his head to rest. The ropes groaned as his weight settled in the feather tick. He gave the covers a yank and they snapped over his head. His breathing slowed. His body relaxed.

How was she ever going to find it in her heart to tell him?

She eased onto her stomach and folded the top edge of the sheet back. Although it was dark, her eyes had adjusted to the shades of black in the room, and she could make out the darker black of his hair scattered over his high brow and the hollow of his closed eyes and the rise of his nose. The cut of his chin as he breathed in and out, lost in sleep.

He was extraordinary. A magnificent man. One that would always be hers. Or, so she had believed.

I'm going to lose him. What would she do then? He was her entire heart. How could she live without her heart?

Pain left her dizzy and weak and she sank into her pillows, burying her face. The soft feather pillow cupped her face, but it did nothing to stop the images in her head. The image of Dillon cradling Mariah Gray's baby in his arms and his desire for one of his own naked in his twinkling eyes.

The image of his hand curving over her low abdomen, above her surgical scar, over her womb. Had he placed his hand there while cradling her close in the kitchen and wished one day that was where his son would grow?

She remembered the town doctor's sadness when he had told her the truth that day she'd lost her baby. *It is certain there will be no more children. I'm sorry.*

Her entire body grew taut, as if she'd taken a blow to the stomach. Pain was a sharp, curved blade cleaving her in two, leaving her helpless and raw, a mortal wound. It wasn't a roof she needed. It was Dillon. She needed his love, his touch, his tenderness in the night.

His undying regard for her.

She slipped from the covers, careful not to disturb Dillon. He lay on his back, his big body relaxed in sleep. His quiet puff of air as he breathed out was endearing to her. He'd stripped down to the skin, and the midnight gloss of it, a strange luster in the dark night, made her fingertips itch to stroke their way across the delineated lines of his chest. To feel the heat of his skin and the thud of his heart and know this man was hers to love.

She kept close to the wall, where the boards did not squeak or groan beneath her feet. The stairwell was as dark as a coffin as she descended to the first floor, where signs of Dakota's visit remained—the scent of cigar smoke and the shadow of empty cups on the hearth. Where the brothers had sipped a bit of whiskey and smoked while they talked through the hours.

It was a room where brothers confided in each other, where a husband and wife found contentment in front of a crackling fire. A room where children should run and play in the sunlight, their laughter echoing like happiness.

Her losses felt reopened like wounds scabbed over and newly bleeding. She stumbled into the kitchen and to the door, where her coat hung neatly on a peg. As if it belonged there, next to Dillon's, hung up and ready to wear on his early-morning chores.

Blindly she jammed her arms into the sleeves of her coat and stumbled outside. The frigid wind sliced through her few layers, straight through her skin to her bones.

Good. She had to stop feeling. She wanted to be like the winter, numb, silent and cloaked with forgetfulness. It hurt too much to do anything else. And what was she going to do? Wake up Dillon from a sound sleep and tell him she was the reason he would never have a son?

Pain cracked her open, left her wounded, left her bleeding. She headed out into the prairie, and let the cold and the darkness claim her.

Katelyn? Dillon woke with a start and saw the pillow beside him empty. The sheets where she should be lying were cool. Where was she?

Probably downstairs. He heard the stove lid rattle, and his fear ebbed. Katelyn was lighting the morning fire, he figured. He had to stop expecting her to change her mind. To find him wanting.

Hadn't *she* held him? Reached up to kiss him? They were a part of each other now. Husband and wife. Lovers and friends. Of one flesh. And he hated to think of her working so hard, when she still needed to take good care of herself. The doc had been clear about his orders. Katelyn had to take it easy for some time to come. She'd done far too much around the house yesterday.

What she needed was a little rest and relaxation. Maybe she would feel up to a trip into town. He wanted to get a look at the last-minute additions at the county auction. It was a good excuse to take the sleigh into town and treat Katelyn to a nice lunch at the diner of her choice and a shopping trip. He'd even go along to hold her packages.

That was proof of a man's pure adoration.

He yanked on his Levi's and tugged on his shirt, buttoning it as he rushed downstairs. He didn't know why he felt a need to tell her his plans. Something was troubling him, and he couldn't put his thumb on it. Couldn't name the odd, jittery anxiety snapping in the dead center of his gut.

The kitchen was empty. A fledging fire snapped and crackled in the stove's belly. The lamp in the center of the table had been filled with oil and cast a bright light to guide him to the door, where the peg next to his was empty. Where had she gone? He grabbed his coat and, on the edge of panic, skidded outside into the frosty morning.

Where had she gone? He followed the small imprint of her shoes on the frosted crust of the snow to the stable. There, just beyond the paddock where the stallion watched, a dark figure in the shadows spread grain from a small silver pail for the five deer in a half circle around her.

Her back was to him, and the delicate shape of her affected him more fiercely than ever before. How could it be that every time he looked at this woman, he desired her more? Thought her more beautiful? More sensual? More amazing?

As if she felt his presence, she stiffened. Turned. How pale she looked. Big circles bruised the delicate skin beneath her eyes. She *wasn't* feeling well. It troubled him. He should have made sure she didn't feel obligated to do too much too soon. Well, he'd take care of her. He always would.

"Good morning, beautiful."

Her smile was tentative. Shadows darkened her angel's eyes. He took the empty pail from her mittened hands and gave her a kiss to warm her to her toes.

The same way she warmed him.

It should have been a beautiful day, but it wasn't, Katelyn realized. Seated beside Dillon in the snug little sleigh skimming the snow behind a matched set of black-and-white pintos should have been the most exhilarating ride of her life. It wasn't.

Was there any way he would want her when she told him the truth? Their love was so new. It wasn't as if they'd spent years together and their bond had been strengthened by time and familiarity. No, her husband of many years had been able to cast her aside. How easy would it be for Dillon?

"I've got to swing by the stockyard." Dillon broke the silence as the prairie road gave way to the first signs of town. "You want me to drop you off at the dress shop?"

"That sounds wonderful. I need a few things."

"You make sure you get whatever you want. I got you some clothes, but that was only meant to get you by. You need more than you have."

"No, I have all I need."

"Me, too."

He snuggled her close, drawing her against him, his arm a pleasant weight on her shoulder.

Her generous, loving husband, who had vowed to always stand by her. To always love her.

What if he knew the truth? Would he still want her?

The main street of town was crowded with horse-drawn sleighs and various sleds. Folks had come in from all over the county because of the auction, Dillon explained as he drew the horses to a slow walk behind a loaded teamster's enormous sled stacked high with crates.

Katelyn was grateful for the chaos. Dillon was kept busy as out-of-town drivers rode through intersections or stopped in the middle of the street to look around and get their bearings. He was too preoccupied to wonder why she was so quiet.

She should just tell him. Say it very matter-of-factly. Open her mouth and let the words roll off her tongue. *Dillon, I can't have children. Will you still love me anyway?*

Her stomach clenched tight. A blurry, agonizing memory shot into her head. Of Brett hauling her to the door, his fingers biting into the soft skin of her upper arm. Angry, so angry. And she'd felt so worthless....

No, don't remember. She squeezed her heart closed, like the lid on a too-full trunk, and did her best to lock it up tight before any other painful images popped out.

Dillon wasn't Brett. She knew that. Dillon was an

incredible man of integrity, everything that Brett was not. But the truth remained, cold and harsh and as unchangeable as the season. As the dirty, beaten-down snow on the street in front of them. Every man wanted a son.

"I can't believe our luck." Dillon drew the team to a halt and waited while an ox-drawn sled skimmed away from the hitching post. "Right in front of the dress shop."

Maybe there was a chance he would want her. He was the most steady and loving man she'd ever known. He accepted her flaws and her less-than-perfect cooking with that easy, lopsided grin of his. Maybe he would still love her. Maybe he would still love her the same way.

As if she were a princess, he took her hand and helped her from the sleigh. He walked by her side up the slick wooden steps, opened the door for her as the overhead bell tinkled and introduced her to the seamstress.

"Have a good time shopping. I know it's what you women like to do." With an approving grin, he laid his palm to her face and kissed her in public, to the sigh of the seamstress and a few nearby shoppers.

He strode away as regal as any prince. A noble, worthy man who deserved to have the son he wanted.

The son she couldn't give him. The injustice of it tore her in two. Could have dropped her to her knees except for the seamstress who took her elbow and helped her to the bench near the window.

"Goodness, you look pale, dear. I'll fetch you a cup of hot tea. That should help cure what ails you."

It was a lovely thought, that something as common and as ordinary as tea would fix the grief inside her.

Her gaze naturally followed him through the window. He yanked on the tether line to make sure it was good and tight, then slipped pieces of peppermint from his coat pocket and let the horses lip the treat from his gloved hands.

He turned, his attention on someone just out of sight. A group of women stood in a small circle, blocking whoever it was Dillon was talking to from Katelyn's sight. Wait, the women were moving. Dillon reached out for something....

A baby. Mariah's baby boy was wrapped in green today. His thick coat and cap and mittens were so small, so dear. Mariah waited, looking pleased with Dillon's obvious compliments, as he cradled the little one, held him close and blew kisses on his plump forehead.

What a good father he would be. Katelyn had *felt* his silent longing when he'd held the infant. Because a part of her heart would always be his. Her last hope died as quietly and as surely as a single snowflake in sunshine. Melting without protest. Because it was inevitable.

Dillon should be a father. He had the right to hold his son one day. She would not stand in his way. She did not want him to live his life alone, without the large family he obviously desired.

The one she could never give him.

The seamstress returned with the tea, and Katelyn sipped it dutifully. She watched as Dillon handed the baby back to Mariah, said goodbye and tromped off across the busy road, cutting between vehicles as he went, until he was out of sight.

Everywhere she looked, she saw children. A toddler cried, "Mine! Mine!" somewhere in the store. Children who were too young for school raced down the boardwalk, escaping from their mother who charged after them. Babies held tight in their mother's arms.

Did these women know how lucky they were? she wondered. Her arms felt empty without a baby to hold.

As empty as her soul.

Every wonderful thing Dillon did cut like a knife. His generosity. His gallantry. He held every door. Took her hand. Carried her packages. Treated her to a delicious meal at the finest diner in town. He helped her into the sleigh and tucked the robes snug beneath her chin.

The image of him holding Mariah's baby troubled her. The way he had lit up. How big and strong he looked, cradling that tiny little boy. He wanted one of his own. Anyone could see it.

I wish I could give you a child. She'd sacrifice anything, do anything, to give Dillon what would make him happy. To give him the child he wanted. If only she could.

Just tell him. It plagued her all the way home, as the afternoon sun chased away the stubborn gray clouds. It burdened her as she added wood to the stove and checked on the pot of simmering brown beans.

Maybe it would be all right. She wouldn't know

until she told him. What happened next—whether she left or stayed, was happy or miserable, loved or not wanted—was all in Dillon's capable hands. It was his choice.

She had to let him make it.

It wasn't easy opening the door and stepping outside. It was hard to make her feet move forward all the way to the paddock. Her spirits didn't lift when she saw the man and stallion together, alone. The wild horse trusting Dillon enough to eat peppermint treats from his hand.

Dillon's low voice calmed the horse and it calmed her heart. She waited, perched on the fence, while Dillon stroked the stallion's face and head. The animal shied and sidestepped, only to return to the delicious treat and the man's enchanting touch.

"That's it, boy, that's all I have. You ate all of it." Dillon held up his hands and the stallion backed away, haltingly, unsure. Dillon spied her and headed straight for her. "Katelyn, I'm glad you're here. His wound is healed, and so I'm letting him go."

"Back to the wild? But what about the reward for him?"

"It no longer exists." He braced his forearms on the fence as he stretched over the top rung and claimed her mouth with his. "You know those ten Arabian mares I bought at the sale? The ones Dakota is going to help me drive home from the livery tomorrow? Those were your stepfather's horses. The ones he paid me to train."

"*What?* He wouldn't sell those horses."

"He didn't. He's bankrupt, and the bounty on our

stallion's head is nullified. He is no longer in danger.''

She felt relief for the stallion, but sadness, too. ''That land was my father's.''

''Your stepbrother managed to appease the bank. The land is his now. At least it's still in the family.''

''Good.'' Memories flooded her. Of family. Of helping her father build the big ranch house. Of so many good times. But not nearly as treasured as the ones she'd made here with Dillon. Now she had more memories to comfort her when she was alone.

There's no reason to wait, she realized. She knew how it would end. She may as well handle it with as much dignity as she could. Even if her heart was dying. ''It's good for a man to have a son.''

''Or a daughter. I'm not choosy.'' He flashed her that slow, lopsided grin, the one that always made her soul smile in return. ''Daughters can inherit land, too. Daughters can learn to train horses.''

She could see his dreams. He wanted to teach a child how to ride a horse and how to handle them. He wanted to pass on the knowledge his grandfather had given him about horses, the land and life. It would make him complete. Make his life come full circle.

''As for this fellow—'' he gestured to the stallion that was standing a few feet away, skittish but demanding more candy ''—you want to come in and say goodbye?''

''Knowing him has been a privilege.'' She climbed through the space between the rungs. The stallion had started the romance between them, that night of the season's first snow. She remembered how Dillon had defended him, and befriended him and saved him.

Just as he'd done for her.

And he had saved her, she realized. If she hadn't come here, if she'd chosen to live on her own, then she never would have known this man. The strength of him that could never break. The integrity. The tenderness.

Knowing Dillon had been a gift. One she would treasure always.

"Goodbye, handsome."

His greatness shone over her like the sun, true and remarkable and, when Dillon opened the gate, that greatness didn't diminish. It swelled and soared as the animal lifted his head, scented his freedom, neighed a warm trumpeting goodbye and trotted off, free. Leaping fences and crossing meadows until the prairie claimed him as its own.

The greatness, she realized, wasn't the stallion's. It was the man beside her.

"You're looking pale, darlin'. Let me walk you back to the house. Get you lying down." His hand lit on her shoulder, a tender claiming touch that left her wishing there was a way.

But she couldn't stay. She couldn't do that to Dillon, to this wonderful man she loved more than her life.

"Did you have a good time in town today?" he asked as he held the back door for her. "Did you overdo it?"

"No. I enjoyed it, very much." She took off her wraps and hung them on the peg by the door.

"You didn't buy hardly anything. I might be a

humble horseman, but I can afford to buy my wife what she wants.'' He drew her against him, folding his arms around her, cradling her close. ''I love you, you know. You weren't getting a taste of town life and wishing you lived there, were you?''

''No. I have treasured my time with you.'' She wanted him to know how she felt. Wanted him to know this great love she had for him was endless.

She lifted up on the tip of her toes to give him her kiss. To lay the palm of her hand against his strong jaw. He was everything to her. Now, and for all time.

He could feel it in her kiss; she was sure. He cupped her head and kissed her in return. A hot, hard caress that matched her own need for him.

''Let's finish this upstairs.'' His intimate suggestion enlivened her. Made all her senses spin. She didn't need to answer. He swept her into his arms and carried her upstairs, raining kisses over her face as he navigated down the tiny hall and into the room where their bed waited.

One more time. She was given this chance to love him once more. It was magic, his kiss, his touch. Thrilling as he laid her across the cool sheets and hovered over her.

''You are overdressed for this occasion, ma'am.'' Flashing her a dimple, he tugged at her collar and freed her from her dress. While he kissed her throat and breasts, he unlaced her corset. The stroke of his tongue grew hot and wet as the lace gave way and his mouth closed over her nipple, suckling hard.

Desire snapped like a tight line through the core of her. She dug her fingers into his hair.

''Oh, yes.'' She wanted him forever, to remember

him just like this. The excited thrill of her body as he kissed his way down her stomach and the white-hot flash of pleasure as his fingers parted her. His low, deep groan when he found her wet and ready and lifting up for all of him. The amazing glide of his thickness stretching her open, filling her, making them one, making them whole.

Two hearts, one soul.

Chapter Eighteen

How was she ever going to find the strength to walk away? Katelyn watched Dillon sleep, his hair tousled from lovemaking, the sweat drying on his brow. She loved him so much her spirit ached with it. She couldn't tell him the truth now. She loved him too much.

As he loved her.

"Katelyn," he murmured in his sleep and reached out for her.

She put her hand in his but didn't let him pull her close. He sighed, holding on to her hand so tight, even in sleep. As if to say he intended to hold her forever.

And at what cost? She had failed him. It was only a matter of time before his love eroded slowly and as surely as sand on an ocean shore, moved by a current too strong to resist. Time would pass, and if Dillon could accept her barrenness, then his desire for a child would go unrequited. Become stronger until one day he would gaze at her with disappointment in his eyes.

The slow death of their love would be twice as

painful. And if she stayed, she would be asking too much of him.

The fear that she wasn't enough, wasn't good enough, rose up hard and fast and blinding. She loved Dillon too much to fail him. She couldn't do that to him. To herself. The end result would be the same anyway.

Walk away. It was the only solution for them both. He would hurt, but he'd get over it. She couldn't take this pain anymore. It rose up like a serpent from the sea, twining around her spine, twisting around her entire being. Crushing her body, heart and soul. There was no escape from the black sorrow.

There never would be.

He will be happier without me. Thinking of all the ways Dillon would benefit from her leaving was the only way she found the strength to let go of his hand. The courage to slip the wedding ring from her finger. The faith to face a future without the love of her life.

She took one look back before she crossed the threshold. Love for him burned inside her as bright as a summer sun, radiant and everlasting and strong enough to bring light to anything. Even to the darkness of her fear and her sorrow.

She was doing this for him. So he would have a better life. So he would be free to find a woman who could give him a son. Her legs trembled as she descended the stairs. The deepest part of her was breaking.

Keep going. She was doing the right thing. Walking through the parlor, her steps whispering around her. This house wouldn't always be empty. Isn't that why Dillon had always chosen to travel, when he had the land and the money and the horses to stay here and build a life?

The yard was sullen and silent, long with shadows as the daylight waned. Dark came early this time of year, and it felt as if it were coming into her. The shadows inside her lengthened, blotting out all the happiness she'd known here.

One day children would run in this yard, shrieking as they played tag and blindman's buff. Little boys with Dillon's dark untamable hair ruffling in the wind as they threw baseballs back and forth. Or wrestled in the grass. Or pulled toboggans along the snowy ground in search of the perfect slope to speed down. Little girls with Dillon's dimples playing with their dolls on the front steps or riding horses in the endless fields.

She could see Dillon seated on the front porch on a summer's evening, reading his ranching magazines, content while his children played around him. And a pretty, kind woman who would bring a tray of lemonade and coffee as an evening treat.

It was a happy picture. The best gift she could give him. Her lifetime of unhappiness without him was worth happiness in his.

Forgive me, Dillon. Guilt assailed her as she padded down the road. She wanted to turn back. With all her soul she wanted to race into his house, fall onto their bed and make binding, passionate love to him. To never let him go. Ever.

Each step she took was agony. Every breath was torture. What if she did turn back? What would be waiting for her? Dillon's rejection? Or his love? And how about the future? No, it wouldn't work. She wasn't enough. She never would be. And she loved Dillon too much.

She *had* to keep going. Although it felt as if she were breaking from the inside out. And leaving little pieces of her heart, of her soul behind her as she went. With every step she took away from Dillon's home, she lost more of herself.

She'd figure out a way to survive. She would exist, grow older as time passed. But live? No, it was impossible. She'd left her heart and soul behind, the deepest and most vulnerable part of her, which was somehow a part of Dillon, too.

She would always love him. Always be grateful to him. He'd given her a gift far more precious than gold. He'd given her love. He'd shown her what true love was. And that she was worthy of it, for one brief time. Being loved had changed her.

She would be able to get through the bleak days ahead because of him. Because of the memories he'd given her. And the love that still lived inside her.

It always would.

Twilight wrung the last rays of light from the day. A somber sunset of storm clouds and darkness descended upon her, oppressive and lonely.

Dillon woke in the heavy shadows and knew she was gone. He could *feel* it. He wasn't surprised to see the wedding ring on the pillow where she'd left it for him to find, as if to prove that he'd been right all along, that tiny fear inside him that could not be silenced. She'd had enough of this life with him and walked away.

Why was she doing this to him? It was raw emotion

that propelled him off the bed. He grabbed the ring, crushing it in his palm, yanking on his trousers and searching in the thickening darkness for his damn shirt. Where was it? He gave up and grabbed a new one from the bureau drawer.

One thing was for sure. Katelyn wasn't going to walk away from him like this. Not now. Not ever. She wasn't going to keep him strung tight like this, full of doubt that she'd leave him. Not after he'd figured she was going to stay. She was settled. She was happy.

Hadn't she lain there beneath him, clinging to him while he pleasured her, moved with him as they came together? Hadn't she given him all she had, all she was, the same way he'd given her? How could she do this to him? First strip him bare and then drive the dagger in when he was as vulnerable as a man could be?

He didn't bother to grab tack from the barn. He called to the brown-and-white pinto, whistling a command to her. She lifted her head from the manger, pricked her ears and took out in a full gallop toward him. He opened the gate, grabbed her by the tuft of her mane and mounted in one easy glide.

Damn, he was angry. So damn angry he couldn't remember the last time he had been this mad. The dark hid her trail on the snow, but he knew where she was going. Away. Just away. From him and his love for her.

He pushed the pinto hard as the darkness claimed the land, but he found her anyway. Walking along the road, head down, hands jammed into her skirt.

Wrapped in nothing more than a cardigan sweater over her blue calico dress.

She glanced over her shoulder at the sound of the mare's hooves on the ice-crusted snow. Her jaw dropped, her eyes pinched and she turned toward town and away from him, her head high. But her shoulders sagged.

What kind of game was she playing? It was likely to kill him, that's what. He urged the pinto to a skidding halt and dropped to his feet. That Katelyn kept walking without acknowledging him drove his fury higher.

He breathed deep, gathered his control and marched right after her. "Going to town?"

She didn't look at him and kept going. "I didn't think you would wake up so soon."

"That's the explanation I get? I want a better one. A good one." He kept stride with her. What was she doing? "I married you. I gave you everything I have. Everything I am. And this is what you do to me? Leave me without even saying goodbye?"

It wasn't what she had expected him to say. Katelyn had anticipated a raging fit. She'd gotten used to her first husband and his temper, but Dillon defied expectation. Fury radiated from him with such force it was a wonder he didn't melt the snow at his feet. And yet he was calm, solid, steady.

Was he always a good man, no matter what? Always the honorable man he showed her he was, even when he had lost his temper? Shame squeezed like an iron band tightening around her chest. Her decision to leave was the right one. "I thought it was best to leave this way. While I could."

"What does that mean?" He raked his hand through his hair. He wasn't wearing his hat.

On closer inspection she realized that his shirt was half-buttoned and his jacket was wide open. He wore no muffle or gloves to protect him from the biting wind, the wind she was too broken inside to feel.

Had he been frantic? She remembered all the times he'd come looking for her, with an edge of panic in his voice, afraid that she would reject him. Did he understand? Was he going to make her say the words that would drive him away from her forever?

"I thought you loved me."

"I love you more than anything, don't you see?"

"No, I guess I don't. All I see is you running off and leaving me because you're, what, tired of being a horseman's wife?"

"Not tired. No." This wasn't how it was supposed to be. He was supposed to let her go quietly. He wasn't supposed to charge after her and make her look into his eyes and see his pain. "I've hurt you. I can see it." She laid her hand to his cheek, rough with the day's stubble, as she'd done before she'd walked away.

If there was any way this could work…she would do anything. Anything.

"Hurt me? You're killing me. You may as well have shot me straight through the chest. If I'm not good enough for you, then you should have the courage to say it."

"It's not you, Dillon. Can't you see?" She swiped at her eyes and hated the wetness she found on her fingertips. "You've made me cry. And I can't cry. Because if I do, then I'm going to feel how much this is tearing me apart, and if I feel that, then I'm going to feel everything else, too. Like how I love you with everything I am. Everything I will ever be. That walking away from you is killing me, too, and I have to. I have to leave.''

''What are you talking about?'' He sounded angry and caring all in the same moment, pulling her close to his chest so he could cradle her to his heart, where she was safe.

So safe. Where she would never belong again.

''Darlin', why do you have to leave?''

''Because.'' She tried to push away from him, but he held her firm. Not cruelly, but gently. As if, even when she was breaking his heart, he kept his vow to take care of her, to never let her go.

She had to tell the truth. ''I can't give you a son.''

He froze, his muscles turning to steel. Here it comes, she thought. Could she survive hearing his rejection? Could she endure it if he *didn't* cast her aside?

''My sweet wife, when I married you, I wasn't looking for a broodmare, some female to breed with.'' He cradled her face, holding her so their gazes locked, so she could look into his eyes and down into his soul and feel what he felt for her. ''The first time I saw you, I loved you. Just like that. The way the stars shine, just because they do. The way the wind blows, because it has to. I love you and nothing will ever weaken that. Not disappointment, not hardships, not death.''

''But you'll come to resent it.'' Her hands wrapped around his, trying to break away from his grip. ''Time will pass and when there's no son, you'll start to blame me. Start to love me a little less. And I can't stand that. I won't ever be able to have a child, and so it's better if I leave now. And you can find someone else, and we can spare each other all that heartbreak and sadness—"

"Darlin', I'm a horseman. I've helped with foaling since I was a little boy. I know the way of things, and I figured there was a chance you couldn't have a child. Why didn't you come to me with this? Katelyn, I know this is a great sadness to you, but you walking down this road away from me has nothing to do with not being able to have a baby. It has to do with your lack of faith in me."

She tore away from him, and he let her go, stumbling on the snow to catch her balance.

"Oh, that you'll sacrifice your happiness for mine, is that it?" Oh, he was angry. He felt cut to the center of his soul, and she'd done this to him. The woman he loved. "I have stood by you. I've been patient. I've been loving, I've shown you over and over the man I am."

"You're a good man, Dillon. But trust me, time is going to change things. You want a son, you can't deny it."

"I don't deny it. I'd like a child. But maybe I'm a man with a big enough heart to love you more. When are you going to realize that? I am one-hundred percent committed to you. Now. Forever."

He's too good to be true. But he was. He was a flesh-and-blood man strong enough to love her without condition. Without end.

"You can walk out on me, you can take the train far from here but you can't break this love I have for you. I'm not going to put this marriage aside. I am not going to find another woman to love. It will be you or no one for the rest of my life."

"But what if—"

"No ifs. I will love you through every trial and every sorrow and every happiness to come. But will you? I can't make you love me, damn it. I've done everything I can, and I've been wrong. It comes down to this. You either trust me to love you or you don't. And looking at you, I think I know what your answer is." He put his hand to his face, as if he were in the greatest agony.

I'm hurting him. How could that be? Could it be possible that he wanted her that much?

Why couldn't she believe him? He *was* right. It wasn't his failing.

It was hers.

He stood like a warrior of old, after the battle was done. Head down, hands clasped behind him, shoulders straight, legs apart. He was like the night, dark and without hope. A man who had lost everything.

She placed her hand in the center of his back. There were heroes in real life, men of both strength and kindness. How could she not have faith in him when he had so much in her? Maybe that's what true love was, a leap of faith. Like swimming out into the ocean and trusting the waves to bring you back to shore.

It was the hardest thing she had ever done to open her heart, to expose the most tender of places and love this man more than she could ever love herself. To love him beyond doubt and fear and uncertainty. To love him as far as her soul could reach.

As if he felt the change in her heart, Dillon pulled

her tight to his chest, where she belonged for the rest of her life.

The silvered light of a sickle moon peered behind the edge of a cloud to polish the dark prairie. Snow sheened like a black pearl for miles in every direction, broken only by a dark majestic form watching on a rise.

"Look," Dillon murmured, against her lips. "The stallion. He approves."

The Spirit Horse lifted his nose, his mane rippling in the restless wind. It was as if he called for the snow to fall in tiny crystal flakes straight from heaven. They whispered like grace over the land and over the two lovers standing hand in hand.

The horseman saluted him as the horse disappeared into the wind and the night.

Epilogue

Seven years later

Dillon didn't think he'd ever felt more relieved than when he heard the tiny mewling cries, faint and muffled but strong. Healthy. Was Katelyn all right? And the baby? Did he have a son or a daughter?

"Stay calm, brother," Dakota advised as he left his wife's side to put wood on the dying fire. "Doc Haskins knows what he's doing.

"He'd better." Dillon paced the floor in front of the stairs, back and forth. Damn it, he was a patient man but he'd waited seven years for this moment. He was likely to explode if this went on much longer.

The instant he heard the bedroom door open, he shot up the stairs and pushed the doc out of the way before the man could speak. Girl or boy, it made no difference as long as Katelyn was all right.

The first thing he saw was her face, radiant and smiling in the golden lamplight. She was more beautiful to him with every day that passed. Relief left him quaking all the way to the bed, where he went down beside her on both knees. His wife, his beloved wife, was safe and well. The fear knotted up inside him began to unravel. He wanted to bury his head in her lap and give thanks.

"This is your daughter."

His daughter. A pure love so strong it could outshine a summer sun at its height blazed through him.

Overwhelmed, choking with tenderness, he dropped to his knees beside the bed, gazing at his wife and his daughter nestled in her arms. He'd never seen anything more beautiful.

"Are you disappointed?" A faint wrinkle burrowed into Katelyn's porcelain brow.

Still, she had worries? After all this time? Tears stood in his eyes. Love for her brimmed over in his heart. "I'm overwhelmed. More grateful for this miracle than I know how to say."

"She is a miracle. I can't believe after all this time. How lucky we are." Katelyn leaned the curve of her face into the palm of his hand as he touched her. Sighed with fulfillment when he kissed her tender and true. "I can't believe this is real. The doctor said long ago this was impossible."

"For seven long years, he was right." Dillon swiped the dampness from her eyelashes before her tears could fall. Happy tears, he knew. Thankful beyond measure. It was how he felt, too. "Sometimes love can make miracles."

"You are my miracle."

"Nope, darlin', I'm simply a man."

"A good man. My man." Katelyn kissed his cheek.

The love she felt for him was endless. He had loved

her faithfully and truly for the seven happy years of their marriage. Every day had been better than the last. True to his word, he'd loved her with everything he was, everything he had.

And she had loved him in return the same way, with her entire soul. Their love together had been enough.

The doc had been clear. This child was miraculous, and they would have no more. This little girl she cradled in her arms was more than a dream she'd never thought would come true. This newborn with her curls and angel's face was Dillon's child. Love, sweet and strong as eternity, glowed within her, for this man and now this daughter, for both were her entire life.

''You know what this means, don't you?'' She paused, savoring his sweet, tender kiss. ''It means now we are really going to live happily ever after.''

''That, darlin', is a certainty. Because we already were.''

Dillon eased onto the bed beside her and his solid, wonderful presence stirred her soul. As he always did. As he always would.

Katelyn savored the comfort of his arm around her shoulder, the closeness of his cheek against hers. And the gift of his love that would shine forever.

FALL IN LOVE WITH
THESE HANDSOME HEROES
FROM HARLEQUIN HISTORICALS

On sale September 2004

THE PROPOSITION
by Kate Bridges

Sergeant Major Travis Reid
Honorable Mountie of the Northwest

WHIRLWIND WEDDING
by Debra Cowan

Jericho Blue
Texas Ranger out for outlaws

On sale October 2004

ONE STARRY CHRISTMAS
by Carolyn Davidson/Carol Finch/Carolyn Banning

Three heart-stopping heroes
for your Christmas stocking!

THE ONE MONTH MARRIAGE
by Judith Stacy

Brandon Sayer
Businessman with a mission

www.eHarlequin.com
HARLEQUIN HISTORICALS®

Savor the breathtaking
romances and thrilling adventures
of Harlequin Historicals

On sale September 2004

THE KNIGHT'S REDEMPTION by Joanne Rock

A young Welshwoman tricks Roarke Barret into marriage
in order to break her family's curse—of spinsterhood.
But Ariana Glamorgan never expects to fall for the
handsome Englishman who is now her husband....

PRINCESS OF FORTUNE by Miranda Jarrett

Captain Lord Thomas Greaves is assigned to guard Italian
princess Isabella di Fortunaro. Sparks fly and passions flare
between the battle-weary captain and the spoiled, beautiful
lady. Can love cross all boundaries?

On sale October 2004

HIGHLAND ROGUE by Deborah Hale

To save her sister from a fortune hunter, Claire Talbot offers
herself as a more tempting target. But can she forget the
feelings she once had for Ewan Geddes, a charming
Highlander who once worked on her father's estate?

THE PENNILESS BRIDE by Nicola Cornick

Home from the Peninsula War, Rob Selbourne discovers
he must marry a chimney sweep's daughter to
fulfill his grandfather's eccentric will. Will Rob
find true happiness in the arms of
the lovely Jemima?